Ski Mask Way

BY

Randy Thompson

Prologue

*S*hit was about to be a'ight for me and my niggaz. It was 6:20 P.M. on a hot and humid summer evening in August 2001, and we was about to come up crazy.

A week earlier, me, Boota and Wise had taken part in a triple heist of the biggest jewelry stores in New York State. It was a six-man job. We separated into three groups of two and robbed three stores simultaneously. Everything went according to plan—forty-five seconds in and out. No shootings. No fingerprints. No assaults, and most importantly, no evidence left at the crime scene. In total we got away with one hundred and twenty-five Rolexes, ninety Cartiers, fifty Movado watches and three trays of engagement rings. To me, robbery was the sweetest hustle in the world. We weren't by far the richest niggaz out there, but we made more money per minute than anyone we knew.

We were riding down Sunrise Highway in Long Island in my Lexus GS, on our way to our man's crib to pick up our share of the money. As we passed by Green Acres Mall, I thought that I should bring something nice back home for my fiancée, Michelle.

Originally, I had turned down Dro's offer for the job, but I was damn sure glad that I went along now. My cut was three hundred grand.

Being twenty-one years old with three-hundred grand, I felt like I was gonna have the world in the palm of my hand. I was surprised that Dro agreed to split the money up evenly six ways because when it came to money, Dro was like a Jew. Dro was my man, but he was so slick and conniving that I always had to keep my eyes on him. With Dro, there was a motive behind every move he made, and his aim was usually to look out for himself. I never held it against him because that's just how he was. After all, we'd been a clique since junior high. We were like family. Nah, we were family.

"Ayo, Wise, what you gonna do wit' your share of the money? Three hundred stacks is a lot of cake. It might take you two or three months to blow all of that paper," Boota said sarcastically from the passenger seat.

"What the fuck is you worrying about me and mine for, nigga? And who the fuck is you anyway to be telling me how long I'mma keep my money? Miss Cleo?" Wise responded angrily, leaning up closer to the front seat even though he didn't have to.

"I know what you need to do. You need to do something about your mouth. Yo, Ski. What's that shit called when ya breath stink even after you brush ya teeth?" Boota asked, barely able to conceal the smile that was emerging on his face.

"Halitosis," I answered, not wanting to be dragged into the conversation because my mind was on something else.

"Yeah. Halitosis. Ya mouth needs medicine, son. Ya mouth smells like three-day-old shit. Put a Pamper on that, nigga. If you was smart, you'd take ya share of the money and buy a new tongue. Lean back, nigga. You the only pretty boy in America wit' stink-ass breath." Boota said, snapping on Wise and getting him more upset with each remark.

Boota was three years older than me. He was a big funny nigga. Boota could make a joke out of anything. He was six-three and 250 pounds of pure muscle. Boota was just a naturally big muthafucka. When I met him in junior high school I thought he was a gym teacher because he looked like a grown man. Boota had dark skin with a bald head, big lips and a large nose. In the face, he and Shaquille O'Neal could have passed for twins. Boota wasn't the sharpest tool in the shed when it came to book smarts, but he was a born hustler. He came from a family of well-known and respected hustlers.

I glanced back at Wise through my rearview mirror, and I could tell he was tight. His entire face was bright red.

"Ayo, I hope Dro ain't take too much shorts on the jewels. I need my whole three hundred and not a penny less. Fuck that son, I need mine," I stated, changing the conversation to what I'd been thinking about the last fifteen minutes.

"Two hundred twenty-five, 250…I don't give a fuck. It's all free money. It's better than sitting on all that shit. I ain't hear you volunteering to hold none of the watches," Boota responded, rolling up a Dutch, spilling tobacco all over himself in my car.

"Yeah. That big lip nigga is right, Ski. We ain't have no other way to get rid of all that shit. If it comes up short we can't be mad. Dro is doing us a favor," Wise responded.

We all had done other jewelry heists before, but the most we ever made off a job was forty grand. We had no way to get rid of that much bulk of jewelry, so we agreed to take it to this jeweler who agreed to sell it wholesale for us. At that time I'd pulled maybe six or seven juxes, otherwise known as jobs.

Boota's two-way sounded, and he pulled it off his belt, flipped it open and read the text message. Afterward, he began giving me instructions. "Yo, Ski, pull over at Ray Noors Cabin. I got a sale to make," he said, putting his two-way back on his belt and removing his phone from his waist.

"Son, what type of time you on? Here we are about to pick up three hundred mothafuckin' stacks, and you wanna stop and make a sale for a couple of hundred dollars? What type of time you on?" I asked again, shaking my head in disgust.

"Nigga, I'm on presidential time," Boota shot back, waving his presidential Rolex in my face. "I'm a hustler. Money is like pussy. I could never get enough of it. I ain't like Wise. I don't trick, I flip," Boota said, winking at me.

We had been in Ray Noors parking lot for nearly ten minutes when a red BMW 325i with three white girls turned into the parking lot and pulled over to us. Ray Noors Cabin was a restaurant around our way that was known for soul food.

"Hey. What's up, Boota?" Thanks for meeting me on such short notice. Lemme get ten Rolls Royces," the brunette requested from the passenger seat.

"Damn, ten E-pills?" Where the party at? What's really good, Laura? Lemme find out you don't remember me," Wise said, smiling as he got out the backseat of my Lex.

"Wise? Is that you? Holy shit. I haven't seen you in years. Come over and give me a hug wit' yo' fine self. The party is wherever you want it to be, sweetie," Laura said, smiling.

"Oh yeah. It's like that? You know I always had a crush on you since back in the day, right?" Wise said, looking Laura up and down like a piece of meat.

"You better stop before you get yaself into something you can't get out of," Laura flirted.

Wise was a pretty boy. Bitches loved him. When we'd go out to clubs, chicks would come and ask him if he wanted to dance and buy him drinks. Wise was light skinned with light brown eyes and wavy hair. He was six feet tall, and his body was cut up like a bag of dope. Not only was Wise a pretty boy, but he also had the gift of gab. He always said the right things around women. Wise was also a rapper. To me he had no business pulling heists with us. He should've been signed with a major record label.

"All we were gonna do was hang out at Patricia's. She has to go back to school next week, and we were gonna get her fucked up before she leaves," Laura offered, flicking the hair off her face with her hand.

We had all gone to high school together at Baldwin Senior High a few years prior. Where we are from in Long Island, the ratio of black to white is fifty-fifty. It's not unusual to see an interracial couple strolling down the street hand in hand. All of us had popped off with a white girl once or twice. Well, maybe more than once or twice.

Patricia was the driver. She was the cheerleading captain back in the day when I was an All Long Island basketball player in high school. We fucked off and on for almost two years. I hadn't seen or spoken to her since we graduated. Any other time I would've jumped at the opportunity to dig her back out for ol' times sake, but that night all I could think about was my three hundred grand. I sat low in my seat hoping that Patricia wouldn't spot me.

"Hey, Isaiah. I see how you act. You don't know us little people anymore since you became a big shot, huh?" Patricia said out the window of her BMW.

"C'mon, Trish. It ain't like that. You know better than that. I'm sorry, but I got a lot on my mind. How could I ever forget about you? Bring ya sexy ass out here and gimme a hug," I said, getting out of the car reluctantly.

"Damn, girl. Look at you. You got thick as hell. What you been eating up there at school?" I asked as I lifted her off the ground and hugged her.

"You're so crazy. What are you doing wit' yourself nowadays? Why don't you guys come over and hang out at my house? My parents are on vacation. Plus, I can show you all of the tricks I learned at school," Patricia said, not giving anyone a chance to get a word in edgewise while she grabbed my crotch.

Patricia looked even better than I remembered. She had on a tank top with no bra and a pair of cutoff jean shorts that exposed the bottom half of her ass cheeks. My dick was hard just looking at her. Patricia was five-three with an athletic build from participating in gymnastics since childhood. She had wide hips and thick thighs and a nice ass. She had long brown hair and hazel eyes. It took all the restraint I had to turn her offer down.

"Yo, Trish, I would really love to but…"

"We would love to," Wise answered cutting me off and smiling at the girls.

In high school, Laura was prom queen, valedictorian and captain of the tennis team. She was bad for real. She was hotter than Pamela Anderson in her heyday. Wise had wanted to smash her for years, but never got the opportunity. But now that he had the chance he wasn't gonna let nothing stop him—apparently not even three hundred stacks.

Boota dropped out of school early, so he didn't know any of the girls except Laura, but as usual he wasted no time getting straight to the point.

"Do you take a dick in ya mouth?" Boota asked casually.

"What?" Allison asked, knowing she heard him right the first time.

"You heard me. Do you or don't you take cock in ya mouth?" Boota replied, slightly raising his voice.

Allison was Laura's and Patricia's best friend. I wouldn't say she was ugly, but she damn sure wasn't pretty. She was at least twenty-five pounds overweight, acne painfully covered her face, and she had a big sloppy gut. Allison knew that Patricia and Laura wanted to get up with Wise and me badly, and she didn't want to spoil the party. Besides, it wasn't every day that a guy gave her some attention. She probably wanted some dick just as bad, if not more than Laura and Patricia.

"Uh, yeah, I guess," Allison answered, dumbfounded.

"Say no more then. Let's bounce," Boota said with an evil smirk on his face as he walked back to my car.

To this day, I don't know how Boota ever got any pussy with that line. If I would've said something like that to a broad, she'd probably smack me or throw a drink on me, but every time he asked that question, it worked. Boota was one of them niggaz who could get away with saying anything.

We hopped in my car and followed Patricia to her house in the ritzy section of town called Baldwin Harbor. Don't get me wrong, I've never be one to turn down pussy, but I had my mind on my money and my money on my mind. It bugged me out how Boota and Wise were acting like we didn't have more important shit to be doing.

"Ayo, don't y'all think we should stop by Dro's crib and handle our business first?" I asked as we passed Dro's block.

"Calm down, son. The money ain't going no-fucking-where. You act like we gonna spend the night wit' these bitches or somethin'. Michelle ain't gonna find out, nigga. Relax. Shorty got you pussy whipped," Wise retorted.

Boota had spit out the juice he was drinking so he wouldn't choke himself to death from laughing.

"You don't even sound right, Duke. I want my paper just like you should want yours. You thinking about pussy, and I'm thinking about money. Get ya mind right, nigga," I stated beginning to get aggravated.

"Yo, Ski. What you think Dro gonna do, skip town with our money? I don't really give a fuck about getting with these bitches either, but I ain't got shit else to do. Our money is in safe hands. You know that," Boota explained, trying his best to pacify me.

"When it comes to my money, no hands are safe but mine," I said clearly seeing I had been outvoted.

They were probably right, but I never had anything close to three hundred grand in my life, and I wanted to feel it in my hands. I have a lot of important things to do with that money.

By the time we made it to Patricia's house on Baldwin Harbor it was 7:15. Baldwin Harbor was the picture perfect looking suburb. Patricia lived in an old colonial-style ranch home overlooking the harbor. As we drove onto the circular driveway, I noticed a white Mercedes Benz, a white Range Rover and a candy-apple-red Porsche. Patricia's parents had money. They had a live-in maid and a cook. As I looked around I thought that I had played the whole situation out wrong with Patricia. I should have had that bitch paying for the dick.

As we exited the car and entered the house, I looked at Patricia's ass in those tight-ass shorts and got aroused again. After about an hour or two, we were high and drunk, and the girls were E'd up, and we all split into three bedrooms.

As soon as we got into her parents' bedroom, Patricia dropped to her knees and started unbuckling my belt and pulling down my Evisu jeans. When she saw that I was already aroused, she licked her lips and took me in her mouth.

"Damn, Trish. I missed this. You treat me good," I whispered, my eyes rolling back in my head.

With the tip of her tongue, using her tongue ring, she started licking the head of my dick in slow, circular motions. My knees were buckling. I've gotten head from a lot of women of all nationalities, but Trisha was the best. She sucked dick like a porn star. Her mouth was so warm and moist that it almost felt like pussy. After she licked my balls, she started sucking my dick—at first, just the head, then half of it. After a while she was deep-throating me hard and fast. If I didn't have liquor in me, I probably would've come immediately. After about ten minutes I was holding her by the ears and fucking her face. I pulled out of her mouth, pushed her on the bed roughly and began taking all my clothes off. From there I began ripping off her clothes, and I even ripped her panties. I got on top of her naked ass and began sucking and biting her neck. Trisha liked rough sex, and my aggression turned her on even more. She liked to be the submissive one. As I was licking the pink nipples of her C-cup breasts, I ran my hand between her legs, and she was wetter than a swimming pool.

"Fuck me, daddy. Fuck me now. I wanna feel you," Patricia cried out in ecstasy as I tried to slide my dick inside of her.

I put her legs on my shoulders and began taking long, hard, deep thrusts. She began climaxing instantly.

"OHHHHHH! YES! YES! OHHH my goodness! Fuck me! Just like that! I'm coming," she cried out.

"Whose pussy is this?" I asked still stroking, putting my finger in her mouth.

"YOURS! YOURS! Oh, right there! YOURS! ALL YOURS, BABY," she shouted.

I turned Trisha over and entered her doggy style. I took hard, short strokes, and she met me each time slamming her ass back into me as I pulled her hair and smacked her tight, firm ass.

"Isaiah. Tell me…tell…tell me when you're about to come," Patricia begged.

"Why?" I asked, not breaking rhythm.

"Because…because…I want you to come in my mouth."

As soon as those words came out of her mouth I felt like I was gonna nut. I pulled out of her, rolled her over on her back, stood over her and put my dick back in her mouth. I came so hard it felt like she had drained the life out of me. Trisha swallowed every drop of my seed. A lesser man would've fallen in love with her. Normally, a session like that would put me to bed, but once again my mind quickly returned to my money.

"Yo, Trish, I hate to hit it and run, but there's something real important I gotta take care of tonight. But yo, I promise I'll get up with you again before you leave for school, a'ight?" I replied, lying real hard as I put my clothes back on.

"C'mon, baby. Can't it wait until the morning?"

"Nah. It's real important. You think I don't wanna stay?"

"Why don't you come back when you're finished?" Patricia asked. She was stark naked as she kissed me with the intent of seducing me to stay.

"A'ight. I'll swing back through. Keep that thing wet for me," I responded, smacking her on the ass and walking out of the room.

As I made my way down the steps, I saw Boota knocked out on the sofa while Allison watched television. Boota was a one minute man. All a bitch had to do was talk about touching his dick and he'd come. He'd probably been sleep for hours.

"Lemme guess…two minutes?" I asked Allison already knowing the answer to my own question.

Allison nodded.

"Where are Wise and Laura at?"

As soon as I asked, the noise answered my question for me. Laura and Wise were upstairs going at it. Every time we had sessions with bitches, Wise always tried to outdo me. I sat on the couch with Allison for almost half an hour waiting for him to finish. As Boota started to wake up, Wise came walking down the steps.

"Who the fuck you think you is, son? Mr. Marcus?" I said to Wise, smiling.

"Yeah, nigga. You heard my work? I was punishing that bitch, right?" Wise asked, feeling proud of his bedroom accomplishments.

"Sounded like she was punishing you, the way you were up there moaning like a little bitch. I heard you, kid," I shot back.

By the time we got back in my car, it was close to one in the morning. Everybody was in good spirits. When we turned down Dro's block, one of the guys from around our way flagged me down. I pulled over.

"Breezy, I ain't got no money to give you. I ain't dropping you off nowhere, and I ain't givin' you no weed," I said sarcastically. "Does that answer all of ya questions?"

Breezy explained the situation sounding out of breath, "Nah son. Listen. The Feds just ran up in Dro's crib. He banged it out with them. I think he's dead. Danielle tried to jump out the window but she got bagged."

Boota anxiously asked, "What time did all of this happen?"

"About eight o'clock. You should have seen it. It was…"

By the time Breezy finished telling the story we were approximately ten blocks away. We drove to Grand Avenue and parked in the bowling alley parking lot. It was only a few blocks from our strip.

"I told y'all we shouldn't have fucked them bitches. I told y'all. I told y'all. I told y'all." I yelled as I slammed my head into the steering wheel.

Wise yelled back, "Son, if we were there, we would be dead or in jail right now."

Mad at myself for not following my first instinct, I continued, "I expect a ho-loving nigga like you to say some shit like that. It was six-thirty when we were on our way there. We would've been in and out by the time the Feds rushed the crib."

Getting out of the car to take a piss, Boota retorted, "It could've gone either way, but I think them bitches might have saved our lives."

Covering my face with my hands, I yelled, "Damn. Damn. I need that paper, B. What the fuck am I gonna do now?"

Boota, sounding concerned, said, "Damn, son. Listen to you. Breezy said that Dro might be dead, and all you keep talking about is the money. That's some foul shit."

Boota was right. Dro and Danielle were family. Yet here I was thinking about money. The three years that I'd been in the game had changed me. I had become heartless.

After thirty minutes of silence, Wise asked, "So what do we do now? What's the next move from here?"

Boota replied calmly, "Wait. We gotta wait it out and lay low. Yo, Ski. Drop me off at the crib."

That night was the beginning to the end of life as I knew it. To give you a better understanding, I'm gonna have to take you to the very beginning—back when everything was all good.

*T*here were eleven seconds left in the game, and we were down two points in the Long Island High School Basketball Championship in February 1996. I had just gotten fouled after an offensive rebound. Two shots. This was the biggest moment in my life. I was a rail-thin sixteen-year-old junior at Baldwin Senior High. Nassau Coliseum was halfway packed. Eight to nine thousand sets of eyes were all on me as I approached the free-throw line.

Everyone I knew was there. The game was being broadcast live on cable television. My gaze went toward the giant Teletron above the court. I saw my own nervous sweat-dripping face peering back at me. Up until that point, I had an average game of fifteen points, five rebounds and six assists. Nobody thought we'd make it this far.

A week earlier, we had upset the number one seated Hempstead Tigers in the county finals. I was the best free-throw shooter on the team, but I was so nervous my hands were shaking. Before I stepped into the line, Snoop put his hands around my head, looked me in the eyes and said, "Take ya time, Ski. We need this. This is when all the practice pays off. Knock 'em down. I love you, boy."

After he said that, I felt like the whole world had been lifted off of my shoulders. I couldn't let Snoop down. He had practically gotten us there single-handedly. It was his senior year, and his last chance to make it to the state finals at Glen Falls. Snoop was our starting point guard and the quarterback for the varsity football team. He was also my best friend. Snoop was a natural-born athlete. I had to practice every day and shoot thousands of jump shots to get good. He never practiced. That playoff season he averaged twenty-nine points and eight assists. Snoop was brown skin, five foot ten and 170 pounds. He had corn rows with a slim build, sort of like Allen Iverson. In the face, he resembled Method Man from the Wu-Tang Clan.

When the referee threw me the ball, I had tunnel vision. I couldn't hear the roar of the crowd, see my mother or my little sister in the stands wearing replicas of my jersey or anything else. All I could see was the basket. I took a deep breath, three dribbles, spun the ball on my hand, released and followed through.

Swish!

The ref said that the ball was live after the next shot and handed me the ball. I repeated the same free-throw ritual that I had done since I was four years old. Released and followed through. Picture perfect.

Swish!

Cold Spring Harbor took the ball out underneath our basket. There was eleven seconds left in the game, and neither team had a timeout left. They inbounded the ball to their All-American point guard, Wally Talereco. Wally was the Long Island player of the year the two previous seasons. He already had declared he was going to Duke on a full scholarship. That white boy had game.

Wally went between his legs, around his back and between his legs again as he crossed the half-court line. He faked left, went right and tried to cross over when it happened…

Snoop stole the ball.

Snoop raced toward our basket going a million miles an hour as Wally hurried to catch him.

Four…three…two…

Snoop took off from the dotted line and dunked just as the time expired.

We won. The crowd erupted with cheer.

We did it. Balloons and confetti fell from the ceiling. It was the first time in our school's seventy-five-year history that we'd ever won anything. The whole crowd rushed the floor.

The first person I saw running toward me was Patricia. She was captain of the cheerleading squad. We had a little something going on, but cameras were everywhere and I didn't wanna get caught on TV hugging up on no white girl, so I ran the opposite way toward my mother and little sister, Sable. We danced and acted a fool for what seemed like forever. Snoop was at half court embracing his high school sweetheart, Natalie. After a few minutes, we took turns cutting down the net and doing interviews for all the local sports television and radio stations. A scout from Florida State had guaranteed Snoop a full scholarship and a starting position. We were on top of the world. After the post-game activities were over, Snoop and I sat in the locker room alone and spoke for the first time since the game.

Snoop began the conversation, taking off his jersey. "Yo, Ski. You should've seen ya face after you got fouled. You was shook. I doubted you for a minute."

Lying, while keeping my composure, I replied, "Who me? I got ice in my veins. You heard the reporters."

Not believing me, Snoop shot back, "Yeah, Whatever, son. Yo. You know how much pussy we gonna get tonight? Every bitch in Long Island wanna give us some pussy."

Shaking my head, I said, "Damn, son. All you think about is bitches."

Unfazed by my remark, he said, "What else am I supposed to think about? You act like you don't care about nuffin' but basketball. You gotta lighten up, son. You take this shit too seriously."

"I ain't tryin' to let none of these stink-ass bitches stop me from doing what I gotta do. This is my only way out the hood, son. I ain't tryin' to end up like my brother."

My brother, Dave, was an All Long Island basketball player in the late eighties. Every school in the country wanted to recruit him. One night Dave was at his girlfriend, Linda's house, and her other boyfriend walked in the house and caught them having sex. The dude went crazy and shot Dave fifteen times, killing him instantly. After that, I promised myself that I was gonna make it to the pros. Not just for me, but for my older brother, and most importantly for my mother. Dave's death killed a part of her. My dream wasn't just my dream…it was our dream.

Understanding my feelings, Snoop said, "I know, son. I know. You doin' the right thing. Dave would be proud of you tonight, son. That three pointer you hit started the run. And the free throws were big. In a couple of years we gonna be in the NBA makin' millions. I can see it now. I'mma marry Nat. Get us a big-ass crib and buy my mom and pops a crib."

Snoop was a dreamer. He loved to talk about accomplishing things, but didn't like putting the work in to get them. He thought success was just gonna come knocking at his door. I didn't mind it that day. Sometimes it's good to dream.

Putting on my old beat-up Timberlands, I agreed, "Yeah, I'd love to get my moms a crib too. I hate that she works so hard and we still ain't got shit."

"You know my pops is sick as hell, fam. His insurance don't cover half that shit he got. Chemo and radiation is expensive as hell. I'mma have to leave school early and go to the draft." Snoop explained.

Snoop never talked about his fathers ailing condition. He had been diagnosed with stomach cancer and it was killing Snoop. It bothered him to see his father like that, especially since he couldn't do anything to help.

"I feel you, my nigga. I feel you," I said, sympathetically.

Snoop grabbed his car keys. "Ski, you ready? Let's bounce. We got a party to attend."

□□□

My mother shouted at the top of her lungs from the bottom staircase, "Isaiah! Isaiah! Snoopy is down here. Bring ya narrow ass downstairs."

As I made my way down the steps, she continued, "Listen, Isaiah, you know I don't got money for you to be wasting time at some party, but since tonight is a special occasion, here…" My mother handed me five crumpled one-dollar bills and a couple of dollars in change. I counted the money up in my head and put it in my pocket.

Kissing her cheek, I said, "Thanks, Momma. If everything works out like I plan, we ain't gonna have to live like this no more."

My mother responded by kissing me on the cheek and hugging me, "I know, baby. I know."

As me and Snoop were walking out my front door, I slipped the money back into my mother's pocket. I knew that my mother gave me her last, and if I took the money she gave me, she would have to walk all the way to work. Even though I could've used it, I couldn't do my moms like that. I didn't like taking anything from her. People from New York City always assumed that everyone in Long Island was rich, but that couldn't be further from the truth. There are ghettos and poor people everywhere.

Snoop looked me up and down as we walked to his car. "Ayo, Ski, how are you going to the party wearing that shit? I'mma take you to my crib and give you something of mine to wear. You can't be my man going to a party looking like that. How you gonna bag bitches?"

Climbing into the backseat of Snoop's car, I said, "It's all I got, son. You know my moms is struggling. She ain't got no money to be wasting, buying me two-hundred-dollar sweaters and shit."

Natalie intervened, cutting her eyes at Snoop, "Leave him alone, Snoopy. You look fine, Isaiah." Natalie turned around to the backseat and flashed me a big smile.

Snoop and Natalie had been together since we were in junior high. Natalie was an Amazon at five foot ten, with olive skin and jet-black hair that fell down the middle of her back. She had light brown eyes, high cheekbones and was thick in all the right places. She was a dime for real.

Snoop came back with his matter-of-fact attitude, "Naw, Nat. I can't let Ski go out like that, wearing all that bootleg shit."

I shot back, "This ain't bootleg shit."

Snoop responded with an eruption of laughter, "Yo, Ski. When did Jansport start making button downs? They make book bags. Not clothes, nigga."

Snoop had an older brother who hustled, and he made sure that Snoop stayed fly. Snoop had enough clothes to wear for three months without wearing the same thing twice. Me, on the other hand, I could barely go a week without wearing the same outfit twice.

We pulled up at Snoop's crib at about eleven-thirty that night. Snoop didn't live in the town that we lived in. He lived in the neighboring town called Hempstead, in one of the worst projects in Long Island called Terrace. After Snoop's family moved to the projects, he used my address and kept going to school in Baldwin because the whole crew went there. Not to mention that Natalie did too.

Snoop was going through his closet and said, "Ski, put this on and you'll look official. This is Iceberg right here. Now maybe you'll get some pussy and stop stressing over Kim."

"Leave him alone, Snoopy. You're always picking on him," Natalie shouted.

Snoop shouted back, "And you're always taking up for him."

"And, so what? Are you guys ready?" Natalie asked, tired of waiting.

Everybody in our clique treated me like their little brother. That shit used to annoy the hell out of me. True, I was the youngest and most inexperienced, but they took it to the extreme. They were only a couple of years older than me, if that. At that time I had just turned sixteen. I was darkskin, six feet two inches and 175 pounds soaking wet. My hair was wavy, I had coal-black eyes and long eyelashes that everyone used to make fun of when I was younger. I was in an awkward stage back then. My voice was changing, my feet were too big for my body and my wardrobe was terrible. The only place I felt comfortable back then was on the basketball court. I was no model by any stretch of the imagination, but if I dressed right, I could have been considered good looking. At the time though, the last thing on my mind was my appearance. I thought about basketball sixteen hours a day, and dreamt about it the other eight while I slept.

We pulled into the South Beach parking lot at a quarter past twelve. Outside of the club, Wise was battling this kid named 100 Proof who had just moved around our way from Queens.

Wise rapped…

They say love is blind
Well it must be dumb and deaf too
'Cause everybody heard I'm fuckin' ya broad except you
You out there maxin' ya Visa packin' her freezer
Treatin' her special
Meanwhile I'm wearing her out like an old pair of dress shoes

Boota shouted, putting his arm around Wise and pulling him away from the cipha, "Ayo, Wise, that's enough, son. This bird-ass nigga can't fuck wit' you! Where's my money? That was no contest."

Seconds later, Boota saw me, Snoop and Natalie walking up.

Boota teased, "Oh, shit! If it ain't the Long Island–muthafuckin' Globetrotters. Can I get an autograph?"

Snoop responded, giving Boota dap, "Don't start ya black-ass Amistad-lookin' muthafucka."

We shook so many hands that it felt like I was the mothafuckin' mayor. Everyone had seen the game. I was a celebrity in the hood.

Boota and his hustling partner at the time, Hand, convinced Hand's pops to let them throw a party in his club if we won the game. Boota had dropped out of school two years earlier to sell drugs and take care of his pregnant girlfriend, Shamika, who had gotten kicked out of her parents' house. Boota and Hand weren't at all what you would consider big-time hustlers, but for me, at the time they were like Frank White and Nino Brown from King of New York and New Jack City. They stayed in the hottest gear. They had every pair of Jordans and name-brand item the week they came out. They had Cuban links with iced-out Jesus pieces and their own apartments. A lot of niggaz were dropping out of school to work for them. At the time, that was the last thing I'd ever think about doing. Out of our crew, the only ones who were still in school were me, Wise, Snoop and Dro.

Snoop went to school for two reasons…sports and girls, and not in that order. Snoop was on the block so much with them, that everyone assumed he hustled, too, because every time beef popped off, Snoop was right there squeezing his hammer like he had work on the block too. Me, on the other hand, I rarely went to the block. Standing on the corner smoking and drinking was a waste of time. I wasn't into that life at all.

"Damn, Wise. You wilded on Proof in front of everybody. When you started talking about fucking his girl, I thought we was gonna have to beat his ass," I said to Wise as we entered the club.

Wise responded, giving me dap and laughing, "Fuck Proof. His flow is like his girl's pussy…trash."

□□□

The party was jam-packed. Everybody who was somebody was there. People were treating me like I was a star. And prior to that night, most of them didn't even know I existed. All eyes were on me. Big-time hustlers kept sending over bottles of champagne, and mad females were coming up to me asking me to dance.

Me and Wise were standing on the balcony looking down at the dance floor when Wise said, "Don't turn around, but Kim is coming this way. And she got her faggot-ass man with her."

Kim was holding her new boyfriend's hand looking me up and down when she spoke. "Hi, Isaiah. Nice game."

Ghost was a new nigga who moved to our school from Brooklyn. He was a grimy-looking dude. He had missing teeth and all types of scars on his face. He didn't even keep his hair cut. He also sold drugs.

Up until a couple of months ago, Kim had been my girlfriend, but when Ghost came to the school, all of Kim's hood-rat friends jumped on his dick because he was getting money. Somehow they convinced Kim to break up with me and hook up with him. Kim gave me an ultimatum. She said that if I didn't start hustling so that I could take care of her, she would find someone who would. I thought about it, but couldn't do it. I told her to find someone else, and she did just that. Kim was a gold digger in the making. I acted like I didn't care, but inside I was steaming.

"Thanks, Kim," I said, trying not to be salty.

Before Kim walked off arm and arm with Ghost, she had more to say, "Look at you. You look nice. I know those can't be your clothes. Whose shit you flossing? You need to hit the block wit' ya friends. You too old to be playing basketball and ain't shit gonna ever become of it."

As they walked away, Wise looked at me and said, "I don't know how you put up with that bitch's shit. I would've spit in her face. We should stomp that nigga Ghost out, B. I'm telling you."

Telling half the truth, I answered, "Nah, B. Fighting over a bitch is lame. Fuck her. I don't want no bitch who don't want me."

Wise raised his voice, "Nah, nigga. Letting some new nigga walk around wit' ya bitch is lame. That's why she keeps playing you. Not only is you makin' yaself look like a sucka, you makin' all of us look like suckas." Wise walked away and left me standing at the balcony watching Kim and Ghost dance.

Nothing could put me in a bad mood that night. The party was jumping. Girls were practically throwing the pussy at me. One of the many females who approached me was Maria. Maria was twenty-four years old. She was Dominican and Black, five feet two inches with long hair, big titties and a fat ass.

As we were dancing, she whispered in my ear, "I wanna take you home with me tonight and see if you move as good as you do on the basketball court in the bedroom."

Maria put her tongue in my ear, and my whole body shivered. My dick got rock hard instantly.

In the VIP area, Boota, Dro and Wise were all pissy drunk. Wise, always the player, had two bisexual chicks sitting on his lap kissing each other. Snoop was in the corner hugged up with Natalie and Dro was with his high school sweetheart Danielle. Boota was bugging the fuck out. He was on the dance floor bumping, pushing and ice-grillin' every nigga in his path. At one point I saw him pulling random girls' hair.

Curious, I walked over to him, "Yo, Boota, what's going on, son?"

Boota responded, "What does it look like I'm doing, nigga?"

"Why you pulling girls' hair?"

"I wanna see who got real hair before I holla at these bitches. A lot of them be havin' weaves, B, I'm telling you."

"What? Who the fuck is you? The hair inspector, nigga? C'mon and sit your ass down before you start some drama over nuffin," I said, walking Boota back to the table.

As we were making our way back, we noticed a small crowd forming where we were sitting. We pushed our way up to the front and saw Snoop beefing with some cat. Apparently, Snoop had left Natalie for a minute to take a leak, and when he came back duke was trying to holla at Natalie who shut him down, and told him she had a man. The cat even apologized to Snoop, but Snoop wasn't trying to hear nothing.

Snoop twisted his face in his trademark scowl. "Nigga, stop trying to act like you ain't know I was wit' her. I saw you staring over here earlier."

The kid responded, sticking his hand out to give Snoop dap, "My bad, son. I ain't know that was ya wifey. Pardon self, fam."

Snoop smacked his hand away.

Natalie pleaded, "Snoopy, let it go. You're overreacting. He apologized. Let it go."

By that time, damn near our whole hood was surrounding duke. If he had any of his people with him, they must've been ass, because ain't nobody come to hold him down. Just when I thought Snoop was gonna let it go, he pulled out an Ox and buck fiftyed the kid on his left cheek. The kid was in shock. His whole left cheek was dangling off his face. He covered his face with his hands and tried to back outta the circle, but Boota snuffed him with a two piece to the jaw that knocked him out. As soon as he hit the floor, me, Dro and Wise began kicking and stomping the kid into oblivion. Snoop was so caught up in the beef that he ain't even notice that Natalie had left the club.

After a few minutes, the bouncers came running from the back and broke it up. They were five minutes too late. Hand's father came out from the back as well and deaded the party. He was mad at us because he knew the police were gonna show up, and he had underage people drinking.

Wise left with the two bisexual chicks he'd been chillin' with all night while Dro and Danielle bounced together. I was on my way out the door with Maria when Snoop said, "So I guess you don't need a ride home, huh?"

Maria responded by grabbing my nuts, "No, papi. He's in good hands. I'mma take him on the ride of his life."

What I didn't know then was that Maria was a stripper at one of Hand's father's strip clubs and the fellas had paid her to fuck me. She was supposed to turn me out, but she ended up getting open off me. The two hundred and fifty dollars they paid her and then some, she ended up spending on me down the road.

Though we all walked outta the club in one piece, shit was about to go down in the worse fucking way. All because one nigga had a bad temper and the rest of us were young and dumb. If I knew the problems that lay ahead, I would have cherished every second of it.

*M*y niggaz decided it was time for me to get hooked up, and it didn't matter if we had to beg, borrow and steal to make that shit happen. It just so happened we were gonna steal.

Me, Dro, Wise and Snoop were packed in Snoop's mother's Mazda 626 outside of Macy's department store at Roosevelt Field Mall, in Garden City, Long Island in June. Roosevelt Field is one of the biggest malls in New York State. Generally, the parking lot was packed and it took anywhere between fifteen to twenty minutes just to find a parking spot. We all got up early that Friday morning to boost clothes. I'd never shoplifted before, but I couldn't imagine it being difficult. To tell you the truth, I didn't even put too much thought into it. I was tired of walking around looking like a poster child for the Salvation Army.

Dro explained to me, "Make sure you stay close to me, B. Grab as much shit as you can in ya size and when I give you the signal, bounce out the side door. Make sure you the first one out, B. A'ight?" Dro repeated himself. "A'ight?"

Aggravated from the backseat, I replied, "Yeah, nigga. Damn! I ain't no fucking baby, nigga. How many times are you gonna tell me the same shit?"

Dro shot back, "As many times as it takes until I'm sure you got it, nigga. I ain't trying to be the one who gets you in trouble. Not only would I have to hear my mom's mouth, I'd have to hear my girl's mouth too."

Snoop agreed, "Word!"

"Yeah. Whatever, yo. Y'all niggaz ready or what?" I asked.

Like I said before, I hated the way everyone in our clique always treated me like a kid. Looking back, I realize it was because I was the youngest. Aside from that, everyone thought I was gonna make it out the hood and be something. I got good grades. I didn't hang out on the block, plus everyone knew how much it would hurt my mother if something happened to me after my brother's death.

As we all got out the car and headed toward the back entrance of Macy's, Dro said, "Yeah, let's go. Mall security just passed. We got ten minutes until they swing through again. Let's make it quick."

Dro was five-feet-ten and 225 pounds. He was light skin with a baldhead and a football player's build. He was our high school's star running back. He turned down scholarships to some of the biggest and best football programs in the country. School just wasn't his cup of tea. Dro was a paper chaser. He was always scheming on something. He was also an introvert. People took his quietness for shyness, but I knew better. It was arrogance. He didn't talk much because he felt he was smarter than everyone else. He had this sneaky look about him, like he was always up to something, and he usually was. Dro did whatever for the dollar. He sold drugs, stole cars and even boosted clothes. Dro came up with the whole plan to hit Macy's. Normally, everyone would grab clothes for themselves, but on this day, everyone was grabbing clothes just for me. They were tired of me looking like a bum, and I was ready to shine.

We entered Macy's one by one. I was the last one to walk in. As I went into the men's section, I caught eyes with Dro's girlfriend Danielle, and she glanced in Dro's direction.

Danielle was in the same grade as Wise and me. She was full-blooded Puerto Rican, but she looked and acted like a straight-up white girl. She was short and thin, with a short Halle Berry hairstyle, with big nerdy glasses. Danielle was beautiful in the face, but she had no body at all. To this day, I don't know what Dro and Danielle saw in each other. They were complete opposites.

Macy's was empty just like Dro said it would be. Besides Danielle working in the perfume department, there were only two employees on the whole side of the store we were on, and they were older women. No way were they gonna be able to catch us. Snoop stayed outside in the car as the getaway driver. In approximately six minutes he was to park the car in front of the exit and pop the trunk.

With ten Tommy Hilfiger shirts underneath my arm, I asked, "Yo. What the fuck is this? I thought we were only getting clothes for me?"

Dro answered in his usual arrogant voice, "Shhhhhhh! You talking loud as hell, son. Why don't you just tell the whole store we boosting? And these are for you. These shirts is hot, B. You don't know nuthin' about clothes. You ain't got no style, son. I'mma have you dressing fly like me."

At six minutes to the second, I looked out the door, and out of the corner of my eye I saw Snoop pull up and pop the trunk.

Dro was looking around the store, "Yo, where's Wise?"

Wise was standing behind Dro. "Right here, son. Y'all ready?"

Dro shouted, pushing toward the door, "Oh, shit. Ski, go. Go, go, go. Security is coming."

A white man with jeans and a walkie-talkie shouted, "Hey, you guys. Stop right there."

We bolted out the door like the Olympic track team. By the time the security guard came running outside we were halfway out the parking lot. We made it. I was gonna be fresh to death.

☐☐☐

The next day, me, Snoop, Wise, Dro and Danielle were all at Natalie's graduation party. The party was weak. No smoking, no drinking and no music. Earlier that day, Snoop, Natalie, Dro and Boota's girlfriend Shamika all graduated. Five minutes earlier, Natalie's mother told her to make Boota leave. Boota tried to leave early, telling Shamika that he had to hit the block because he was missing sales, but she insisted he stay. So, instead of going to the block, Boota brought the block to Natalie's crib. Boota had ten cars full of fiends lined up in front of Natalie's house. Natalie's mother was square, but even Stevie Wonder could see that Boota was selling drugs. She immediately demanded that Boota leave the party. Unfortunately for us, that was the only entertaining thing that happened. It seemed like the entire graduating class of '96 showed up. Black, White, Spanish, Chinese…they all loved Natalie. She was just a naturally good person.

I came to the party fly as hell. I had on a white-and-red Polo shirt, black Polo jean shorts, a white fisherman's hat and some white-and-red Jordans. I had so many clothes that I didn't even have enough hangers to place them on in my closet. After we came back from boosting, Boota and Hand picked me up and brought me a thousand dollars worth of boots and sneakers. You couldn't tell me I wasn't the shit. I was in Natalie's backyard sitting on a foldout chair talking to a crowd of chicks. When we went to the state championship at Glen Falls, I made a name for myself. We lost, but I played the game of my life. I finished with forty-two points. I got invited to all the major camps that summer—Nike camp in Chicago, Adidas camp in Massachusetts, and the ABCD camp in Maryland. All the girls were riding my dick.

A brown-skinned girl named Alisha asked me, "So, Isaiah, what NBA team do you think you're gonna go to?"

I put my arms around her waist, "I don't know. It's too early to tell. First, I gotta go to college for at least a year, then I can apply for the draft. What you trying to do, have my baby before I make it to the pros?"

Alisha sat on my lap. "I hadn't thought of that, but it doesn't seem like a bad idea now that you mention it. Where did you get all these new clothes? Who brought them for you, your coach?"

I turned around and saw Natalie standing behind me with her arms folded, dispersing the crowd. "A'ight, girls, break it up. That's enough. I need to talk to my li'l brother."

As Alisha got off my lap, I tried to hold her by the hand, but Natalie nudged her away.

Alisha looked like she was ready to go.

"Nat, what's good? You fucking up everything," I whined.

"Where did you get these clothes from?" Natalie asked.

I tried to lie, "These clothes? Uhh...I been had these."

Natalie hit me on the head. "Don't lie, Isaiah. I know ya mother ain't buy you those clothes."

Natalie was only a year older than me and a grade ahead of me, but she treated and talked to me like I was five years younger than her. Natalie's mom and my mother were close friends, so after my brother passed, Natalie always came around the house to baby-sit my little sister. We weren't blood, but we treated each other like brother and sister. In addition to being the girlfriend of my best friend, she also helped me with school projects and looked out for me. As crazy as it sounds, she was like my second mother.

Nonchalantly I answered, "It ain't no big deal. I went with Dro and them to Macy's and we boosted them."

"You did what? What is wrong with you? Why couldn't you wait? Didn't I tell you I was gonna take you shopping with my check from the recreation center before school started? What if you would've got caught? Did you think about that? Your mother would have a heart attack. You gonna wait until ya senior year to start fucking up? Huh?" Natalie demanded an answer.

"Nah. I was just tired of walking around looking like an orphan. I wanna wear some fly shit sometime too. I'm tired of everyone whispering about my clothes when I walk by."

Natalie was concerned. "Isaiah, listen," she said emphatically. "I know how you feel, but you've come too far to mess up now. You're not like the rest of ya friends. You have a 3.0 grade point average. If you weren't gonna get a scholarship for basketball, you could get one for academics. Your mother is trying her best to support you and Sable. She couldn't take it if something were to happen to you. You know that. Don't go down the wrong path, Isaiah. Don't let Boota, Wise, Dro or even Snoopy get in the way of your dreams. You hear me?"

When I looked up, Nat was crying.

I pleaded, putting my arms around her, "C'mon, Nat. Don't cry. I'm sorry. It won't happen again."

Natalie punched my stomach. "It better not. I decided to stay home and go to NYU, so I won't be far. Don't think I ain't gonna be checking up on you 'cause I will be." Natalie got up and walked away.

"Hey, Nat, one last thing, yo."

"What?"

"Tell Alisha I said come back here. Why don't you lemme take her in your room so I can beat that."

"Nigga, is you stupid? You're doing too much. Stay out of trouble, ya hear?"

"I will, big sis. I will."

☐☐☐

I'd been home a week and a half and still hadn't got up with anybody. Not that I didn't want to, but I'd been balling for two months straight at basketball camps across the country. I was tired. I spoke to Snoop and Wise a couple of times over the phone, but other than that, I'd been in the crib. Everybody seemed to be doing their own thing.

While I was gone, a lot of things had changed: Boota put down on a house for him, Shamika and the baby; Dro opened up a weed spot in North Baldwin; Wise was working at Dro's weed spot; Danielle moved upstate to Poughkeepsie; and Snoop was getting ready to leave to go to Florida State University.

Snoop was leaving to go to school Sunday morning, so we all decided to hang out on the block Saturday night.

"Who wanna bet a hundred that I roll a five or better?" Boota asked as he shook the dice.

A voice shouted from the back of the crowd that was standing in a circle around the dice game, "I got a hundred on it."

Boota looked at Michelle. "Kiss the dice, baby."

Michelle was a bad bitch. She was Panamanian. She was short, brown skinned, with thick thighs and a fat ass. Michelle was a ride-or-die chick for real. She was a straight hoodrat. She transported work, could bag up, held hammers and everything. Michelle knew Boota had a girl, but she played her position.

She kissed the dice, and Boota rolled a four, five and a three.

Boota picked up the dice and shook them again. "Yeah." Y'all bird-ass niggaz see what it's about to be. I hope y'all know it's double if I roll head cracks."

One of the betting voices shouted out, "It's double if you ace out too, nigga. Don't forget that."

Michelle kissed the dice again, and Boota rolled them off the curb. He rolled a one, two and a three. He aced out. Basically, he lost four hundred dollars.

"Yeah! Lemme get that off you, Boota. I needed that," Malik said, grinning ear to ear.

Boota angrily picked up the dice, rolling them again, "Get what? That one was stuck in the crack? I get another roll. What the fuck is you talking 'bout, nigga?"

Malik picked up the dice as soon as they hit the ground.

Boota stood in front of Malik with his fists balled up. "What the fuck is good, nigga? Niggaz done died for that shit right there, son."

Malik was defiant. "You could get killed for that clown shit you tryin' to pull. I'm from the Bronx, nigga—BX borough. We don't play that sucka shit. I don't know about this other nigga, but I'mma get mine one way or the other."

Malik was a clown-ass, fake tough nigga who moved around our way a year prior from the Bronx. He was a straight-up bitch nigga.

Niggaz always moved to Long Island from the city and tried to get on some Tough Tony shit thinking we was soft. I knew as soon as he started talking that BX shit, we was gonna end up stomping his face in.

Boota calmly explained, "Check this out, you fish nigga. This ain't no BX. This is Long Island. Fuck you and ya borough. Now we can handle this two ways. You could let me roll the dice again or you could get ya jaw broke and still lose ya money. The choice is yours."

Malik shouted, pulling a revolver off his waist, "Oh, nah, B, it ain't even going down like that. Get mine or get naked. Matter of fact, all y'all niggaz lay down."

We all had our hands in the air when Michelle knocked the gun out of his hand. Dro rushed Malik and slammed him into the pavement. Boota stomped him in his face with his size ten-and-a-half Timbs and picked up his revolver.

Boota let off a warning shot in the air. "Strip, nigga."

Malik pleaded taking his clothes off, "A'ight! A'ight! Hold up, son. Don't shoot!

"What? You can't hear?" Boota belted while popping off more shots.

Boota stood over him and shot him twice in the stomach. The whole block cleared out. Boota was drunk. He ain't know how to act when he had that Henny in his system.

Boota screamed, staggering up the block, "Where y'all going?" We ain't even go to the strip club yet. Yo, Snoop, don't leave. Don't go, son. Fuck that basketball shit."

By the time me and Snoop made it to his car, sirens could be heard approaching in the distance.

Snoop started the car. "Where's Boota? We gotta go back and get him. Get in!"

We found Boota in an alley between the bodega and the bar. He was beating Michelle's ass.

Boota backhanded Michelle in the mouth. "It's all ya fault. I was gonna convince Snoop to stay. If you ain't blow ya stink-ass, dick-sucking breath on the dice, everybody would still be here, ya bad-luck bitch."

I yelled from the passenger window, "Boota, what is you doing, son? Don't you hear the fucking sirens?"

"Ski! Snoop! My niggaz," Boota exclaimed before he passed out.

We hopped out the car and dragged Boota into the backseat. Michelle got in on the other side. I don't know who was crazier, Boota or Michelle. This nigga was beating her ass for saving his life, and there she was getting in the car like nothing happened. Before we pulled off, Snoop wiped off the revolver with his T-shirt and threw it in the sewer.

We dropped Boota and Michelle off at a motel and parked in our high school parking lot. After a brief silence, Snoop said, "Yo, Ski, I don't wanna leave."

"What? Why not?" I asked in disbelief.

"I don't wanna leave Nat, son. I know if I leave, we gonna end up breaking up. Long-distance relationships never work out."

"C'mon, nigga. You sound crazy. Nat loves you, B. She ain't no chicken head. She wants you to go to school. What are you talkin' 'bout?"

"It ain't just that, son. My pops is getting sicker every day. I ain't got time to be wasting dreaming, trying to see if I'm gonna make it to the NBA. My pops need treatment now, not in a couple of years. I've been talking to Boota, and I could make that money in a month hustling. Basketball is a dream, but I gotta deal with reality."

"Yo, you buggin', B. You don't even sound right."

"Ski, I don't love this basketball shit as much as you do. I wish I did. I barely touched a basketball all summer. I'm ready to say fuck this shit and get money. I'm too short to go to the pros anyway," Snoop said.

I sat in the passenger seat shaking my head in disgust. I couldn't believe my ears. I'd never heard Snoop doubt himself before.

After a short silence, Snoop asked, "Yo, Ski, Coach said you was putting that work in at them camps. What up wit' dat? Gimme the scoop."

"You should know what it is. A li'l bit of this and a li'l bit of that. You should know how I do from all these years I've been bustin' yo' ass."

"I still got the key to the gym on my key ring. What's up? What you wanna do?" Snoop asked as if I was gonna say no.

We went inside our high school gym and played one on one for hours. Who won? Well, that's up in the air. We argued about that night for years. He said he won, and I said I won.

The next day I woke up at nine in the morning and called Snoop's crib to see if he left or not. His mother said that he was gone, and I felt relieved. I took a deep breath and went back to sleep.

ise was impatient as he tried to open a locker with the master key. "Yo, hurry up, nigga. I told you to let me do it."

I handed him the key. "Damn, nigga. If you wasn't all in my mothafuckin' ear, I would have been had it open a minute ago."

It was a couple of weeks into our senior year of high school. The day before school started, Dro passed down the master key to all the lockers to us. We could open up any locker in the whole school. The previous year, Dro was breaking in a locker every other day. Don't ask me how he got possession of the master key, because I don't have a clue. Dro was just that type of nigga. He was always plotting on something. Since school had started, Wise and I didn't let a day pass without breaking in at least one locker.

Earlier that day, we were at McDonald's at the shopping center by our school on Grand Avenue during lunchtime. We saw a Chinese kid pull a knot out of his book bag to pay for his food. We had to get him. We followed that Chinese kid around for three periods. He took his book bag with him everywhere. Finally, at the end of the eighth period, he put his book bag in his locker. This was our only chance.

I whispered to Wise, pretending to get a drink of water, "Yo, chill. Ms. Margolis is coming. Put the lock back on."

Wise did as I said.

In unison as she walked by, Wise and I said, "Hi, Ms. Margolis."

Suspicious, Ms. Margolis asked, "What are you two doing in the hallway? I hope you two have hall passes."

We both reached in our pockets and pulled out the hallway passes we had stolen from the dean's office.

"Well okay, fellas. Don't stay out here talking much longer." Ms Margolis left, going up the steps to her classroom.

After she was out of sight, Wise got the lock open again, and we searched the bag frantically until we found what we were looking for.

"I got it. Let's roll." Wise put the book bag back in the locker the way he found it and locked it.

We walked into the bathroom and divided the money. "Three-hundred ninety-two, three-hundred ninety-three, three-hundred ninety-four dollars, son. That was a come up," Wise stated, smiling as he passed me my half.

Wise was a kleptomaniac. He stole and sold everything he could get his hands on. He stole cell phones from Radio Shack, frozen food from Pathmark and even food from our high school cafeteria. He said he did it for the money, but I think he did it for the thrill. If he wasn't stealing, he was bagging a honey. And if he wasn't bagging a one, he was rapping. At the time, that's all his life consisted of, and he was the best at all three.

I counted my money again for the hundredth time. "Damn, son. I ain't never had this much money before in my life."

"You never had one hundred and ninety-seven dollars before? That's crazy! You need to come work with me at the weed spot. Dro pays me like fifty dollars a day. All I do is play video games, get pussy and smoke for free," Wise spoke proudly.

"I would never do that. If I ever decided to hustle, which I'm not, I'd hustle for myself. What I look like working for Dro?"

Wise laughed. "I don't know what you'd look like, but you wouldn't be broke. I'd rather work for Dro than to be taking money from my moms and Natalie. And, as a matter of fact, if it wasn't for Dro, you'd still be walking around here looking like Salvation Army kid!"

Wise wasn't lying. If it weren't for Dro, I'd have no gear. I was fly every day now. Tommy Hilfiger, Eddie Bauer, Nautica, Polo, Guess, Girbaud, DKNY—anything that was hot, I had it. I went from hand-me-downs to popping tags every day. At the rate I was going, I was gonna be voted best dressed at the end of the school year.

Wise looked at his watch. "Yo, you going to ninth period? I'm about to head to the studio. You coming through?"

"Nah, I got a math test. I'll get up with you after school."

Wise laughed as we went our separate ways. "A'ight, you lame-ass nigga."

Wise was using all the money he made for studio time at Supreme Sounds Studio in North Baldwin on Grand Avenue, down the block from the 7-Eleven we used to post up in front of. His demo was turning out to be hot. Everybody in our hood was bumping it. Supreme, the studio's owner, started letting Wise record for free. Supreme had a lot of connections in the music industry. He said he knew some people at Def Jam and was gonna take the demo up there when it was completed. Wise damn near lived in that studio. In a week's time, he completed six full songs. Supreme was feeling the songs so much he signed Wise to a management deal. He was shopping the demo to anyone with ears.

A couple of weeks after he finished the demo, I was in the gym shooting around with my coach when Wise came running in the gym.

"Yo, Ski, lemme holla at you for a minute, son," he said, out of breath.

"Hold on, coach. Lemme get a five minute break." I took one last jump shot and ran over to Wise.

Out of breath, I asked, "Yo, what's good, son? We got beef?"

Wise explained, "Nah, son, nuffin' like that. Supreme got me in this talent show at York College in Queens. Mad record labels gonna be there. Mad artists too."

"Word? When is it?"

"This weekend, son. It's the Camp Cool J Talent Show. I need everybody there to gimme support. Don't make no plans for the weekend, a'ight?"

"C'mon, son. That's mandatory. I wouldn't miss that for the world, B."

Wise gave me dap and a hug, "A'ight, son. I'll let you get back to getting ya Michael Jordan on. I'll holla at you later. I gotta go tell Dro, Boota and the rest of the crew."

It was raining the Saturday evening of the talent show. York College auditorium was jam-packed. The line to get in was two blocks long. Supreme rented two stretch limousines for the occasion. When we pulled up to the front of the college, people thought we were stars. Everybody who was anybody was there—Puff Daddy, Busta Rhymes, Funkmaster Flex, Mister Cheeks, Russell Simmons and Kid Capri, just to name a few.

Wise was dressed better than most of the celebrities. He had on a silk black-and-red Versace shirt, black Versace dress pants and red gators to match the design in his shirt. Boota and Dro went half on the outfit and let Wise borrow their Cuban links and Jesus pieces. He looked like he was a multi-platinum rapper.

All of us were there. Me, Boota, Shamika, Dro, Danielle who came down from Poughkeepsie, Natalie and even Snoop came all the way back up from Florida for the weekend to show support. None of us would have missed that show for the world.

Our seats were about fifteen rows up. Tracy Morgan was the master of ceremonies. After he cracked jokes for a while, LL Cool J came to the stage and spoke. "I just wanna thank everybody for coming out tonight. This is one of the ways that I like giving back the most. These are all hungry unsigned artists who up until tonight have never been seen or heard before. There are some new stars back there who are gonna do some big things, and I'm glad that I've had the opportunity to bring them to you first. So without further ado, let's get this show poppin'."

The crowd roared, the lights dropped, and the first artist took the stage.

The show was about an hour and a half long. Wise and Supreme went backstage to prepare for the performance. Luck was on Wise's side that night. He got the best slot to perform. Last. Before he went backstage, Wise looked at all of us and said, "Hold me down y'all. This is gonna be a night that none of us will ever forget for the rest of our lives."

Wise was right. None of us would ever forget that night.

Wise came on stage like he owned it. He did excerpts from two of the songs of his demo. After that, he cut the beat off and freestyled a cappella. He freestyled about everything from the artists and celebrities in the audience to other artists who performed. The allotted time for each artist was only five minutes, but they let Wise go for fifteen. LL had to come on stage and snatch the mike from him.

The crowd gave him a standing ovation.

After the show there was an after party at Club Mercedes on Jamaica Avenue in Queens. Wise and Supreme were talking to executive after executive. We didn't even get a chance to talk to him after the show.

I was drunk as hell. I was stumbling, bumping into people, and stepping on people's shoes. Natalie must've seen me stumbling around and walked me back to our table.

Natalie asked in a motherly voice, "Isaiah, are you okay? You look sick. Sit down and drink some water. You don't even drink. What are you doing? Maybe we should take him home, Snoopy."

Snoop was aggravated. "That nigga is a'ight. Stop babying him. If he wanna drink, he can drink. Who the fuck is you, his mother?"

Natalie ignored Snoop's previous statement. "Isaiah, do you want to leave?"

Snoop looked at me, looked at Natalie and then took a deep breath. I wanted to go home, but I ain't wanna ruin Snoop and Natalie's first weekend together, so I said, "Nah. Good look, Nat. I'm starting to feel a li'l better already. Why don't you and Snoop go dance or somethin'? We suppose to be celebrating, right?"

"Only if you're sure you are all right," Natalie replied.

"I'm good," I said, lying through my teeth.

Natalie pulled Snoop by the hand. "Come dance with me, Snoopy. This is my song."

Snoop, still mad from their exchange said, "Come on, Nat, chill. I don't feel like it right now. Leave me the fuck alone."

Natalie stuck her tongue out at Snoop. "Forget you then, punk."

Natalie walked to the dance floor and started dancing by herself. As she was dancing, some brown skin older dude with dreads and a suit on started dancing with her. It started off innocent at first, but after a while he started grinding on her.

Snoop got up, ran straight to the dance floor and pushed the man who was so big he didn't budge. I immediately got up out of my seat and ran toward the dance floor.

Snoop yelled, pointing his finger in the man's face, "What the fuck you doin' grinding on my girl like that?"

The older man said calmly fixing his tie, "Chill out, youngblood. We were just dancing. It was all innocent. Besides, I ain't hear ya girl complaining."

Natalie shouted, "Snoopy, calm down. Let it go. Let's just go home."

Snoop ignored Natalie's plea and swung. The older man weaved it, rushed Snoop and slammed him on the floor like a rag doll. I kicked the man in the back of the head, but he still had Snoop in a tight headlock and wouldn't let him go. I kicked him several times, to no avail. The man was just too big. The bouncers broke it up before he managed to put Snoop to sleep. The bouncers were holding the older man with his arms behind his back, so when Snoop got up off the floor, he punched him in the eye with a left and drew blood. The older man started going crazy. It took four bouncers to hold him back from getting at Snoop.

The man screamed as he was being escorted out the club, "This ain't the last you gonna hear of me, youngblood. You don't know who you fucking with, you young punk."

"Eat a dick," Snoop replied.

Natalie smacked Snoop and ran away in tears. Snoop followed her.

Natalie shouted frantically at the top of her lungs, "It's over, Snoopy. I'm tired of all this bullshit. You always find a way to embarrass me. I hate you." Tears were pouring down her face. "If I wanted a thug, I'd get one. I don't know what I ever saw in you. You ain't shit, and you ain't never gonna be shit."

Snoop tried to explain his actions, "Nat, what do you mean? That nigga was out of pocket. I had to defend you."

"I'm grown, Snoopy. I can defend myself. You never listened to me."

Snoop begged, "Nat, I'm sorry, baby. Listen to me. Just let me talk."

Natalie shot back, "I don't have anything to say to you. It's over, Snoopy. I'm taking a cab home. What kind of father would you have made anyway?"

Snoop was dumbfounded. "What?"

Natalie pushed Snoop and headed out the club. "I'm pregnant, Snoopy. Damn. Are you that stupid?"

Snoop ran after Natalie and caught up with her in the parking lot. It was pouring rain.

"Nat, you can't leave me. I ain't shit without you. You're the only good thing I have in my life. Do you know how much stress I'm under right now? My pops is getting sicker every day. I'm all the way in Tallahassee, Florida, miserable because I'm away from you. It's killing me, Nat. I'm under so much pressure right now. I'm going crazy. I promise you I won't spazz out like that no more. Just don't leave me."

Snoop placed his hand on Natalie's stomach. "I love you. I want us to be a family. Let's go back inside and get our coats and call a cab. We gonna catch pneumonia standing out here in this rain like this."

Snoop put his arm around Natalie, and they started walking back toward the club holding hands. Natalie loved Snoop, and even though she always threatened to leave him, she wasn't going anywhere. They were about twenty feet from the entrance when they heard tires screeching.

A voice called out from the car, "Hey, youngblood. I know you ain't think it was over."

Snoop turned to see who it was and saw that it was the older dude from the club. He was driving a GMC 1500 truck with the windows down and had niggaz in the front and backseats with guns pointed in their direction.

Snoop yelled to Natalie, "Natalie, go. Hurry up."

Snoop was about to start running behind her when shots rang out.

The first two shots were direct hits. They both landed directly in the back of Natalie's head. Natalie didn't even have the chance to scream. Brain fragments fell on the pavement, and Natalie's lifeless body slumped to the ground.

"No! Nooooooo," Snoop yelled, running over to Natalie.

The people in the truck started letting off shots crazy. As Snoop was running over to Natalie, he was spun completely around by a bullet to his shoulder, and then another hit him in the chest. Another shot hit his leg. Snoop dropped to the ground right next to Natalie. When he hit the pavement, he laid on top of Natalie to shield her from the bullets, but it was too late. Bullets continued to hit Snoop in his arms and legs.

By the time we made it outside, we saw Snoop and Natalie lying in a pool of their blood. Somehow Boota had managed to sneak his gun inside the club, and as the truck was zooming out the parking lot, Boota emptied his whole clip at the truck to no avail.

I ran straight over to Snoop and Natalie. Remarkably, Snoop was still conscious.

Dro screamed, "Yo, Snoop? Snoop? Hang on, son. An ambulance is on the way."

Snoop cried out, "Nat's dead! She's dead, B. Oh my God. They killed my baby."

I stood over him, and the first thing I noticed was the wound to his leg. His knee had a hole in it the size of a fist. It looked like his leg was gonna fall off at any minute.

I shouted, "Snoop, get off Nat so we can see where she's hit."

Snoop yelled with a mouth full of blood, "She's dead, son! She's dead! It's all my fault. It should be me instead of her!"

Dro and Boota rolled Snoop off Natalie, and that's when I saw it with my own eyes. Natalie had a hole inside her head so big, I could actually see inside it. Her eyes were wide open. Up until that point, I had never seen a dead body that close. I threw up. It was all surreal. I stood in the same spot in shock crying. I couldn't believe it. Natalie was dead, and Snoop didn't look far from it. Wise was right. I'd never forget this night for the rest of my life. Natalie was like my sister.

That night, Snoop lost three of the most important things in his life, Natalie, his unborn child and basketball. He didn't know it then, but he'd never be able to play basketball again. I knew at that moment that Snoop would never be the same. None of us would. Especially me.

A year after Natalie was murdered, in October 1997, Boota was still hustling selling cocaine, and he and Shamika had their second child—a baby girl they named Natalie. Snoop had been out of the hospital for about six months. He'd been in a coma for three months and had sustained two punctured lungs, one of which had to be removed; a lacerated liver and four broken ribs. One gunshot wound was inches away from his heart. It was a miracle that he was still alive. While Snoop was comatose, he lost more than twenty pounds. His knee had to be surgically reconstructed, and he had to go to physical therapy to learn how to walk again.

Dro shut down his weed spot and started robbing everything with a safe. Roach and Dro were on a robbing spree. Boota's older brother Roach had just come home after a year and a half bid at Sing Sing for burglary.

Ski was upstate New York at a junior college named Ulster on a basketball scholarship. Natalie's death hit him hard. After Natalie died, Ski stopped going to class and started drinking and smoking heavy. Most days, Ski spent the whole day visiting Snoop in the hospital. No one could get through to him. His best friend was in a coma, and Natalie, who Ski looked at like an older sister was dead. Ski snapped into such a deep depression that he failed off the basketball team and had to go to summer school to get his high school diploma. All of the major division one schools who were interested stopped sending letters, and Ski was forced to go to Ulster to get his grades up. The coach there got Ski and a couple of other players apartments off campus in a nearby town called Kingston. After Snoop got out of the hospital, Ski started to snap out of his depression.

Wise was in Nassau County Jail on a rape charge. He was dealing with a girl named Melissa who was madly in love with him. She did anything and everything he asked of her, including fucking his friends. When Wise got tired of her and stopped returning her calls, she cried rape. Everyone knew the charge was bullshit. It wasn't a matter of if he got off. It was all a matter of when he got off.

A chubby kid at the jail that everyone called Harlem was talking, "Ayo, Wise. You kind of nice wit' the rapping shit."

"Good look, son! I'm from Baldwin Long Island," Wise answered, sitting in his cell brushing his hair.

"Baldwin? I ain't never heard of that shit! By the way you rhyme, a nigga would think you was from Harlem or Brooklyn, kid."

Wise had just finished battling some kid from the Bronx who everybody claimed was the best in jail. Everyone thought that the kid was gonna eat Wise up, but to their surprise, Wise got out on him. Harlem was the only one on the tier who heard Wise rhyme before that. Harlem took bets with everyone in the entire unit. When Wise won the battle, Harlem won more than a thousand dollars in commissary.

Wise explained, "Yeah, son. Baldwin is right in the middle of Hempstead and Freeport."

"Yo, you ain't never try to get a deal or nuffin'? If I could spit like you, I would be a millionaire."

"For a minute I was trying to get on, but it ain't really all about how you spit, it's all about who you know. It's a lot of politics in that shit, son. Na'mean?"

After the talent show, Wise had meetings with a few labels, but nothing came out of them. They kept sending him to the studio to make new songs for his demo, but when he did they kept postponing his meetings. Wise ended up getting sick of the whole waiting process and gave up.

"You should've got a manager. My man Smalls got a lot of connections. He could get you on. I'm telling you, fam, he'll get you plugged in. I'll introduce him to you. He'll have you doing shows and the whole nine," Harlem suggested.

Wise became disinterested in the direction of the conversation. "Good look, son, but I ain't really trying to fuck wit' it like that no more. I already been through all of that. I had a manger, did shows and all that, B."

"Say word? Where you did shows at?"

"I did the Lyricist Lounge, Camp Cool J Talent Show and—"

Harlem cut Wise off midsentence. "You performed at Camp Cool J? When?"

"Last year."

"Oh shit, son. My man Smalls was there last year. He probably heard of you before."

Wise continued proudly, "Anybody who was at that show would definitely remember me. I tore that shit down."

"Yeah. I know you heard what happened at the after party? Some niggaz tried to stunt on my man. They ain't know who they was fucking wit'. My manz and them caught one of the niggaz and his bitch in the parking lot. Straight aired 'em out. I'm telling you, B, I run with killers. Niggaz in here be thinking I'm frontin'. That night dem niggaz ain't know who they was fucking wit'."

Wise spoke sarcastically, giving Harlem dap, "I bet they know now."

"Damn right they do. Smalls is the king of Harlem."

Wise could not believe how lucky he was. "Smalls sounds just like the type of nigga I need to get on. Lemme get ya information before you go home, son. I'mma give ya man a shot at managing me."

"No doubt, fam, I got you! I'mma call him tonight and let him know that I'm in here with you. It's a small world, ain't it?"

Wise answered, handing Harlem a sheet of loose-leaf paper, "Damn sure is, my nigga. Damn sure is."

☐☐☐

Boota shouted from the living room of his and Shamika's brand-new three-bedroom house, "Hey, Ayana, come here for a minute. Daddy needs to talk to you."

Ayana smiled brightly looking up at her father. "Yes, Daddy?"

Ayana was Boota's oldest daughter. She was three years old, but could sit and have a conversation with you like she was a grown woman. Boota was doing good for himself. He traded his '96 Maxima for a brand-new '97 Lexus GS and bought Shamika a '97 Acura Legend. Boota was also putting Shamika through school to become an LPN. Life couldn't be better for Boota. The only problem Boota had was that he spent too much money. For as long as he'd been hustling, he should've been re-ing up with multiple bricks, but he wasn't. He kept re-ing up with the same big eighth time and time again.

Boota grinned across the room to Shamika. "Ayana, when you grow up, promise Daddy you won't be a ho like your mother."

Ayana's eyes, big and bright focused on her father, hanging on every word. "Okay, Daddy, I promise, but what's a ho?"

Boota responded, laughing, "What's a ho? Yo' momma is a ho. Don't be like your mother or your aunties. They had kids when they were in their teens. That's a ho."

People would get offended by the things that came out of Boota's mouth, but with Boota, they had to accept it as a joke. He was a comedian.

When the phone rang, Boota answered on the third ring, "Yo."

"This is a call from…Wise. The cost of this call is three dollars and forty-five cents for the first minute and fifteen cents each additional minute. To accept this call, say yes at the tone. To decline this call, hang up…"

Boota said yes at the tone.

"Boota, what up you, black-ass nigga?" Wise asked from the other end of the line.

"Shit, I'm just sitting here with my three favorite bitches."

"Word? Who you got over there?" Wise said.

"Shamika, Ayana and Natalie."

"You a bugged-out nigga, son. How you gonna call ya daughters bitches, son?"

"It is what it is. So what's crackin'? You need some more money?"

"Nah. I got information on who's responsible for that Natalie situation. I know who did it."

Boota was so excited, he almost dropped the phone. "Word?"

Wise continued, "Yeah, this big-mouth Harlem nigga slipped up and told me. He gonna introduce me to him when I touch back down."

Boota asked, "Yeah?" That's what's up. What ya lawyer talkin' about?"

"I'll be home in a minute—no more than two months. Come check me this weekend so I can tell you everything. Tell everybody what's up."

Boota joked, "No question, my nigga. Stay up. Don't drop that soap, son, please."

"Yeah, a'ight. Fuck you, nigga. One."

"One."

Meanwhile, Dro and Roach were blacked out in a stolen Honda Accord two blocks away from the check cashing spot they were about to rob.

Dro spoke from the passenger seat, "Yo, Roach, spin around the block one more time."

"For what? Let's get it over wit' now. This shit is sweet."

"Just spin around the fucking block, B. I wanna see if them people left that was in the Dodge Neon," Dro said, frustrated.

Roach put the car into drive. "The people in that Neon are kids smoking weed. They ain't worried about us, so why are we worried about them?"

Roach was Boota's older brother. He was nothing like Boota. He was even quieter than Dro. He rarely spoke a word. People took Dro's shyness for arrogance, but people took Roach's quietness for weirdness. Roach was a straight criminal. He was Dro's right hand man, and he was the one who taught Dro how to steal cars and put him on to doing robberies and burglaries. Roach stole cars, did home invasions, pulled street stickups and robbed businesses. Roach even robbed banks by himself. Roach was down with anything that could make him a dollar. He was a live wire. Roach and Dro were tighter than OJ and AC. Roach was brown skin with sharp, keen facial features. He was five feet ten inches tall with a slim build and wore a short afro. Roach was the oldest out of the whole clique, but you couldn't tell by looking at him.

Dro spoke to Roach as they watched a police car pass the spot, "Yo, I bet you happy we took another lap now."

Roach spoke more to himself than to Dro, "I watched this spot for weeks. Cops been patrolling every twenty minutes on the hour. What the fuck are they doing here?"

The cop car passed and went down the block.

Dro was ready. "Roach, you ready?"

"Been ready."

Dro cocked back his .45 and got out of the car. "Let's go get it then."

The plan was simple. There were two employees behind the registers and another employee in the back with the safe—two females and one male. Dro and Roach were gonna enter through the front door bare faced posing as customers, two minutes apart. When Roach entered, he was to brandish his nine-millimeter and lay down the two employees who were behind the register and tied them up. While Roach was doing that, Dro was to go to the room with the safe and do the same to the male employee.

After all three employees were tied up, Roach was to clean out the registers while Dro emptied out the safe and took the videotape. Even the getaway was smooth. They were gonna leave out the employees' exit in the back of the store, run down the alley and enter another stolen car that they had parked in a nearby Kentucky Fried Chicken parking lot. From there, they were gonna drive straight down Sunrise Highway to the Lynbrook train station, switch clothes and drive home in separate cars taking different routes. All of this would be done in ten minutes time. Dro was a perfectionist.

Roach shouted as he entered the store, "Ayo! Everybody lay the fuck on the floor. Y'all know what it is. Don't try to be a hero, 'cause I will put you on the front page of tomorrow's paper. Don't be the dumb black bitch who died for some white people's money."

Dro was at the counter pretending to be scratching off a lottery ticket when Roach came in. As soon as he saw Roach enter the store, Dro hopped over the counter and ran straight to the safe.

Dro, with his nickel-plated .45, calmly said, "I'm gonna ask you one time, and one time only to gimme the key."

The man replied, handing him the key, "Please don't shoot. It's right here."

Dro took the key from him, pushed him back to the floor and duct taped him.

Meanwhile, in the front, Roach had both girls taped up and had just finished cleaning out the first register.

Roach shouted, "We have one minute and three seconds. Hurry up, fat boy."

As soon as Roach finished cleaning out the second register, Dro came walking out the room with the safe and a book bag full of money.

Dro asked Roach if he was ready.

"Let's move," Roach screamed.

They left out the employees' exit, ran down the alleyway to the stolen car in the KFC parking lot and drove down Sunrise Highway to Lynbrook train station.

As they were throwing their black hoodies and jeans in a Dumpster, Dro turned to Roach and asked, "What's the time, B?"

Roach responded to himself as if he could not believe they pulled it off, "Nine minutes and forty-eight seconds. You're a genius, B."

Roach and Dro got away with fifty-five thousand dollars in cash.

*S*malls spoke to Wise as the engineer finished running the play back. "Hey, youngblood, that was fire. You gonna make me a whole lotta money, Wise."

Wise smiled. "Good look, my nigga. You heard me big you up on the second verse?"

Smalls laughed, shaking Wise. "You know I did. That was the best part of the song."

That January, Wise and Smalls were at the Hit Factory in Manhattan working on tracks for Wise's debut album. Wise's case had been dismissed, and he had come home from the county jail the first week of November. He and Smalls met for the first time in person two weeks after that. Since the met, they were inseparable. They hung out in Smalls' hood around 145th Street in Harlem, they went to countless industry parties, and Smalls even took Wise with him to Las Vegas for New Year's. Smalls not only liked the way Wise rapped, he also liked Wise as a person. Hanging out with Wise made him feel young again. Wise was the son Smalls had never had.

Smalls handed Wise his jacket. "Youngblood, let's go for a ride. I got a surprise for you."

When Smalls asked Wise to go for a ride with him, Wise's heart dropped. He knew Smalls was a dangerous man. He heard Smalls say that to a man before and the man was never seen or heard from again. Wise's biggest fear was that Smalls was on to him. He knew he'd surely kill him.

Wise was scared. "Yo, Smalls, I gotta finish up my ad libs."

Smalls raised his voice a little. "I ain't asking you, youngblood. I'm telling you. I'm the boss. You can finish up tomorrow."

"You the boss, B. Let's roll then," Wise answered tapping his feet nervously.

Wise was terriried. He couldn't stay still and he was avoiding eye contact with Smalls because he couldn't stop his lip from twitching.

Smalls was born and raised in Harlem. He got his name in the early eighties extorting and killing drug dealers. His name was well known and feared in all five boroughs of New York City. Smalls had a ten-block kingdom from 135th to 145th streets. He had his hands in everything from Coke, crack, dope, weed, ecstasy, guns, gambling houses and prostitution. It was rumored that he made close to two million dollars a month. Smalls also owned several legit businesses such as Laundromats, liquor stores and dollar stores, but he really wanted to break into the music industry. He wanted desperately to be a celebrity.

Smalls was brown skin, six feet three inches tall, three hundred pounds and as big as a house. Smalls was in his late thirties, but he looked and acted much younger.

Smalls and Wise jumped into Smalls' Range Rover and headed to a house in Scarsdale, New York, a suburb just outside of the Bronx.

Smalls looked to Wise as he turned off the ignition. "Youngblood, I know what you're up to. Nothing gets passed me. Do you know why I brought you here tonight?"

Wise was so scared that he could have pissed himself, but he remained calm.

Wise looked around nervously. "Smalls, what you talking 'bout?"

"Get out the car, youngblood. It's time I gave you this. Come with me."

Wise took a deep breath and got out the truck and walked down the dark driveway with Smalls to the front of the garage. As they stood there, Smalls reached into his suit jacket pocket and pulled out a garage opener. When Wise saw him reach into his jacket he flinched and put up his hands.

Smalls began to laugh and smacked Wise on the back. "Relax, youngblood. I ain't gonna hurt you."

Smalls pressed down on the garage door opener and unveiled a brand-new CLK Mercedes Benz with a red ribbon on top.

Smalls passed the keys to Wise. "That's all you, youngblood."

"What? Get the fuck outta here! You serious?"

"Youngblood, I've been noticing that you've been giving me a lot of signals that you need some transportation, so I got you this. You represent me now. I can't have you taking the train to Harlem."

"Smalls, I don't know what to say, B."

"Just keep making them hot records. Look at this as a signing bonus. Now listen, Wise, I brought you to my house tonight. I got guys who have been down with me over fifteen years who don't know where I live. Nobody knows where I live. That's how much love I got for you, Wise. Don't ever cross me, you hear?"

Wise responded by giving Smalls dap and a hug. "Never, my nigga. Never."

Smalls placed his hands on Wise's shoulder and walked him to the garage. "C'mon, youngblood, don't get all mushy on me. Come inside and meet my old lady and my two daughters. I've told them a lot about you."

Wise had the break he'd been waiting for for months, and it was sooner than he expected. Payback.

￼ ￼ ￼

When a phone rang, everyone in the Caravan reached for their phones.

Snoop pulled out his phone. "It's me, y'all. It's me." Snoop answered, "Yo, what up?"

Ski was on the other end. "Yo, where y'all at?" I've been at the train station waiting on y'all niggaz for almost an hour. What's poppin'? We got a change of plans or something?"

"Ski, I ain't even gonna do you like this. Get back on the train and go to school," Snoop replied.

"What? Why? Niggaz ain't handling that tonight?"

"Yeah, *we* handling it tonight," Snoop said.

"What you mean?"

"Exactly what you heard, Ski. You ain't ready for the shit we about to do, son, trust me. Go back to school, son."

Ski shouted into the phone, "Yo! Fuck y'all niggaz, B. Nat was like my sister. If anybody is supposed to be there, it's me! Come pick me up, Snoop."

The line disconnected.

Ski took the bus all the way from Kingston in Upstate New York back to Long Island to partake in running in Smalls' crib. Boota, Snoop, Dro and Roach didn't think Ski was ready to go all out like they planned. Ski was a basketball player in their eyes. They all looked at him as if he were their kid brother. Ski had plenty of fights in the hood and was far from being soft, but he never busted his gun before. He had never put any major work in. They had all planned to keep what they were about to do a secret, but Wise slipped up and told Ski on the phone, and he insisted on coming. They told Ski to meet them at the train station, but they had no plans whatsoever on picking him up. Ski was irate. He wanted badly to seek revenge on the person who took Natalie's life.

Roach angrily bit on his bottom lip and nodded his head. He wasn't pleased at the circumstances, but gave his consent. "Fuck it! If he wanna come through, let him come through. That nigga is a grown man."

Snoop looked furiously at Roach. "Nah! Fuck that shit. I don't want Ski involved in none of this."

"If Wise ain't open up his big mothafuckin' mouth, Ski wouldn't even know," Boota said from the backseat.

When the phone rang again, Dro looked at Snoop. "You know who it is. You might as well just turn ya phone off."

Boota added, "Nah, don't do son like that. Don't have him waiting on us all night."

Snoop picked up his phone on the tenth ring and shouted in the phone, "Yo, Ski, I told you you can't come. Take ya ass back to school, man. This ain't for you."

"Warren? Is that you?"

"Mom? What's up? What's wrong? What you doing up this late?"

Snoop was shocked it was his mother on the other end and not Ski.

"Warren, I need you to come home right now. I got bad news. Your father passed away tonight."

"What? I'll…I'll be there in a minute."

Snoop hung up the phone.

Wise looked to Snoop with concern. "Yo, was that ya moms? What happened, son? Everything a'ight?"

Snoop was somber, covering his face with his hands. "That was my moms…my pops just died, yo."

Boota sighed. "Damn, son. Yo, Dro, we gonna have to do this another night. Drive to Snoop's crib."

Dro shot back, "No kidding! C'mon, B, that's obvious."

Snoop pounded his fist in his other hand. "I gotta take this shit out on somebody, B. This nigga is gonna pay tonight."

Dro looked back at Snoop from the rearview mirror. "Chill, Snoop. You need to have a clear head. Go home and be wit' ya family. They need you right now. We'll get this cocksucker another time."

Snoop shouted back with tears welling up in his eyes, "Nigga, did I fucking stutter? Tonight is the mothafuckin' night, with or without y'all niggaz. He killed Nat, B. He gotta pay."

The whole crew was silent. Dro made a U-turn and got on the Southern State Parkway headed to Smalls' crib in Scarsdale.

It was about 1:45 A.M. when Smalls pulled up in front of his house in his 600 Mercedes Benz. Smalls put his car in park, turned off the headlights and popped his trunk to retrieve the shopping bags of clothes he had brought for his wife and daughters earlier. As notorious and infamous as he was on the street, Smalls was a family man at heart. The only time he ever felt at peace was when he spent time at home with them.

Smalls thought he heard footsteps behind him in the distance, so he dropped the bags, grabbed his .38 off his waist and spun around quickly with his gun out. No one was anywhere in sight. Smalls shook his head, took a deep breath and put his gun back on his waist.

Smalls thought out loud to himself, "I'm buggin'! Nobody even knows where I live."

Smalls was paranoid. He was always on point. That paranoia was what had kept him from being in the ground or in a prison cell for the last fifteen years. He closed the trunk, grabbed his bags and walked to his front door. After he unlocked it, he bent down to pick up his bags and felt a sharp pain in the back of his head. As he regained his balance, he looked up and saw three guns pointed at him.

"Don't move faggot," Dro said.

Smalls lunged for one of the guns, but Dro managed to shoot him once in the stomach, dropping Smalls on his doorstep.

Dro and Boota carried Smalls in the house by his arms and left him on the living room floor. Roach gave a signal to the crew in the Caravan, and Snoop and Wise came running out, each with garbage bags. Boota and Dro proceeded to stomp Smalls out, while Snoop and Wise ran through the house looking for his wife. Boota, Dro and Roach picked Smalls up off the floor and sat him in his dining room oak wood chair and duct taped him. Smalls' white dress shirt was soaked in blood, and his face had several wounds that were also bleeding.

Snoop was upstairs in Smalls' mansion opening every door searching for Smalls' wife. Smalls' house was huge. He had seven bedrooms and four-and-a-half bathrooms. The last door that Snoop checked on the west wing was the one he was searching for—Smalls' bedroom. Smalls' wife had somehow slept through the whole ordeal and was on top of the covers nude.

Snoop let off three shots in the air, and Smalls' wife woke up screaming and scared for her life.

Snoop dragged her out of the bed by her arms. "Shut the fuck up, bitch. Don't say shit. Make another sound and I'll really give you something to scream about."

When he finally made it down the steps, Smalls' wife was barely conscious. He dragged her right in front of Smalls' feet and left her there.

Smalls shouted, "Please, man. Please. You can have the money, the drugs and even kill me, but please…please don't harm my family. They have nothing to do with this." Looking up and noticing Wise, he continued. "Wise, how could you do this to me? I would have given you anything you wanted!"

Snoop gun butted Smalls in the jaw, knocking out three of his teeth. "Shut the fuck up, nigga. Remember me, faggot? Huh? Remember me?" Snoop waved his gun in Smalls' face.

Smalls looked at Snoop and recognized him immediately. He knew then he was a dead man.

"You killed my girl and my baby, nigga. Yeah! It's me nigga! Payback is a muthafucka, ain't it? What happened to all that tough shit now, huh?"

Snoop shot Smalls in both of his feet.

Smalls yelled in pain, trying to wiggle out of the tape to no avail. "You mothafucka. Untie me and fight like a real man. Punk."

Snoop gun butted Smalls again. "Nah, nigga. Ain't shit fair. You in my world now, nigga. You gonna meet God tonight, muthafucka, but I'mma make you suffer first."

After Snoop gun butted Smalls again, Smalls' wife got off the floor and lunged toward Snoop, reaching for his gun. Snoop backhanded her with the gun and sent her back to the floor.

Theresa strongly resembled Phylicia Rashad from the Cosby Show. She and Smalls had been married for ten years. They attended high school in Harlem together and she was the mother of his two daughters.

Snoop grinned. "Oh! You got a feisty one, huh? I know what she wants. I know what'll make her calm down."

Snoop picked Smalls' wife up off the oak wood floor and bent her over the dining room table, right next to Smalls.

Snoop began unbuttoning his jeans. "I know what you want, bitch. You want this dick, don't you? I seen the way you've been looking at me. Hey, Smalls? Lemme borrow ya wife for a test drive. Do you mind?"

Helpless and in pain, Smalls cried out, "I'mma kill you, mothafucka. You're a dead man.

Snoop pulled out his dick and entered Smalls' wife roughly from behind. She shouted out in agony begging for Smalls to help her as Snoop pounded away in her.

"Ahhhhh!" Theresa screamed in pain and horror.

"Yeah! That's it, girl. I knew you wanted me. Hey, Smalls. Ya wife got some good pussy," Snoop said as she screamed.

Smalls tried to get out of his chair, but he couldn't move. He couldn't do anything but look on helplessly as Snoop raped his wife two feet away from him.

Snoop yelled, "Take this dick, bitch. Take it."

Smalls' wife cried out again, "Help! Help! Do something! Owww! Uhhhh! Uhhhh!"

Boota, Dro, Wise and Roach all looked on in shock. They all thought Snoop was taking it too far, but were scared to say something.

"Yeah! Here it comes. Look at me, bitch. Look at me while I'm giving you this dick. Uhhhh," Snoop shouted as he came inside of her.

Once he was done, Snoop shot her three times in the back of her head. His dick was still inside of her when he killed her. Brain fragments flew all over Smalls' face. Snoop pulled out and the woman's lifeless body fell to the floor.

Smalls cried out with tears running down his face, "Oh God! Theresa! Theresa! Theresa! Nooooo!"

Snoop pulled up his pants. "What you crying for, big man? Her pussy was trash anyway.

Smalls shouted in anger, "You're dead. Your family is dead. You'll never get away with this."

"Pass me that knife Wise." Snoop demanded.

Dro grew impatient. "Yo, Snoop, just kill the mothafucka so we can get out of here, B. Enough is enough."

Snoop had a demented look in his eyes. "Wise, what the fuck are you waiting for? Pass me the mothafuckin' knife, nigga."

Wise looked around and didn't know if he should or not.

Boota spoke up. "Give it to him, Wise. Yo, Snoop, you got ten more minutes. If he ain't dead by the time we finish searching this house, I'mma kill him myself."

Wise passed Snoop the knife and he, Boota, Dro and Roach ransacked the house in search of money, drugs and jewelry.

Snoop tortured Smalls who was in and out of consciousness from the shot he took in the stomach and the two shots he took to his feet. Snoop cut Smalls' fingers off one by one, stabbed him multiple times in the legs and arms and shot him in the balls. Smalls was still breathing, but was unconscious. When Wise, Dro, Roach and Boota came back in the dining room, Snoop opened Smalls' mouth and shot him three times. Smalls was unrecognizable at this point.

Boota found ten kilos of cocaine and a little over sixty thousand dollars in cash and some jewelry. As they were walking out the door, one of Smalls' daughters came running down the steps crying, "Mommy! Daddy!"

Dro turned around. "Yo, Wise, I thought you tied them kids up."

Wise looked away. "Nah, I couldn't tie them up, so I just locked them in the bathroom."

Snoop was pissed. "Damn. Now we gotta kill the kids too."

Boota looked at Snoop angrily. "What? Kill the kids? Nigga, is you buggin'?"

Snoop was serious. "A witness is a witness. That li'l girl could fuck around and get us life."

Snoop tried to run and pick the girl up, but she ran up the stairs. Snoop followed her, and Boota followed them. The little girl reminded Boota of his daughters. He had watched Snoop rape a woman, but he wasn't gonna allow him to kill a kid. When Boota made it to the bathroom, it was too late. Snoop had the gun to the little girl's head and pulled the trigger.

"Damn, son. My shit is empty. Boota, lemme see ya hammer."

Boota dragged Snoop out of the bathroom and out of the house, "Come on, son, let's get the fuck outta here. You going crazy, son. Let's go."

They drove to Long Island in silence. No one could believe what Snoop had done. To them, Snoop had gone crazy. If it weren't for Boota, Snoop would've killed the two little girls. Nobody knew what to do next. They had avenged Natalie's death, but nobody felt better because of it. Not even Snoop.

*M*ichelle gazed into my eyes. "Don't these candles make dinner so romantic?"

I was a bit annoyed. "What are you talking 'bout? I ain't got these candles lit to set the mood. I got these candles lit because I ain't got no electricity. Tell me, Michelle...what's romantic about having no electricity? Eat ya food."

It was April 1998, and I was in the living room of my three-bedroom apartment with a girl I was dealing with from school. College was nothing like I thought it would be. Halfway through the season, the athletic director at my school cancelled the remaining twelve games of the season and fired our coach because eight of the twelve players were academically ineligible. I was in the middle of having an All-American season. I was starting to gain attention from all the major Division I schools again. To make matters worse, our coach didn't even call to tell any of his players he'd been fired. We found out through the newspaper like everyone else. Our coach abandoned us. Not only did my roommate not have a way to pay the rent for our apartment anymore, but when we went to register for school for the second semester, we were told that we never had scholarships. Most of the players didn't care, but since I was one of the two players who passed my classes, I was heated. All of the other players went back home, but I no longer had a home to go to. My mother had gotten laid off from her job and couldn't pay the rent, so she had gotten evicted. She and my sister were living in a shelter in Brooklyn. I could've moved back to Long Island and stayed at Boota or Snoop's crib, but I decided against it. I was used to having my own place. Besides, I was still tight at them for not letting me go with them to ride on Natalie's killer.

Michelle spoke after a brief silence. "Isaiah? What are we?"

Angrily I threw my fork onto the plate, "Here we go again. What do you mean, what are we? We're two humans sitting in the dark eating dinner. C'mon, Michelle. Don't start up, please. I ain't in the mood."

Michelle was a girl I had met at school who was deeply in love with me, and I knew it. Since my coach had gotten fired, Michelle walked three miles to my apartment every day with a plate of home cooked food to make sure I ate. She found me a job at a telemarketing agency and even helped me pay rent when I was short. Michelle was a good girl. She was everything a girlfriend was supposed to be, but at the time I didn't know it. Michelle was honey complected with light brown eyes and shoulder-length hair. She had huge double D titties and thick thighs. She was pretty, but she wasn't my type. At the time I thought that wifey had to be model material.

Michelle stood up and folded her arms over her chest. "Well, I hope you're not seeing anyone else, because I couldn't deal with that. I hope you're at least giving me that much respect."

"Or what? What if I am?" I shot back intentionally to provoke an argument.

"Then we couldn't have sex anymore. We'd just have to be friends."

"A'ight, then…well I guess we'll just have to be friends."

"Oh, my God! I can't believe this! I can't believe you! How could you do this to me?" Michelle screamed as tears began to run down her face. She angrily bolted out the door.

After seeing Michelle's reaction, I immediately regretted my last statement. Michelle was a good girl and didn't deserve to be treated that way. I quickly caught up with her outside.

"Michelle," I called. "Come here. I'm sorry." I pleaded and she stopped. I wrapped my arms around her. She continued to cry in my arms.

"What's wrong with me? Why don't you want me? I'm trying my hardest to show you that I care. What am I not good enough or something?" she asked.

"Michelle, stop crying. It's not you. It's me. I'm sorry for saying what I said. It's not true and I didn't mean it. I'm just going through a lot right now and I need to get my head together. A'ight? But I do appreciate everything you've been doing for me. And, for the record, I'm not ready for a girlfriend right now, but if I was you'd be my number one pick." I lied.

Michelle smiled.

"C'mon, let me walk you home."

After I walked Michelle home, I took a different route instead of returning to my apartment to clear my head. I was at the lowest point of my life. I didn't have a dollar to my name.

My moms and my sister were in a shelter, and I couldn't do anything to help. I was tired of being broke and I needed a plan.

After walking around a fiend stepped to me and asked if I was working. I was so green; I told him I had the weekend off. Then minutes later another fiend approached and within twenty minutes six of them had come up to me asking for drugs. I finally put it together. Initially, I kept telling them no, but then my senses kicked in. Instead of telling them no, I started to ask what they wanted. In an hour's time, I counted that I could've made five hundred dollars. This was more money that I'd ever had in my life. I had a plan.

On my walk back, I heard someone calling my name. It was Rule.

"Yo, Ski, what's good son?" he asked as he gave me a pound. "You ain't hear me calling you? You walked by me like ten times."

Rule was from Brooklyn, but we met upstate. I met him through various chicks that I had messed with in the past. It seemed like every broad I messed with he had either slept with their roommate, cousin or best friend. We kept bumping into each other and eventually just got cool.

Rule was six foot one with brown skin and curly hair. He wasn't skinny, but he wasn't big either. He was cut up from doing time most of his life. We used to tease him and say that if he shaved his head bald he'd look like Damon Wayans. Rule moved upstate to stay out of trouble, and up until then, he was doing a good job of it. He worked with me part time at the telemarketing agency.

"Word, my bad son. I ain't even hear you. I was in a zone." I replied.

"Yeah, I see you getting that paper, dawg." He thought that I had made some transactions and I didn't bother to correct him.

I looked at Rule in amazement. "Yo, I didn't know there was money out here like this."

Rule, not fazed, said, "You been up here all this time and just figuring that out? This shit is a gold mine."

"Word?"

"Yeah, nigga. This shit is sweet. These niggaz is soft as hell. Outta town money is the best money."

I couldn't believe it. "How come you ain't getting none of it then?"

"I was trying to fall back from that, but now I see you up here doing ya thing, I might as well get it poppin'. So what, you pushing hard or soft?"

I was dumbfounded. "Hard or soft? What you mean?"

"Damn! I forgot you was a college boy. What you out there selling? Weed? This must be your first time hustling. Hard is crack, and soft is Coke. Which one you pushin'?" Rule asked.

"I ain't pushin' nuffin' right now, but I'm about to go around my way and holla at my manz and them—try and take this shit over. Na' mean?"

Rule became serious. "Yeah. I feel you. Yo, I'm trying to get money too. Put me on."

"I got you, son. I'm taking the bus to LI tomorrow. Yo, lemme hold twenty dollars for a bus ticket."

Rule handed me two crumpled-up ten dollar bills from his pocket. "Make sure you holla at me when you get back, son."

I gave Rule dap and headed back to my apartment. "I got you, nigga."

I was jumping head first into a game I had never played before. The decision I made that day was gonna change my life forever. Good-bye, hoop dreams, and hello, street dreams.

□□□

Dro and Roach hopped out the window and ran through the back-yard, each holding a duffle bag full of drugs. When they made it into the front of the house, there were two cops knocking on the front door they just burglarized. Dro and Roach didn't even see them.

The black officer reached for his gun. "Hey, you two, freeze."

It startled them at first, but they both broke for the stolen Nissan Sentra parked across the street.

The cops fired at them, but they managed to make it to the car without getting hit.

It was two-thirty in the afternoon and Dro and Roach were on Murdock Avenue in Queens burglarizing a drug dealer's stash house. Roach told Dro that he'd been watching the spot for two weeks, but he had lied just so Dro would do the job. A neighbor saw them going in through the window and called the cops.

Dro looked out the window as he saw two cop cars in pursuit. "Un-believable. Unfucking believable."

Roach floored the Sentra. "Be easy, nigga. I'mma get us outta here."

The job they had just done was a waste. All they found was ten pounds of weed and a couple of thousand dollars.

"Yo, Roach! What the fuck happened to all the money that you said was in the house?"

Roach began laughing. "I lied. I had beef with this cat a while back, and I knew the only way you'd come along was if I told you there was mad paper there."

Two more shots were fired. The third one hit the front tire and the Sentra swerved off the street and ran into the telephone booth on 193rd Street. Dro and Roach hopped out the whip, leaving the money and weed and ran in opposite directions down Murdock Avenue. One cop followed Roach and the other two followed Dro.

Dro ran four blocks up to O'Connor Park, threw his mask in the garbage and ran straight through the basketball court. He took off his hoody and threw it on the side and pretended he was a part of the full-court game going on.

Dro was out of breath. "C'mon, y'all. Somebody pass me the ball and somebody sit down."

The niggaz in the park saw the police chasing Dro and continued to play as if Dro was already there. When the police made it to the court, they looked around for a minute and ran up the block in pursuit.

Roach didn't have the same luck. He got busted four blocks down from where he crashed the car. When they caught him, the police beat him like he was Rodney King. Roach was going on an iron vacation…again.

000

The next night I was on the block hollering at Boota about my new plans.

Boota began laughing. "Oh, so now you wanna hustle, huh? What you gonna sell, basketballs?"

Repeating what Rule had told me a day earlier, I said, "I'm telling you, son. It's money up there. It's a goldmine, B. We could make millions up there if we locked it down right."

Boota changed the subject. "Yo, how come you ain't tell me about ya moms losing her crib? You know I would've helped y'all out."

I started to become impatient. "I don't want none of ya money. I want my own money."

Boota was making more money than he'd ever made in his life. After he found the ten kilos, he thought he was the king of Long Island.

Instead of stepping his game up and selling weight, he continued selling grams. He finally stopped hustling his drugs himself and got three niggaz from around our way we called the three stooges—Dog, Slink and Shabba. All Boota did all day was spend money just as fast as he got it. Sometimes he'd go to the strip club and spend five thousand dollars. He loved tricking his money on strippers and prostitutes.

I was fed up at this point. "Yo, Boota. What you gonna do, son? I'm trying to get this money."

Boota practically brushed me off. "Gimme a couple of months. I'll come up there and see what it look like."

"A couple of months? Son, you buggin'. I ain't tryin' to wait a couple of months. I need money now."

Boota reached in his pocket and handed me a grand and smiled. "That oughta hold you down for a minute. You probably never had that much money in your life," he said as his two-way vibrated.

It was Dro telling Boota to pick him up at the train station.

"Yo, Ski, come through. I gotta take care of something real quick. Come through."

Dro was sweating when we pulled up to the train station. "What the fuck took you so long, B?"

Boota joked, "I'm here, right? That's all that matters, you mango-head nigga."

We were at Baldwin Train Station an hour and a half after Boota got the two-way. From all the stops that Boota was making, you would've thought that he was in no rush to hear about what happened to his brother. Not only did we pick up Snoop, we also picked up one of Boota's girls, Shantel.

After Dro told us the story of the burglary, we decided to get out the car and smoke some trees. It was then that I got my opportunity to holla at Dro. "Yo, Dro, you need to come upstate and get this money with me. It's mad paper up there."

In between his pulls of the L, Dro looked at me like I was crazy. "Ski, when did you become a hustler?"

"Listen, son, not even I could pass this shit up. It's so much money up there that I stopped playing ball."

This piqued Dro's interest. "What's selling up there?"

"What's not selling up there? The prices is ridiculous too. A dime bag of garbage is like thirty dollars up there. No bullshit."

"Oh, so you tryin' to push weed?"

"Nigga, I'm trying to push everything—hard, soft, whatever. Whatever you can get, you need to get it and come up there with me."

Dro was getting serious now. "Yo, where did you stay at up there?"

"Kingston. Why?"

"How far is that from Poughkeepsie?"

"Twenty-five or thirty minutes."

"Ski, I think I might fuck wit' you up there. You know Danielle stays in Poughkeepsie, right?"

"Oh, yeah. I forgot about that."

Dro passed me the L. "I go up there to visit her all the time. You heard what happened earlier today? Shit is getting hot around here. I need a change of scenery. Yo, Ski, get a pen and take my number. I'm definitely coming."

"How long?"

Dro thought about it for a moment. "Gimme two weeks, B. That's my word. I hope you know what you talking 'bout, B."

Smiling, I gave him dap. "Listen, nigga, I put this on my mother. This is going to be the best move you ever made in ya life."

Dro hugged me back after giving him dap. "A'ight. We'll see."

□□□

I had been on the block for an hour, and I hadn't made a sale yet. I was heated. I just came back from re-ing up. I was tired, broke and hungry. After I left Long Island, I was so hyped to get in the game that I stopped uptown and copped an ounce of hard for $650. Raul, the Dominican dude that I copped from, took an instant liking to me. He could tell that I never hustled before. He could've given me anything for any price and I wouldn't have known better, but instead he looked out for me. In three days, I had already gone to cop from him twice. I went from one ounce to three ounces in three short days. Rule taught me how to bag up five twenties out of every gram. I was making a killing. I almost didn't care if Dro ever came through on his promise. I was seeing more money than I had ever seen in my life.

Across the street from where I was posted up were three niggaz and two bitches sitting on a porch getting every sale that came through. I made up my mind that the next sale that came through was mine. Fuck it. Just then a chubby, light skin woman came around the corner on a ten-speed headed straight to the crowd on the porch. I got up and walked over there.

"Ayo, what you looking for, ma? I got big twenties. What up?"

I opened my hand and showed the fiend my work as she was copping from someone else. She had two crumpled bills in her hand. I snatched the two ten dollar bills out of her hand, gave her one piece and walked away. I didn't know it then, but I had just cut my first throat. I ain't know the seriousness of what I did, but I knew it was wrong, so I put my hand on the glock Dro had given me through my windbreaker.

One of the cats on the porch called out to me, "Ayo."

I tightened my grip on my ratchet. "What up?"

"Yeah, dawg. That's Yolanda. She's good for like a hundred dollars a day."

One of the girls spoke up. "You ain't gotta do it like that. It's enough money out here for all of us to eat. You wanna smoke wit' us?"

"Nah. I'm good. But next week, I'mma have some smoke for sale. Make sure y'all come and see me."

I turned around and walked away. Those upstate niggaz was sweet. I later found out that I could've got killed for that shit I pulled on a real block. At that moment right there, I realized that hustling upstate was gonna be very lucrative for me.

7

"Ayo, Scrap, turn that shit down, man. I feel like I'm hustling in the sixties or something," I said smiling.

Scrap got up and did various old dance moves. "This is good music right here. Y'all young boys don't know about this right here. This is the type of music y'all was made off of."

Dro and me burst out laughing. In June 1998 in Kingston, they didn't have any hip-hop or R&B stations. All they had was the oldies but goodies station.

Scrap continued to dance. "That's the problem wit y'all young niggaz. Y'all can't recognize good music when y'all hear it. All y'all wanna hear is that bang, bang shoot-'em-up shit. This is real music right here."

Dro got up off the couch and turned the radio off. "Yo, Scrap. Sit ya old ass down and finish cooking my shit, 'cause if everything don't come back, you don't come back."

Dro and me were in hustlers' paradise. We had just opened shop out of Scrap's crib a month before, and we were already making five thousand dollars a day. Scrap was the biggest and most popular fiend in Kingston. He was also the best chef. By the time Dro came upstate, I was already re-ing up with a quarter of a brick. Raul, my connect, convinced me to start buying powder instead of ready rock and cook it up myself. By doing it that way, I made my work more potent and I started snatching up customers.

Dro came upstate with two bricks of hard. The work was trash, so we sold ounces for six hundred to get it off quick. Them upstate niggaz loved it. They were getting New York prices without having to go all the way to New York. After we moved one brick and ten of my ounces, I took every cent of the money and went uptown and copped two bricks of raw powder.

This time we weren't selling halves, big eights or even ounces. We broke it down to twenties and forties. With Scrap on the stove, we couldn't lose. We had that Star Trek crack.

Dro stood at the doorway of the bathroom. "Yo, Ski, I don't think you understand how much money we're about to make."

I was brushing my hair in the mirror. "Didn't I tell you that this was gonna be the best move of your life?"

"This shit is crazy, B. If we get a good six-month run, we gonna be set."

"When I go back to Long Island and Boota sees me shining, he's gonna be sick that he passed on all this paper."

Dro sounded annoyed at what I said. "We need to keep doin' what we doin'. Don't spend nuffin'—just stack and flip. Yo, Ski, you listening to me?"

"Ayo, Dro, is my waves spinning crazy or what?" I asked, ignoring his first statement.

"What?"

"You heard me, nigga, is my waves spinning?"

"How the fuck did we start talking about ya hair? We were talking about this money."

"Nah, nigga, you was talking about money. You're like a fucking robot. You say the same shit all the time, over and over. What you need to do is come hit some of these skins wit' me."

Dro rarely left the spot. If he wasn't going to get something to eat or to use the phone, he was in the spot. He took the phrase *business before pleasure* to the extreme. He ain't never holla at one broad from upstate. Night and day all he did was sit up in the spot. When I came back from Long Island, I had an eviction notice on my door. I took all my clothes and went to Michelle's house for the night. Every night since then I was on the block or in the spot grinding. I really didn't need my own apartment, but every night, I'd get a room at the Super 8 Motel. No way was I sleeping in a crack house. Dro, on the other hand, slept there. He thought niggaz was gonna try to run up there and rob it if he left. He wanted to be there if they tried.

"I'm on the grind, B. I ain't come up here for pussy. I came here to get money."

"I'm up here trying to get money, too, but while I'm here I might as well get some pussy too." I smiled and put my du-rag on. "Yo, you should see the chick I'm fucking with tonight. Shorty is a dime."

"Word?" Dro replied, showing some interest.

"Yeah. I'mma bring her through here one of these days. Yo, that's my cab beeping the horn, son. I'm out. Page me if you need me," I yelled as I ran out the door.

Paula was a bad bitch. She was light skinned with long hair that fell down the middle of her back. She was a green-eyed mulatto. He mother was Italian and Irish, and her pops was black. Paula didn't have a fat ass or big titties. She wasn't thick, but she had some meat on her bones. None of that mattered because her face was flawless. She was so beautiful that I could stare at her all day long.

I met her through her cousin Jessica. We clicked instantly. Not only was she beautiful, she was also cool as hell. We got up that night for the second time. The first time we chilled, I didn't even touch her.

"So, Ski, tell me some of the girls you messed wit' since you've been up here."

Trying to avoid answering, I said, "Damn, girl. What kind of question is that?"

"I'm asking because ya fine ass is probably a ho."

"Oh. So now I'm fine, huh?" I put my arms around her.

"Yeah. You a'ight," Paula said, smiling.

Kissing her on the cheek, I said, "Stop frontin', girl. I must be more than fine to bag ya beautiful ass."

"Ski, I hope you ain't out here selling drugs. You are gonna go back to school, right?"

"Damn. I feel like I'm on *Jay Leno* the way you asking me mad questions. Nah, I don't sell drugs, but what if I did?"

Paula playfully pushed me away. "Then I wouldn't be your girl-friend."

"You move fast. How do you know I want you to be my girlfriend?"

Paula pushed me on the bed and began to kiss me passionately. First, she kissed me on my mouth, then she made it to my ears and then my neck. From there she got up off the bed and took off every piece of clothing she had on slowly and seductively. Paula looked beautiful na-ked. Her body had more curves than I thought it would. She straddled me and continued kissing and sucking my neck as she removed my T-shirt. Paula was seducing me. She pulled out my dick, put both of her hands around it and said, "I want you to be my man. Can I have you?"

That was the stupidest question I had ever heard in my life. I whis-pered to Paula, looking deeply into her green eyes, "I'm all yours, baby."

After I said that, she put my dick in her warm, moist mouth. It wasn't that the head was all that, it was the fact that I had this beautiful girl with her mouth on my dick.

Paula wanted to be in total control. She pushed me back down on the bed and placed my dick inside her tight, dripping-wet pussy. Instead of taking my whole dick inside of her, she only put a quarter in at a time. She had me at her mercy. I was damn near moaning.

Feeling so good, I managed to whimper, "C'mon, Paula. Stop teas-ing me. You're driving me crazy."

She continued to ride my dick in short strokes, sometimes going as much as halfway down. She was driving me insane. After a half an hour of teasing me, she sat down and let my entire dick enter her.

Paula cried out while she rode me slowly, "Ohhh, Ski, you feel so good. Make love to me."

I moved my pelvis up and met her as she came down in a slow, steady rhythm.

Paula whispered in my ear and began kissing me as her body shook. "Oh my God. I'm coming. I'm coming."

When she said that, I couldn't hold back any longer. We came together. I wasn't wearing a condom, and I put every drop inside of her. I was hoping that she got pregnant.

We lay in bed practically stuck to each other in the same position, kissing and sharing pillow talk for almost an hour. I could have laid there forever.

"Ski, you're so different from the other guys I've been wit'."

"How's that? Is it because I'm three years younger than you?"

"No. It's because you're you. You're the first boyfriend that I've ever had who I didn't have to worry about going to jail."

Smacking Paula's booty, I said, "Shit. I'm black. They might throw me in jail for being wit' ya high-yellow ass."

"You know what I mean, stupid. You aren't like these other niggaz selling drugs, trying to be a thug."

My two-way was going off.

Paula folded her arms and pouted. "Who's that?"

"That's my man Rule. Chill. Why you buggin'?"

"Because you mine, right?"

I ignored her and called Rule on my cell phone. Rule answered, "Yo, what's good, fam?"

"What up? This shit couldn't wait 'til morning?"

"I got a sale for a 62. I need you to come wit' me. Dro ain't trying to leave the spot."

"Why don't you have them meet you at the spot?"

"Nah, son. I don't want niggaz knowing where our spot is."

I replied, annoyed, "What the fuck you talkin' 'bout? Everybody in

Kingston knows where our spot is." I became silent.

Rule figured out what was up. "Money over bitches, nigga. Don't fall in love on me, son. Shorty ain't going nowhere. We'll be back in half an hour."

"Tell Dro to let you borrow the whip. I'm in Room 428." I hung up the phone.

Paula watched me as I dressed. "Where are you going?"

I began putting on my shirt. "I gotta do something real quick. I'll be right back. Take a shower. I got a surprise for you when I come back. You ain't the only one who knows how to be seductive."

Rule showed up at my motel door in five minutes. If I ain't know better, I would've thought he was in the parking lot when I spoke to him on the phone. Just as Rule walked in the room, Paula came out of the shower with nothing on but a towel.

Rule looked Paula up and down. "Damn, Ski, I see why you ain't wanna leave. This bitch is bad."

"Who you callin' a bitch? Ya mother is a bitch," Paula shot back.

"No. My mother is not a bitch. She's a crack head. You're a bitch and a ho."

"Ski, how you gonna let him talk to me like that?"

"Bitch, who you think you is? You ain't nobody."

I stood behind Paula and kissed her on her back and neck, trying to calm her down. "Yo, Rule. Chill, son. This is my baby Paula."

Rule grinned. "Oh, so you Paula, huh? My bad. I heard a lot about you. Yo, Ski, she definitely gets my stamp of approval. Shorty got a little thug in her."

I started walking to the door. "Yeah. That's my baby. But yo, let's bounce. Paula, I'll be back in a minute."

By the time we made it to the Walgreen's parking lot, it was almost two in the morning. Besides us, there was only one other car in the lot—a '98 Nissan Sentra with dark tints. When we pulled in, they hopped out. It was three dark-skinned cats with dreadlocks.

I joked as Rule parked, "Yo, who the fuck these niggaz supposed to be? Boot Camp Clique?"

Rule began backing the car up. "Damn, son, I forgot my hammer. We gotta go back to the spot. I don't feel comfortable without my hammer."

"Son, you wildin'. I got the glock on me. Take it. The last thing I'm worried about is these fake-ass Wu-Tang niggaz trying to rob us." I handed Rule my ratchet.

Rule cocked back the glock and put it on his waist. "You better stop sleeping on these niggaz, Ski."

We got out the car and walked over to the Sentra to handle business.

"What up, Rule? And you must be Ski. I heard a lot about you, dawg—all good things. I'm Thirsty, and this my man, Murder Marv, and this is—"

I cut Thirsty off, "Yo, son, you can save the introductions. I don't give a fuck who none of y'all is. Where's the money?" I was in a hurry to get back to Paula at the motel.

"In the trunk," Thirsty replied.

"Y'all niggaz put thirteen hundred dollars in the trunk? Y'all buggin'. You could've put that in ya pocket. That ain't trunk money, that's pocket money." I laughed, looking at Rule.

Thirsty sounded demanding. "Let's see the work first."

I started getting nervous. "Let you see the work first? Rule, where the fuck you find these niggaz at? All y'all buying is a 62. Y'all acting like ya buyin' ten bricks or some shit. Y'all the police or something?"

"Nah, dawg, we ain't police. We just don't know you," Thirsty responded with an attitude.

I began walking back to the car. "Y'all niggaz is wasting my time. Keep y'all thirteen hundred dollars. Rule, let's bounce."

Thirsty reached for his gun. "Hold up, dawg. You ain't going nowhere with that work."

Shots were fired.

Rule shot Thirsty twice in the chest and his body slumped to the ground.

More shots rang out.

Thirsty's two men started dumping on us. Me and Rule had to take cover behind a garbage Dumpster.

Rule shouted out of breath as shot after shot flew by us, "Didn't I tell you not to sleep on these niggaz? I bet you wish you would've lemme get my hammer now."

Rule stood up and shot back at them, but quickly squatted back down next to me shouting in pain, "Damn, son."

"You hit?"

"Yeah. It just grazed my hand though. These niggaz is trying to kill us." Rule wiped the blood off his hand with his T-shirt. "Ski, you gotta go get the car so we can get the fuck out of here. I'mma hold you down."

"Nigga, is you stupid? How the fuck am I gonna make it to the car without getting my top popped?" I was not feeling his plan at all.

"Didn't I say I'mma hold you down? Trust me, son. It's either this, or we die."

I nodded. My heart was pounding a million miles per second. I had never been in a shoot-out before.

Rule shouted, "A'ight. On three. One...two...three."

The sound of broken glass filled my ears. The front windshield was shattered and glass flew everywhere as Rule hopped in. As we raced out the back of the parking lot, they shot out the back window too.

"Yo, Ski, you bleeding, son."

We pulled out onto Broadway. "Where?"

"Ya wrist. That shit is fucked up. You gonna need stitches."

"It's only glass, son. Fuck all that though. I think that kid Thirsty is dead. He ain't move the whole time. I'm going back to the telly. We gotta get low, son."

Rule slid into the driver's seat. "Yeah, you right. I'mma go back to the spot and see what Dro wants me to do with the whip, then I'mma slide off to Tiesha's crib. I'll page you tomorrow."

"Do that. I'll call Dro and let him know you're on the way. One."

"One."

When I came back inside the room and Paula saw all the blood, she damn near passed out. She must've thought I got shot or something.

"Oh my God. Thirsty shot you?"

"What? No. I ain't get shot. Rule crashed into a pole and the glass from the windshield cut my hand. How you know I was gonna meet Thirsty?" I was curious to know.

"I heard Rule say something like that when you were on the phone."

"You know that cat Thirsty?"

"No, but I know of him. Why? What were you going to meet him for tonight anyways?"

"I was going wit' Rule. I don't know why the fuck he was meeting this bird-ass nigga. We never made it over there."

Paula didn't believe me, but she accepted it. I was more worried about how she would act if she found out Thirsty was dead. I didn't remember Rule telling me Thirsty's name over the phone. That struck me as odd.

Paula and me fucked all night and all morning. Rule dropped the whip and gun off to Dro and went to stay at his girl's house. I had only been in the game a month, but it felt like a year.

By the time I managed to visit home in August, it didn't even feel like home anymore. Everything was different. Natalie was dead. Roach was in jail. Snoop's father was dead, and I had quit playing basketball.

The four months I had been in the game were the best times of my life. The first thing I did was put forty grand down on a house for my mother and little sister in the Poconos. I told her I won the money playing in a one-on-one tournament. Although she knew it was a lie, she was happy nonetheless to have her own place again. I was also renting a one-bedroom condo for me and Paula on the outskirts of Kingston. I let Paula do all the decorating, and she hooked it up real nice. I also bought my first pieces of jewelry. Dro, on the other hand, spent all his money on himself. He didn't believe in saving for a rainy day. If it wasn't jewelry, it was cars. If it wasn't cars, it was clothes. Dro had two thick twenty-four-karat iced-out gold Cuban link chains with Jesus pieces, three-carat diamond earrings in both of his ears, two ten-thousand-dollar bracelets and an iced-out Movado watch. He also traded his '98 Denali for a '98 535 BMW. We originally planned not to spend paper until we started re-ing with ten bricks, but after the first two, it was a wrap. We went on a shopping spree.

Me, Dro, Danielle and Paula were on our way to meet Boota, Shamika, Wise and his new girlfriend Tory at the All Star Café in Manhattan. Me and Paula were getting serious, so I decided that it was time to introduce her to the whole clique.

My cell phone rang as we were arriving in the city. "Hello."

Rule shouted into the phone, "Yo, Ski. What's up, nigga?"

"What's good, my nigga? You got that paper I sent you?"

Rule joked, "Yeah. Good look, my nigga. Stop sending me so much paper though, son. My books is stacked. You keep sending me money like this, and the Feds gonna be investigating me."

Rule had gotten arrested on attempted murder charges a couple of days after the shooting. One of Thirsty's homeboy's ID'd him. I was lucky enough not to be implicated in any of it. The only way I could be involved was if Rule said that I was there, and that was never gonna happen. For that reason, I held Rule down to the fullest. I visited, wrote, sent pictures, accepted collect calls, did three-way calls, paid for his lawyer and sent him one hundred and fifty dollars a week. He kept it real with me, so I had to keep it real with him. Loyalty is everything.

"I'm just trying to make sure you straight, son. What the fuck the lawyer talking about?"

"Right now it's too early to tell. I'm just playing the waiting game. They ain't got nothin' on me. I'mma beat it."

"Shit, he better be doing more than that. I gave that nigga twenty grand."

"Where are you, Ski?"

"Right now I'm in Manhattan, on my way to the All Star Café with Dro, Danielle and Paula."

"Oh yeah. Y'all doing the double date thing?"

"Yeah, son. You know it."

"Yo, I'mma let you go enjoy yaself. Stay up, my nigga."

"One." I closed my cell phone.

Dro spoke moments after I hung up. "Rule is a good nigga, Ski. A lot of niggaz would've folded by now, but son is holding it down."

"Yeah," I agreed, "I got mad love for him. Yo, when he comes home, we should give him a share in the spot."

Dro smiled, looking back at me from the driver's seat. "I ain't say all that. He's a good nigga and all, but I ain't giving him none of my share. You could give him some of yours.

The All Star Café was packed. TV screens with different basketball games and boxing matches were all over. Between all of our clothes, jewelry and women, people thought we were stars. I introduced Paula to everybody, and after a few drinks, Boota was up to his usual cracking jokes.

Boota smirked. "Yo, Ski, you got nerve to be wearing that Avirex turtleneck with that long-ass neck you got."

I placed my arm around Paula. "Son, when you got a chain that costs as much as this and a girl who looks like this, niggaz don't pay no attention to ya neck."

"You ain't never told a bigger lie than that, you giraffe-neck mothafucka. You look like Geoffrey the giraffe from the Toys 'R' Us commercials. I'm surprised kids ain't running up to you asking for discount coupons." Boota had the whole table erupting in laughter.

Paula stood up. "Hold up! Hold up! Y'all ain't gonna just snap on my baby all night."

Boota smiled. "Paula. You don't know me too good. Sit down, 'cause you could be next."

Paula shot back, "I wish you would, blackie."

"What you call me? I know you ain't trying to snap, shorty? Ski, you better tell her about me."

Paula continued, "You fake-ass Shaq. Why don't you get us some free drinks or something? You are co-owner of this place, right?"

"Oh, shit. I know interracial Barbie ain't trying to snap."

"Yeah, I might be. That's why if you stay outside in the sun too long, you'll probably turn into a leather coat." Paula had the table in tears laughing.

Boota gave Paula dap. "I like that one. You got that off. I like shorty, Ski. She's a trip."

After dinner, we all drove back around my way to Long Island. Shamika took the girls to her and Boota's house, and we all went to hang out. We bumped into Snoop at 7-Eleven and ended up standing in front playing dice and smoking. Paula was a hit with everybody. Even Shamika gave her stamp of approval. I couldn't help but wonder if Natalie would've liked her too.

While I was playing dice, a young kid from around my way named Kashaun told me he wanted to holla at me. After I lost about two hundred and fifty dollars, I was done so I hollered at Kashaun. "Yo, K, what's good?"

"You tell me, son. You the talk of the hood."

"I know that ain't what you wanna talk to me about. Stop beating around the bush, nigga."

"Yo, Ski, I'm trying to do this school and basketball shit, but I can't concentrate. My moms is smoking again and me and my sisters be in the crib with no heat and electricity for weeks at a time."

Kashaun was fifteen years old and in the tenth grade. Our mothers went to church together. I knew him and his family since I was peeing in the bed. Kashaun always looked up to me because of the way I played basketball. He was six feet tall, dark skin with a thin frame. Everybody always said we could pass for brothers.

I pulled a knot out of my pocket. "So what you telling me? You need money? C'mon, son. That's nuffin'. How much you need?"

"Nah, son. Keep ya money. I want you to put me on so I can make my own money. I need you to put me down. This school shit is for the birds, B. If I don't step up and take care of my family, then no one will." Kashaun was defiant in his response.

"Damn, son, you puttin' me in a fucked-up situation. I don't wanna pull you outta school and into the street."

"It don't make a difference if it's with you or the next nigga. I already done made up my mind that this is what I gotta do. The reason I wanna fuck wit' you is because I like your style. You just got in the game and you already shittin' on all the niggaz ya age. You smart, son."

I could hear the hunger in his voice. He sounded just like me four months ago. I looked at Kashaun as a little brother, and I hated to see him in the street, but I'd rather he come upstate so I could keep him out of jail.

"Ayo, K, you know I live upstate, right? If you wanna fuck wit' me, you gotta be ready to move up there." I was hoping that would change his mind.

"I don't give a fuck where we go, just take me wit' you. I'm ready to leave right now."

"A'ight. I'mma take you wit' me, but only for six months. After that, you should have a nice piece of change stacked up."

Kashaun hugged me. "Yo, good look, Ski. You ain't gonna regret it. I'll go all out up there for you."

"Hold up, son. I got one condition. You got to enroll in high school up there and be passing all of ya classes."

Kashaun was excited. "I got you. No problem. Good look, Ski."

"A'ight. Pack ya shit. I'm coming to get you tomorrow."

Boota passed me the L. "Ski, I don't know why you fuckin' wit' that li'l-ass kid. You barely know what the fuck you doin'. You gonna get that kid put in jail or killed. Remember I told you that."

"It's better he fuck wit' me than you. At least he'll make some paper. Oh yeah, I almost forgot." I reached in my pocket and peeled out twenty hundred-dollar bills. "That's ya G back with interest."

Boota snatched the wad out of my hand. "You frontin'-ass nigga. I'mma spend all that shit on weed."

Meanwhile, Snoop was losing every penny he had in the dice game. Every time Boota gave Snoop some work, Snoop fucked it up. He just wasn't a hustler. Selling drugs wasn't his thing. Ever since Natalie and his father passed away, Snoop was like a madman. Everywhere he went he started trouble, and he usually finished it too.

Boota looked at a high school kid standing near the store. "Ayo, shorty, you got weed?"

"Yeah. I got a little bit."

"However much you got, give it to me."

"I got twenty-four dimes, son. That's 225."

"Nah, nigga. That's 240. How you a hustler and can't even count?"

Just then, Snoop walked up to the kid, pulled out his Desert Eagle and gun butted him in the mouth, knocking one of his teeth out. "What I tell you about selling weed around here?"

The kid balled up and started crying.

"Yo, Snoop, leave shorty alone son. Let him live," I called out to Snoop, hoping he wasn't gonna pull the trigger.

Snoop ignored my plea and kicked the kid in the ribs. "Nah. Fuck that. Niggaz need to know that if they ain't from Baldwin, they can't make money here."

Boota attempted to reason with him. "A'ight, Snoop. Enough is enough. Li'l man has learned his lesson."

Snoop continued in his rage and stomped the kid in the face. "Li'l man ain't too little to hustle, is he? He ain't too little to take money out of my pocket, is he?"

Boota shook his head. "What the fuck is you talking about, Snoop? How is he taking money out of your pocket? You don't even sell drugs."

Until then I heard stories of how crazy Snoop had been acting, but I had never witnessed it for myself. Snoop had gone crazy. I felt like I didn't even know him.

Snoop kicked him in the mouth, stomped him in the head with his boots and punched him in the face repeatedly until the kid was unconscious. The kid's eyeball was almost completely out of his socket.

Wise couldn't stand watching anymore and pulled his Desert Eagle on him. He grabbed Snoop by the shoulders, shook him and said, "What the fuck's wrong wit' you? You buggin' the fuck out, son."

"Wise, back the fuck up off me. Don't ever grab me like that again. Who the fuck you think you is, captain save a nigga?" Snoop shouted as he cocked back his hammer.

Dro pleaded, "Snoop, don't do it. That's Wise." He pulled out his own .38 and pointed it at Snoop.

Boota pulled out his gun and pointed it at Snoop too. Snoop stood there with his gun pointed at Wise, staring at Dro and Boota.

I walked over to Snoop with my hand out. "Yo, Snoop, Natalie wouldn't wanna see us out here beefing like this, and you know it. We like family. Gimme the gun."

Snoop never let Wise out of his sight. He continued as I eased my way closer to him. First, I put one hand on the gun, then both hands. As Snoop let go of the gun, he kicked the boy's unconscious body and went into the kid's pockets and took the little bit of weed and money he had.

Boota was mad. "Damn, man, this nigga Snoop could fuck up a wet dream. Let's bounce."

We all left in separate cars. Boota and Dro drove Snoop home in the Beamer, and me and Wise went to Boota' crib to get the girls in Boota's Lexus. It was the first time that me and Wise had been alone in a year.

I looked at Wise as we parked in front of Boota' crib. "Yo, that nigga Snoop done lost it, Wise."

Wise agreed, "Yeah. Snoop is on some bishop shit. He ain't been the same since Natalie died."

"Yeah. I heard how he's been acting. I thought he was gonna pop you tonight."

"He ain't got no excuse for that one. Nigga ain't drunk or nuffin'. He did that shit on the sober tip. But yo, fuck all that. Look at you, son, you doin' good, fam. You wearing that money well, my nigga." Wise smiled and gave me dap. "Yo, shorty is bad too. You gotta keep her. Shorty is wifey material for real."

"Yeah, Paula is one bad bitch. She got the total package. She's fly as hell, cool as a fan and the pussy is blazing. I think she's the one."

"That's what's up, son. I'm glad you found a good one."

Wise sounded sincere.

"Son, you don't even know the half. Every time I give her money to spend, she spends it on me. She don't even like me hustling."

"You need to hurry up and put a seed in that."

"You think I'm not? I'm trying hard as a muthafucka."

We laughed and shared dap and got out of the car.

"Baby. What are you doing?" Paula spoke to me half sleep as I went underneath the cover and between her legs.

I teased her first by licking the inside of her thighs, then with the tip of my tongue I began to lick her clit in slow, circular motions. Paula took the cover off my head so she could watch. "Ohhh! You are so nasty."

I whispered to Paula as she slowly spread her legs. "You love it though."

I spread her lips with both of my thumbs, stuck my tongue in her already dripping wet pussy and probed her insides as if I was the Coastguard searching for a body.

Paula shouted in ecstasy, "Ohhh! Ohhh! Mmmm! Ohhh!"

I took my tongue out of her and gently bit her now pulsating, erect clitoris. After that, I licked her clit in fast, vertical strokes as I slid my finger in her pussy and moved it as if I was telling someone to come here.

Paula cried out as she wrapped her legs around my neck and began grinding my face, "Ohhh! Ohhh! Yes, baby. Right there. I'm about to come."

When I saw that she was reaching her climax, I sucked her clit as her love juice dripped down my face. Paula whispered with a devilish grin, "Oh my God. Damn. Whoo. Thank you, baby. Come give me a kiss."

"How you know I wanna kiss you? You ain't even brush ya teeth yet, stink mouth!" I joked as I stuck my tongue in her mouth. There was never a time that Paula's breath or pussy stunk. Her pussy always tasted like honey. I gave her the nickname Sweet P.

Paula stared at me with her beautiful green eyes. "You wanna kiss me because you love me."

"You sure are feeling confident this morning, ain't you?"

Paula began trying to pull my pants down. "C'mon, baby. Take ya pants off. Gimme some before I take it."

"Nah. I got a surprise for you." I picked up her naked body and carried her into the bathroom. When we got there, I had thirty candles lit around the tub and her favorite Bath and Body bubble bath and Chanel perfume in it as well. I gently placed her in the warm water, turned on Brian McKnight's CD and washed every part of her body slowly and sensually. After the bath, I dried her off, laid her on the bed and lotioned her body from head to toe. I put her in her housecoat, sat her up on the bed and brought her her favorite breakfast, two sausage biscuits with cheese, a hash brown and tea. Paula was overwhelmed.

Paula gave me a big kiss and a hug. "Isaiah, you make me feel like the most special woman in the world. Nobody has ever done anything like this for me before. I love you so much."

I grinned. "Damn. If I knew a couple of sausage biscuits would have you acting like this, I'd get them for you every day."

"Shut up, stupid. You're so silly." Paula continued to enjoy her food.

We stayed in bed all morning watching TV and smoking weed. The Lifetime movie that Paula forced me to watch had just ended when she started up with me.

The Lifetime movie depicted a woman whose husband was caught for dealing drugs. After his incarceration she turned to drugs and lost everything. When the husband finally returned, they were no longer the same couple as they were before he was incarcerated.

"Isaiah, did you see that? That could happen to us. I told you from the beginning that I didn't want a relationship with a drug dealer."

I pulled the covers over my head. "Damn, P, here we are having a nice morning and you wanna start up? How many times do we have to go through this?"

Paula pulled the covers off my face. "As many times as it takes to get it through ya head. I love you, Isaiah, but I'm not gonna let you fuck up my life."

I took her hand in mine. "Paula, I'm doing this for us. How do you think we living the way we live? I want us to be comfortable."

Paula pleaded with me as her eyes began to water. "Isaiah, I don't care about these material things. I'd love to be with you if you lived in a cardboard box. I'm twenty-one and you're eighteen. We're doing better than most middle-aged couples. Damn, how much more money are you trying to save? You paying off ya mother's house. We got that brand- new Lexus sitting outside, and we got money put away. It's time to stop now. Let Dro keep the spot to himself, Isaiah. If you love me then you'd do it."

"Yo, P, gimme a couple more months and I'm out. Trust me. After that, it's you and me, baby. I promise. I'mma go back to college and play ball and everything…A couple more months." I wasn't sure Paula was too convinced, but I was relieved when the doorbell rang.

Saved by the bell.

It was Kashaun. The last thing I needed was Kashaun coming over asking me about drugs. I got up to answer the door and Paula followed me.

I gave him dap as he entered. "K. What's good, son?"

"Ain't shit, Ski! What up, P? Why you look so mad?" Kashaun looked at Paula not getting a response. "Dro told me to tell you to come to the spot and help him bag up."

"Why ain't he call?"

"You know how that nigga is. He be on some paranoid James Bond–type shit."

It was November, and Kashaun had been upstate for three months. I had him selling weed in the high school. He locked it down quick. He was making close to four hundred dollars a day. I took half the money from him, but I only did that so he wouldn't spend all of his money. Kashaun was doing real good. He went home often and paid his family's rent and utility bills.

Paula placed her hands on her hips. "How come you ain't in school?"

Kashaun shook his head. "It's half a day, P. Damn! Y'all two is worse than my moms."

I wrapped my arms around Paula as she rolled her eyes at me. "Yo, P, I'll be back later. I'mma see what's up with Dro. Yo, K, stay here and I'll come get you tonight. Tell me you love me, Paula."

"Remember what I said, Isaiah. I ain't gonna be here forever."

I was halfway out the door. "I love you."

Paula watched me get into my new Lexus. "I love you too."

I saw Dro as I walked to the window. "I don't know how the fuck you stay here 24/7. This smoke is killing me."

"It's easy, B. You see that Beamer outside? You see this jewelry I'm wearing? That's what makes me stay here. Money. You act like you satisfied with the little paper you made already."

"Nah, I ain't satisfied at all. I ain't been able to stack nothing real big yet. I just put another forty-five grand on my mother's crib and I have to give Rule's lawyer another fifteen grand. Plus, I just copped that Lex."

Dro joked, "Damn, I thought I had a lot of bills, but at least all of my money gets spent on me."

"If I get a hundred and fifty to two hundred grand in the stash, I'm out. I'mma go back to school and play ball."

Dro pulled his fisherman's cap down over his eyes. "Get the fuck outta here. Maybe Paula believes that bullshit when you tell her, but I know better." Basketball is a thing of the past. You hooked now. You too used to having money. You're a paper chaser now."

"Yo, let's get the fuck out of here, son. Let's go get haircuts and get something to eat."

"Why would I wanna get a haircut when all I do is stay in the spot?"

I tried to persuade him, "Just to get outside, nigga. C'mon son, get some sun. You ain't never been in my whip. Let's go for a ride."

"Nah, B. I ain't goin' nowhere. Who's gonna look out while we're both gone?"

"Scrap is. Who the fuck looked out for two days when we went home to visit? C'mon, son. Let's bounce. I'll pay for the haircuts and the lunch."

Dro finally stood up. "A'ight, but only for an hour, B. We gotta get back so we can bag up."

Dro and me got haircuts, ate lunch at Applebee's and chilled for the first time in a while by ourselves. We talked about everything from Snoop going crazy to money plans and our girlfriends. By the time we made it back to the spot, it was damn near four o'clock in the afternoon. We'd been gone for three hours. As we pulled up to the apartment complex where we had the spot, we saw at least ten to fifteen police cars.

I was scared. "Oh shit, son, they running up in the spot."

"Ski, you got something on you?"

"Hell no."

"Good. Park down the block and let's walk back up here and see what's going on."

"See what's going on? I can see that now. Why would you wanna watch the police rush our spot?"

"Trust me. Just do it."

I parked around the block, and we both took off our jewelry and walked to the complex. As we got closer, I saw a plainclothes officer walking Scrap to a squad car. When his eyes caught ours, he started wildin' out screaming, "Dro, Ski, they got me. They got everything…the drugs, the money and the guns. Make sure y'all bail me out and get me a lawyer."

The police heard that and ran at us like we just shot an officer. They threw us to the ground and frisked us. After they couldn't find anything, they handcuffed us and brought us to the police station in the same cop car.

I whispered to Dro from the backseat of the cop car, "Yo, you've got to be the dumbest mothafucka in the world. Nah, scratch that. I'm the dumbest muthafucka in the world for listening to you. We should've just bounced. I knew it."

Dro was unbelievably calm. "Chill out, B. I told you they ain't got nuffin' on us. We'll be out in an hour."

Dro turned out to be right. They had absolutely not a single shred of evidence on us. They separated us and put us in questioning rooms. I felt like I was in a movie. They put the bright light on, played good cop, bad cop, and even told me that Dro was telling on me in the other room. It was my first time being arrested, but I wasn't nervous or scared. Every time they asked me a question, I sat there and stared at them like I was a deaf mute. That seemed to get them even more pissed off. They left me alone for about thirty minutes and when they came back, they let me go.

Dro and I were outside waiting on a cab when I tried to call Paula. I knew she would be worried if she heard what happened, I was surprised that she wasn't at the station.

There was no answer. *Maybe she's in the bathroom,* I thought.

I tried again a few minutes later, but she didn't pick up.

"Damn. Where the hell is she at? She ain't answering the phone."

Dro was cool. "She probably stepped out for a minute."

"Nah. If she was leaving the house, she would've called and told me."

"She probably did, nigga. Remember, they took our phones?"

"Nah, son. Something is up. She would've left a message on my phone." The cab finally pulled up. We hopped inside and got dropped off at our car parked a block from Scrap's house.

By the time we made it to my house, it was nine-thirty at night. The screen to the front door was open, and when I put the key in the lock the door was already opened. "Paula, I'm home."

I was about to flick the light on when I saw it. The whole crib was trashed. Someone robbed my house. Couches were flipped over, mattresses were cut open, and there were holes in the walls.

Dro was concerned. "Damn, B. Niggaz did you dirty! Is ya safe still here?"

"My safe is buried in the backyard. Nobody knows where my shit is. Not even P."

When I walked into the bathroom, I nearly threw up. Kashaun's lifeless body hung from the ceiling by a rope. His eyes were bulging out of his head and his neck was slit from ear to ear.

I yelled at the top of my lungs, "Damn, son. Yo, Dro, come here. They killed K."

"Oh shit" was all Dro managed to say when he walked into the bathroom.

I was frantic. I didn't know what to do next. "We gotta find out who did this shit, Dro. These niggaz got to die. I hope they ain't hurt P."

Dro tried to make me feel better. "Calm down, Ski. Paula probably wasn't even here when they came in."

Just then, the phone rang. "Hello, Paula?" I answered on the third ring.

A voice spoke on the other end, "Listen up, mothafucka. We killed the kid and we'll kill ya bitch too. We want fifty grand in two days or your bitch is dead. If I even think you told the police something, she's dead." The person hung up the phone.

I didn't know what to do. I plopped down on the couch and put my face in my hands. I was helpless. Kashaun was dead and someone had kidnapped Paula. All I could think about was if something happened to Paula, it was gonna be my fault. I should've listened to her.

hat do you mean you lost the three bricks?" Boota yelled angrily, pacing up and down his living room. "How the fuck did y'all lose my drugs? Three bricks don't just get up and walk away. People lose keys. People lose their wallets. People just don't just lose three mothafuckin' bricks. Somebody better start explaining right now."

Dog stuttered, putting his hands on Boota' shoulder, "Yo—Yo, Boota, let me explain, son. Just calm down. It ain't no need to yell. It's not our fault."

Boota knocked Dog's hand off his shoulder. "Calm down? Who the fuck is you talking to, Dog? Y'all niggaz got some nerve. First you come in my house and tell me you lost my work, then you got the nerve to tell me to calm down."

Boota turned around, grabbed Dog by the collar of his shirt and smacked him in the mouth, knocking him to the floor. Boota then stood over Dog and kicked him in the ribs and choked him until he passed out. Boota sat on the couch out of breath. "Now, I'm gonna give y'all two niggaz a chance to tell me what really happened to my work. I swear on my kids that if I think that y'all are lyin', I'mma kill all three of y'all bitch ass niggaz."

Dog, Slink and Shabba were all at Boota's house having a meeting. Dog, Slink and Shabba had been hustling for Boota almost three years. Two days prior, Boota had dropped off three keys of cocaine at their apartment. Boota gave them specific orders to bust down one into ounces and sell it and for them not to touch the other two until he gave them the word. Somehow or another, they managed to lose all three bricks.

Dog, Slink and Shabba were wannabes. They all came from good two-parent, middle-class families. They had no business hustling. They could get anything they wanted from their parents. Everyone in the neighborhood knew them as the three stooges, each one dumber than the other. They sold drugs, but they were far from hustlers.

Shabba stepped up, "A'ight, Boota, I'll tell you what happened. Me, Dog and Slink were out in Lakeview at this bar and we met this broad. She was a fiend, but she was bad. We took her back to our crib to pop off. All we gave her was five grams. This nigga Dog trying to be big Willy around the bitch shows her all the work, bragging and shit. That bitch was damn near hypnotized when she seen all that work. She stripped down out of her clothes and started sucking Dog off right there in the living room in front of us. She sucked and fucked us for hours, Boota. She might have been a fiend, but her pussy was the best I ever had. After we was finished, we all went to sleep—"

Boota interrupted and smacked Shabba in the face, "When y'all woke up the work was gone. Y'all three are the most ignorant niggaz in the world. Y'all let a fiend rob y'all? Didn't I tell y'all not to touch the other two bricks? Didn't I?"

The three bricks that the Three Stooges lost were Boota' last. Since Boota got the ten ki's from Smalls' house, he didn't have to re-up, so he was spending money just as fast as he got it. Boota was buying everything with a price tag on it. He put down fifty grand on a three-hundred-thousand-dollar house in Baldwin for him, Shamika and the kids. He bought two brand-new cars—a Lexus GS and Maxima—a speedboat, three dirt bikes and countless clothes and jewelry. He spent three grand every time he went to the strip club, and that was at least once a week.

Boota didn't believe in stashing any money, and now that his last three bricks were gone, he was broke. He didn't even have enough cash to buy half a brick.

Boota pulled out his gun and made Shabba, Dog and Slink strip ass naked and lay on his front porch on their backs. He then took all of their clothes and threw them in the garbage in his kitchen. When he came back, he pulled his dick out of his pants and pissed on their chests.

Boota was disgusted as he let a shot off in the air. "You bitch-ass niggaz. I should kill all three of y'all. Consider yaselves lucky. I don't know how all y'all gonna do it, but y'all faggots gonna pay me back my money. If I was y'all, I'd go back to that bar, try to find that bitch and kill her. Y'all gonna work this money off doing anything and everything I say. Now get the fuck off my porch."

Twenty minutes after they left, Boota's phone rang. "Yo."

"This call is from a New York State correctional facility. The cost of this call is four dollars and ninety-five cents for the first minute, and seventy-five cents each additional minute. Press 5 to accept the call. To decline the call, hang up…"

Boota pressed 5. It was Roach.

"What up, li'l brother?" Roach said.

"What's good, my nigga? How you? They ain't trying to take yo' ass up there yet?"

"Nah. Never that. What up wit' you? You still ballin' out there or what? I heard you like Russell Simmons in the hood."

"Yo, Roach, you won't believe what just happened. The Three Stooges damn near fucked up my whole shit. I'mma have to sell my jewelry to get back on."

Roach laughed. "Damn, nigga. How you fucked up after getting ten free ones? You could fuck up a wet dream."

"Yeah, I'm assed out. I got a mortgage to pay. I might fuck around and lose my crib over this shit."

Roach continued to joke, "Damn, son, you on MC Hammer status. Don't worry. When ya big brother touches down, I'll put you down."

Boota took a pull off a spliff. "Yeah, son. Shit is crazy out here."

"Yo, what up with, Dro? I ain't speak to him in months."

"Who, Dro? Dro is upstate getting money wit' Ski."

"Ski? Who the fuck is Ski?" Roach was dumbfounded.

"You know Ski, nigga. Basketball Ski. Young dark-skin Ski."

"Say word? Ski is in the game now? What the fuck is the world coming to?"

"Don't sleep, son. Them niggaz is up there getting big paper, B."

"Oh yeah? Well tell Dro I said to send me some of that big paper he gettin'."

"No doubt, son. I'll tell him. When you comin' home?"

"Probably this time next year."

"Oh yeah. That ain't nuffin', son. You could do that on ya head, but yo son, lemme get the fuck off the phone. I don't need no mo' bills that I can't pay."

"A'ight, li'l bro. Be careful out there. Ya heard?"

"Yeah. A'ight. One my nigga."

"One."

arvin was rubbing on Paula's thigh.

"Damn, ma, you a bad bitch. I might have to sample some of this pussy."

Thirsty angrily pushed Marvin's hand away from Paula. "Marv, what the fuck you doin', man? Ain't none of that shit popping off. This is strictly business."

Marvin walked back over to the bed where they had Paula tied up. "What the fuck is the difference? We gonna kill her anyway, right? If them niggaz shot me up, I'd be raping them niggaz'mothers. Chill out, son. Lemme do this, dawg. Besides, I think she likes me."

Thirsty pulled his revolver out from his waist. "Didn't I just tell you this is strictly business, dawg? Sit ya ass down before I make it so that you can't get up."

Marvin smiled. "Oh, I get it. You trying to be the only one to sample that pussy, huh? Stop being selfish, dawg. Sharing is caring."

Thirsty began shouting, waving his revolver in the air, "Nigga, you just don't get it, do you? This shit ain't no joke. Ain't nobody fucking this bitch. If I find out that you or E raped her, I'mma kill both of y'all bitch asses!"

Thirsty, Murder Marv and E-Money Bags were three small time hustlers from Poughkeepsie. When Thirsty was released from the hospital he began plotting to kidnap Paula. Kashaun was not part of their plan, but when he came out of the room busting shots, they had no choice but to kill him.

After Rule shot Thirsty, Murder Marv went to the police station and snitched on Rule. He gave the officers Rule's description and cell phone number. When Thirsty got out of the hospital and found out what Marv had done, he was livid. Thirsty was a grimy nigga, but he still lived by the code of the street. Ratting was unacceptable. Thirsty had no plans of splitting the money three ways. He made up his mind to kill both Marvin and E after Ski paid the cash.

"Ayo, take off the duct tape." Thirsty was tired of playing games. "It's time to make the phone call."

When E took the duct tape off her mouth, Paula spit in his face.

"You faggot-ass nigga. Keep ya dusty hands off me," Paula shouted after the tape was removed.

With no hesitation, E punched her in the eye and spit back in her face.

Thirsty coolly looked at Paula. "C'mon, Paula, there ain't no need for all of that shit. We've been treating you good, right? Don't get disrespectful. I could make ya stay here more miserable than it has to be. Now look at you, a pretty girl like you with a knot on ya face. Stop crying and walk over here."

E untied her, and Paula got up and sat down next to Thirsty crying loudly and holding her eye.

Thirsty spoke to Paula calmly, handing her the phone. "A'ight, shorty. I'mma let you talk to Ski for thirty seconds. Don't say nothing stupid. If he comes up wit the money, I'mma let you go, a'ight?"

He dialed the number and after three rings, Ski answered his phone. "Hello."

□□□

I picked up the phone and heard Paula crying on the other end. "Isaiah, it's me. Please pay the money. Please. I'm scared. These guys are touching me. I'm scared, baby. Help me. They're gonna kill me."

My heart was racing listening to her plead. "Baby, did they hurt you? Are you a'ight? They didn't rape you, did they?"

Paula's voice became even more frantic. "No, they didn't rape me, but they tried. I'm scared. One of them hit me in my face. Don't let them kill me, Isaiah."

"Listen, Paula, I'm gonna get you back. I'm gonna pay the money. Where are you at?"

"Where am I at? I can't even answer that…they'll kill me."

"Paula, I love you, baby. Hang in there."

A male's voice spoke, "Ain't that sweet. You sound like a real hero— Captain mothafuckin' Save a Ho."

"Yo, who's this? You better not put your hands on my girl again. I'll kill y'all niggaz."

"Don't worry about who this is, and don't ever threaten me again. I'll send this bitch to you in a shopping bag, dawg. You ain't in no position to be telling me anything. We playin' by my rules. I talk. You listen."

"A'ight, son, you got it. What do you want, and when do you want it?"

"Now that's the tone I like to be spoken to in. The price is now one hundred grand, and I want it by tomorrow. Get that money up quick because the more I keep looking at this pretty bitch, the more I wanna fuck her."

I was infuriated. "You better not touch her."

"What? I better not do what? What did I tell you about threats?"

"My bad. My bad."

"Yeah, that's what I thought. If you call the police, she's dead. I'll call you tomorrow…Hey, Isaiah, make sure you have the money."

The line disconnected.

"They want a hundred grand by tomorrow night, or they gonna kill her."

Dro looked at me. "A hundred grand? I thought it was fifty grand. That's a lot of money, B. Yo, Ski, you sure you love this bitch?"

"What? What kind of question is that? Yeah, I love her. Why the fuck would you ask me some stupid-ass question like that at a time like this?"

"Because one hundred grand is a lot of money, and you barely know this chick."

"Would you pay it for Danielle?"

"Of course I would," Dro answered without hesitation.

"A'ight then, nigga. So why wouldn't I pay it for Paula?"

"You know that there's a chance that you pay the money and they still kill her, right?"

"Yeah, nigga. What the fuck you think? I ain't stupid. I'm paying it though. I don't give a fuck. I gotta at least try and get her back."

"Damn, B, why you jumping down my throat? I'm just trying to give you all of ya options. You know I'm wit' you regardless, B."

Dro gave me dap. "Yeah. I know, son. My fault. I'm stressing right now. These niggaz got my shorty."

I never felt more helpless in my life. I was only in the game six months, and I'd already been through so much. All I could hear was Paula's voice pleading with me to stop hustling and go back to school. If something happened to her, I'd never be able to forgive myself. Dro and me hadn't slept in more than twenty-four hours. I felt bad doing it, but we had to dump Kashaun's body in the woods up in the mountains in Woodstock, then we had to clean and scrub every inch of my condo. I had forty grand in my stash and twenty grand in a joint bank account that Paula and I shared. That was only sixty. I needed forty more.

"Yo, Dro, how much paper you got?"

"I only got fifteen. I lost ten when they ran up in the spot."

"So how much of that can I borrow?"

"C'mon, B, you can get it all. I got love for Paula too." Dro gave me dap.

"Good look, my nigga. You know I'mma pay you back, right?"

"Damn right you gonna pay me back. After I give you that, I'm dead broke."

I thought out loud and flopped on the couch, "That's still only seventy-five stacks. Where in the fuck am I gonna find another twenty-five at? Yo, you think Boota got twenty-five stacks?"

Dro was rolling up some haze in a dutch. "I can't call that one, B. I got half a brick at the crib, but there ain't no way we could sell all that by tomorrow."

"Boota? Hell no! That nigga don't believe in stashing. I don't even think that nigga owns a safe." Dro continued.

"Yeah, you right. That nigga is worse than you and shit—spending all his money on jewelry."

Dro had an epiphany. "That's it. That's it, B. You can sell ya chain and watch. How much you spent on that?"

"My jewels ain't worth twenty-five grand. I only spent ten."

"What about that ring you were planning on giving Paula for Christmas?"

"I ain't get it yet. I only put five thousand on it."

"A'ight. Look, son, we gotta go get ya deposit back on that ring. Sell ya chain and watch, and if that ain't enough, I'll sell my two bracelets."

I grabbed my car keys. "Ain't no better time to leave than now."

"Hello."

A familiar voice answered, "You got my money?"

"Yeah, I got ya money. You got my girl? Lemme talk to her and see if she's a'ight."

"What did I tell you about making demands? This is my show. You only do as you're told. Is that understood?"

I had to bite my tongue. "Yeah, that's understood."

"This is how it's going down. Meet me at Coppin's Warehouse on Main Street in Saugerties. Don't try nothin' funny—no cops, no homeboys and no guns. If you bring anyone of those three with you, Paula's dead. Put the money in a duffle bag and keep ya cell phone on.

If a dime of my money is missing, she's dead." The phone line went silent.

□□□

It was 11:59 on a windy November night. My stomach was in knots. I had never been more scared in my life. I had on black Polo jeans, a black Champion hoody, and a pair of black Timbs. I was defenseless. Anything could happen. I didn't have a gun or a knife, so not only was it possible that I go home without Paula, there was a chance that I wouldn't make it home either. But I was with it. I loved Paula, and I felt responsible for her being kidnapped. The day before, Dro and I drove down to the Coliseum in Jamaica, Queens, and sold my jewelry. I got seventy-five hundred for my chain and watch, which was highway robbery, and I got my five-thousand-dollar deposit on the engagement ring I planned on giving Paula for Christmas, and Dro sold his two bracelets for $12,500. I had one hundred grand on the dot.

The warehouse was abandoned. It looked like it hadn't been opened in years. It was the perfect place to kill somebody and get away with it. I was scared as hell, and every sound had me jumping.

When my phone rang, I almost shit on myself.

"Turn ya car off and get out of the car with the duffle bag and the keys to ya whip," the voice ordered.

After I did as I was told, the voice continued to speak, "Throw ya car keys over that fence to your right."

I did.

"Good boy. Now take off each piece of clothing you got on."

I took all my clothes off except for my boxers and stood there in the freezing cold.

"Walk over to the fence and throw ya clothes over it."

I had never felt more helpless. This man had my life in the palm of his hands.

"Good boy. You take directions well. I might give you a job

after this. Now take the duffle bag to the side of the warehouse and wait there until I call you back."

Ten minutes after I walked to the side of the warehouse, my phone rang again.

I shivered. "Hello."

"Push the door open, and put the duffle bag inside then go back and sit in ya car while I count the money to make sure it's all there."

Once again I did as I was told and went to sit in my car. I was in the car almost forty minutes when my phone rang yet again.

"It's all here. You lived up to your end of the deal, and I'mma live up to mine. Stay right where you're at and don't leave. My peoples and me gonna leave. If you try something, Paula's dead."

The voice was gone.

A couple of minutes later, a black Nissan Sentra with dark tinted windows zoomed past me. It was then that I figured out whose voice it was. It was Thirsty and his homeboys. I couldn't do anything but look as they passed me by. I had a feeling that I was never gonna see Paula again. I sat in my car in the warehouse parking lot for three hours crying. I knew Thirsty wasn't gonna call back, but I didn't have the heart to leave.

When the phone rang, it surprised me.

"Hello," I said, expecting to hear Thirsty's voice.

It was Dro calling with concern. "Yo, Ski, what's good, B? You a'ight? What's taking so long?"

"Didn't I tell you not to call me? Didn't I tell you I'd call you? I'm waiting for these niggaz to call me back. Now stop callin'."

I hung up, and the phone immediately rang again.

I yelled into the receiver, "Didn't I tell you not to call me back?"

"Oh, if you don't want ya bitch, that's cool. I'll keep her."

It was Thirsty.

"Nah, son. No, I thought you was somebody—"

I tried to explain before he cut me off.

"Go look in the Dumpster. I wish I was there myself to see ya face when you see her. That's gonna be a Kodak moment. But unfortunately I'm busy spending ya money."

Thirsty hung up.

I took a deep breath and then ran about forty yards to the big green Dumpster in the back of the parking lot. When I opened the Dumpster, I couldn't believe my eyes. My heart dropped, and tears began running down my face.

Paula lay in the Dumpster with one arm behind her head and her legs twisted as if they were broken. All she had on was a T-shirt and sweatpants, and they were both soaked with blood. I screamed at the top of my lungs for the whole world to hear, "Paula! Paula! Baby, talk to me, please. Please. I love you."

Paula London was a beautiful, young, God-fearing woman. She left us at the tender age of twenty-two. She leaves behind two loving parents and countless family members and friends. Not only did she have the face of an angel, she had the heart of an angel as well. Anyone who ever had the opportunity to meet or speak to her could tell you how good a person she truly was. Yes. It is true the good die young, but do not weep. For we know that Paula is now home in paradise in her Father's Kingdom. You may now all get up to view the body and pay your final respects," Pastor Wright preached, wiping the sweat off his brow with his handkerchief.

Everyone stood up and formed a line to view the body as the choir sang, "I'm Coming Up." Paula's mother cried hysterically and clung to the casket. She had to be helped back to her seat by the ushers. There was not a dry eye in the entire church. I walked up to the casket with tears streaming down my face, kissed Paula on her cold lips and placed a white rose in her hair.

As I was making my way back to my seat, Paula's father pulled a revolver out of his suit jacket and pointed it directly at me. "You no good son of a bitch. It should be you in that casket. You ain't nothing but a hoodlum," Mr. London shouted as he squeezed the trigger at point-blank range. "The nerve of you to come to my daughter's funeral. It's all of your fault. Rot in hell."

"It's not my fault. Don't shoot."

He fired twice.

The ringing phone caused me to scream, and I almost fell out of bed. I answered the phone. "Yo." It was Dro.

"Damn, B, what you doin' over there? You ain't hear me knocking on the door?"

"Nah, son. I was knocked out. Where you at?" I asked, still feeling groggy.

"I'm halfway home. I saw your car outside, so I knew you had to be home. I knocked on the door and rang the bell for fifteen minutes. I thought you was in there dead or something, B."

"Nah, I'm still here, my nigga. What up though? What's the emergency?" I looked at the digital clock on the side of my bed. "It's two-thirty in the morning."

"I'll be there in a minute."

"Everything a'ight?"

"Just make sure you open the door. I'll be there in a minute."

Dro hung up the phone.

Two months had passed since the kidnapping. When I found Paula in the Dumpster that November, at first I thought she was dead, but fortunately she was just unconscious from an overdose of sleeping pills. The blood on her shirt and sweatpants were from the hit to her eye and the beating she'd endured. I called Dro on my cell phone and we rushed her to the hospital. Paula got her stomach pumped, and when she came to, she refused to let me visit her. She yelled and screamed and caused such a commotion the doctors requested that I leave. Three days later, she was released from the hospital.

I called her day after day, but she refused to take my calls. Eventually the number changed. Paula didn't want anything to do with me. I fucked up the best thing that ever happened to me—or so I thought.

Dro walked through my front door. "Yo, Ski, sit down, B. You're not gonna believe me when I tell you who I sold a gun to last night."

I was excited to find out. "Who, Paula?"

Dro shot back with an aggravated tone, "What the fuck would I be selling a gun to Paula for? Damn, B, is that all you think about? Snap out of it."

"I don't know, nigga. Just tell me. It's too late to be playing the guessing game."

"I sold a gun to a cat by the name of Murder Marv. Do you know who that is? Don't that shit ring a bell?"

"Yeah, I heard that name before. That shit sounds real familiar."

Dro sat back on the couch, putting his hands behind his head. "I bet you it does. He's one of the niggas that kidnapped ya bitch. He's got two men named E Money Bags and Thirsty. Is it a small fuckin' world or what, B?"

I didn't believe him.

"Get the fuck outta here, son. You lyin'! How did you bump into them niggaz?"

Dro sat up as he explained, "Check it, Danielle got a friend named Karen. Danielle been buggin' me for months to double date with Karen and her man. Last night I was bored, so we all went out. At first, Murder Marv was quiet, but as soon as he got a couple of drinks in him, he started running off at the mouth. He told me how him and his two men had Poughkeepsie on lock, and how they were looking to buy guns. As soon as I heard the name Thirsty, I knew it was them, and I sold him my nine and my baby mac."

"So you know where they rest at?"

"Nah, B, I only know where Murder Marv lives. He stay with his girl. I went inside and everything. So what you wanna do?"

I was defiant, "What you mean what I wanna do? I wanna get at them niggaz."

"I don't know if you are ready for all that, B. Let me, Snoop and Boota handle this."

Dro's suggestion was not an option.

"Hell no. They kidnapped my bitch, and they killed Li'l K. This ain't nobody's beef but mine. Them niggaz gotta die." I stood and pounded hand to fist to emphasize my statement.

Dro gave me a serious look. "Yo, Ski, I hope you know how big a step you about to take, B. There ain't no coming back after this one. You sure you can live with a body?"

Dro stared back at me for a while as if trying to detect some weakness. "A'ight, B, I'm out. Tomorrow I'mma come get you, and we gonna start watching Marv's crib. Get some rest." Dro headed for the door and left.

I wasn't in the game a year and already had more drama and problems than I had in my entire life. If it wasn't one thing it was another. I wasn't looking for trouble, but it seemed like trouble had a way of finding me. The more money I made, the more problems I ran into. If I knew then what I knew now, I would've never agreed to ride on Thirsty and his homeys. Sometimes finding out the truth hurts worse than a lie.

□□□

It was Valentine's Day 1999, and Dro and I had been watching Murder Marv's crib every day for a month straight. E Money came over a couple of times, but we never saw Thirsty. It was as if Thirsty had disappeared off the face of the earth. That was until earlier that day when we followed E and Marv to a big house in the nice section of Poughkeepsie. Our mouths were watering when we saw Thirsty open the door and greet his homeboys. This was the opportunity we'd been waiting for, all three of them in one place. From E Money Bags and Murder Marv's body language, it looked like it was their first time at the house too. The sun had just set. We were outside the house for almost two hours. I was starting to get impatient.

"Yo, Dro, what the fuck are we waiting for? Let's get these niggaz."

"Just chill, B. It ain't as easy as it looks. We gotta find a way inside. We've never been here before. We don't know who or what they got inside waiting on us. It could be a deathtrap for all we know."

I didn't care. "I say we ring the bell and body whoever answers the door. From then, it's on. We got vests on, and our hammers got silencers on them. These niggaz ain't prepared for no shit like this."

"The purpose is to kill, not be killed. I ain't going in there blind."

"A'ight. Cool. Stay here and hold me down then." I began getting out of the car and cocked back my chrome .45.

After Paula had left, I stopped caring about everything. To me, if they never kidnapped Paula, we'd still be together and for that, they had to pay.

Dro pleaded with me, hopping out of the car. "Get the fuck back in the car, B."

I ignored Dro and continued to walk toward the house. "Fuck all this waiting shit, son. I've seen enough. If you scared, wait in the car, I'm going in there."

Dro pulled out his Desert Eagle and followed me to the front porch and waited while I rang the doorbell.

E Money Bags looked through the peephole. "Who that?" He didn't see anyone. E Money Bags opened the door and stuck his head out and looked both ways. When he looked in our direction, Dro shot him in the head two times with his .50 caliber Desert Eagle.

E Money Bags' head fell completely off his shoulders. We closed the door behind us gently and walked down the narrow hallway to what looked like it lead to the living room where we heard voices.

Marv turned around, sipping on his Heineken. "Ayo, E, who was that?"

My first two shots missed him, but when he got up and reached in his waist, Dro shot him three times in the chest. His whole insides splattered on the sofa. Thirsty came down the steps and ran back upstairs.

We shot at him, but missed. We reloaded our clips and followed him up the steps and managed to shoot him in the leg just as he entered the bedroom. That's when I saw her. I couldn't believe it. Paula was standing on top of the bed in her panties and bra. I was in complete shock. "Paula! What the fuck are you doing here?"

"What you think she's doin', nigga? She's getting fucked. Paula's my bitch. Always has been and always will be. She was down with everything from the jump. I know you ain't think she really loved you?" Thirsty looked at me from the floor laughing and holding his leg. "You've been played, nigga. Nobody knew about it, not even my road dawgs. You actually did me a favor. I was gonna off both of them soft niggaz myself tonight."

I yelled, kicking him in the mouth, "Shut the fuck up, nigga. Don't say nuffin'."

Thirsty continued to laugh as blood filled his mouth. "Don't hate the player, hate the game."

I shouted at Paula, "You ain't got nuffin' to say? You just gonna stand there and look at me?"

Thirsty interjected, "This is some straight Hollywood shit. Paula, you should get an Oscar for this one, baby."

"Yo, Dro, shoot that nigga, son."

"You kill him. It's your beef. It's time for you to put some work in."

My nerves were shot, and my whole body was shaking. When I pointed my .45 at Thirsty, I looked like Muhammad Ali holding the torch. Thirsty saw my apprehensiveness and started laughing, daring me to shoot him. I took a deep breath and shot Thirsty in the face at point-blank range seven times.

Thirsty's face was mutilated beyond recognition. His mother wouldn't be able to recognize him.

Paula screamed at the top of her lungs, crying.

Dro looked over at me. "What you gonna do wit', Paula?"

Paula jumped off the bed and fell to her knees in front of me. "Isaiah, I love you, baby. It's over now. Thirsty is dead. Now we can be together. The only reason I left you is because he said he would kill my mother," she pleaded, grabbing my legs and staring at me with those gorgeous green eyes. "Isaiah, you have to believe me, we're soul mates. What we have is real. I can't live without you. I've been miserable this last month."

I started crying too. "I missed you so much, P. I never loved nobody like I loved you." The tears rolled down my face.

"Isaiah, I'll never leave your side again. From here on out, it's all about us, baby."

I picked Paula up off the floor, kissed her passionately, wrapped my arms around her and whispered in her ear, "I love you, Paula."

As I was hugging Paula, I put my .45 to the back of her head and blew her brains across the room. Her lifeless body slumped to the ground at my feet. Up until that point I had never felt more betrayed in my life. It hurt to kill her, but it had to be done. I felt no remorse. She deserved it. She took away my innocence. I was never gonna be the same again. One thing I learned about myself that night was that I didn't have a problem killing someone. I knew that I'd do it again if I had to.

"amn, girl, slow down," Wise begged as he was thrown into the wall of the mop closet.

"I want you so bad right now, Wise. Fuck me, daddy. Fuck me." Michelle seductively jammed her tongue down Wise's mouth.

Wise whispered in Michelle's ear while palming her ass with both of his hands, "Shhh! You loud as hell. You gonna get us caught."

Michelle dropped to her knees, pulled Wise's dick out of his pants and began sucking his dick sloppily. Wise guided her head with his hands. "Yeah! Just like that, Michelle. Don't stop. Right there."

Michelle cried out, "I need some dick today, daddy. Don't come. I wanna feel you." Michelle got up off her knees, pulled down her pantyhose, lifted her skirt and bent over the sink in the tiny closet. "Come on, Wise. Put it in. Fuck me, daddy. Fuck me," Michelle screamed out, rubbing her clit as she looked back at Wise.

Wise smiled, smacked his dick on her fat, chocolate ass cheeks and entered her from behind.

"Ohhh. Yes. Yes. Yes. Fuck me," Michelle screamed at the top of her lungs.

Wise and Michelle were on lunch break at their job as sales operators at Cablevision. Wise had gotten the job from his live-in girlfriend Rachel, who was the territorial manager of the Long Island office. Since his girlfriend was the boss, Wise seldom worked. As long as he kept fucking Rachel good, he didn't have to do anything.

Rachel was seventeen years older than Wise and fresh off a divorce. She loved having such a young boyfriend. She bought Wise clothes, jewelry and anything else he asked for. Wise was playing the part of a gigolo. He was living the life in his eyes. He drove all of her cars, had keys to both of her houses and a thirty-five-thousand-dollar yearly salary. Wise felt like he had the best hustle of the whole clique.

Michelle screamed out again in pure delight, "Oh yes! Fuck me, Wise. I'm coming. Don't stop."

Just then, the closet door opened.

Rachel looked at them fucking with fury in her eyes. "Wise! You no good son of a bitch, how could you?"

Wise continued pumping like she wasn't even there.

Rachel screamed at the top of her lungs. "Haven't I treated you well? How could you do this to me? Say something. Say something."

Wise looked at Rachel coldly still stroking Michelle. "Close the door."

"You're fired, both of you. Wise, it's over. I want all ya shit out of my house," Rachel cried, smacking Wise in the face and slamming the door.

"What did you that for? I can't lose my job, Wise. I got kids to feed. I gotta go explain."

"I told you to keep quiet. It's ya fault. She was gonna fire us anyways."

Michelle pleaded with Wise, "Wait. Stop, Wise. Let me see if I can go talk to her."

Wise stroked faster. "Hold up...I'm about to come."

After Wise climaxed, Michelle ran into Rachel's office to explain while Wise went to his cubicle, gathered his things and headed for the door. He knew he fucked up a good thing. Now he was broke with nowhere to go but his parents' house.

When Wise got to the parking lot, he couldn't believe his eyes. His CLK was sitting on cinder blocks. The dashboard and back window were smashed, and there was shit smeared all over the car. On the driver's seat, there was a note.

Fuck you, Wise! Since you don't love anything but yaself and this car, I decided to total your baby. Consider yaself lucky it wasn't you. You shitted on me and now I'm shitting on you. Punk bitch!

Wise stood in the parking lot for fifteen minutes staring in disbelief. He loved that car. It was the only thing that he owned. To make matters worse, he couldn't even begin to guess which bitch it was who had totaled his car. Off the top of his head he could think of ten women whom he'd shitted on in the past month.

Wise put on his book bag and walked across the street to the bus stop. As he was waiting on the bus, a carload of women from the office he had fucked at one time or another drove by taunting him.

"Good for you."

"Drive that home now."

"Broke-ass nigga."

One of the women even threw a bottle at him. As the car passed by Wise said to himself, "I gotta find a new hustle. One of these crazy bitches is gonna end up killing me."

"Yo, you niggaz ain't tired of playing that video game?" Dro asked, bored.

"Nah, I ain't tired of playing this game. I'm tired of you asking me if I'm tired of playing this game. Yo, Dro, you know what I'm really tired of? I'm tired of being broke." Rule continued to play the game without missing a beat.

Dro shot back, "I can't tell that you're tired of being broke. You ain't doing nothing about it. Since you came home, all you've been doing is sitting in front of that TV playing that game and smoking weed."

Rule laughed. "Don't forget about all the bitches that I've fucked."

Dro got up from the sofa he was sitting on. "Nah, B, I'm serious. We need to stop sitting around and go make some paper. Money just ain't gonna fall in our laps, B."

"You ain't trying to get no cake. You've been scared to hustle ever since they ran in the spot. You just talkin', nigga. Sit yo' ass down," I replied angry because I was losing to Rule at NBA Live.

Me, Dro and Rule were at my apartment on a Friday night doing absolutely nothing. Rule had been home for two months. After we bodied Thirsty and his homeboys, the DA had no case on Rule. Murder Marv was the only witness they had, and he was in the dirt. Rule's lawyer got the case thrown out the first day of trial. Since he came home, none of us were doing much of anything. I was flipping an ounce or two here and there to pay bills, but I wasn't focused. That whole situation with Paula had fucked me up. I didn't know how I truly felt about it. I was walking around in a daze. You're never the same after you take a life.

Dro walked up to the entertainment center and turned the PlayStation off.

I yelled out, "Yo, what the fuck you doin', son? I was just about to come back. I was only down by three."

Dro was unfazed. "Fuck NBA Live, B. I got a way we can make some serious paper fast."

I was still angry. "How, nigga? What the fuck you being all dramatic for? Spit it out."

Rule added his two cents. "Yeah. This shit better be good, son."

Dro slammed his fist into his palm. "All we gotta do is start going hard."

"What do you mean going hard?" Rule asked, confused.

"You cut the game off to tell us that bullshit." I said angrily.

"What does it sound like? Fuck trying to make some money, B. Let's start taking money," Dro said seriously, "The ski mask way."

Rule was curious. "Take it where?"

Dro shot back quick, "Everywhere and anywhere, nigga."

Rule smiled. "Oh! So now y'all wanna start robbin' shit, huh? Y'all Long Island niggaz is crazy."

Now I was intrigued. "What type of shit you wanna rob?"

Dro had the answer. "Leave that up to me, B. So are y'all niggaz wit' it or what?"

Rule had no problem. "Fuck it, son. I'm wit' it. Ain't nobody ever gave me shit in my whole life. Everything I ever got I had to take."

"What about you, Ski?"

"Yeah, I'm wit' it. Why not? Let's go hard then. Fuck it."

Dro rubbed his hands together. "Good. That's exactly what I thought y'all would say. I got the perfect spot."

I ain't know it then, but that conversation would turn out to be one of the most important of my life. At the time I had nothing going for me. I felt I had nothing to lose and everything to gain.

□□□

"Yo, Ski, you ready?" Dro asked.

I hopped out of the backseat. "Yeah, let's get it."

Dro, Rule and I were in the parking lot of Blockbuster Video, blacked out with hoodies and ski masks. Dro was watching the store for a month straight. He had everything mapped out. He knew how long it was in between the cops' patrols, where the safe was, how many cameras were in the store and how many employees were working. This nigga could even match the employees to their cars. Dro was a professional. He said that it was a two-man job, and naturally he chose me to go with him. Rule, being the trouper that he was, chose to come along for the ride and watch.

The plan was to enter through the back exit while the manager was on a smoke break. He usually smoked with a young blond chick who worked the register. As they were going in from their smoke break, we were to approach them and force them into the manager's office to open the safe. While I emptied the safe, Dro was to handcuff the man and woman foot to hand. The getaway car was to be parked in the alley, right in front of the back exit door. From there, we were to hit the highway and head straight back to Dro and Danielle's crib.

Everything was going just as planned. The manager was outside the back exit door with the blond girl smoking and talking. Dro and I hopped out the whip, pulled our masks down and backed out on them.

The blond girl started to scream, but Dro went behind her and put his hand over her mouth and his gun to the back of her head. She shut the fuck up quick.

We pushed them into the manager's office and shut the door.

I yelled, putting my .38 to the back of the manager's head, "Open the safe. Don't make me ask you twice."

He followed my orders and opened the safe. After he did that, Dro laid both of them on the ground and handcuffed them foot to hand while I emptied the safe.

"Yo, you ready, son?" I asked after I cleaned it out.

Dro shouted, "Get the tape. Don't forget the tape."

I walked to the VCR, pressed the eject button and threw the tape that may have recorded evidence of the robbery in the bag. "Let's move."

Dro and I walked out the back exit. We pulled our masks up and ran to the car. Rule saw us running. He opened the doors for both of us and started the car.

Dro smiled as we pulled out the parking lot. "One minute and thirty seconds on the dot. You can't beat that. I bet y'all niggaz ain't never made money this quick."

Rule put his seat all the way down and I laid on the floor of the backseat for the entire thirty-minute drive back to Dro's crib. It was the easiest money of my life. Not only was it easy money, it was a mean adrenaline rush. The one minute and thirty seconds that I was in the spot felt like an hour. As I laid down on the floor of the backseat, all I could do was laugh. I kept playing the robbery over in my head. I knew that I was addicted. I was like a crack head getting his first hit.

We made it to Dro's crib about ten minutes before nine o'clock at night. I couldn't wait to get my hands on that money.

"…Nineteen thousand six hundred, nineteen thousand seven hundred, nineteen thousand eight hundred, nineteen thousand nine hundred…twenty thousand. Twenty thousand dollars, B. How's that for a minute's worth of work, B?" Dro was impressed as he divided up the money.

Dro handed me ten thousand. "So how much of that ten grand you gonna give me? I know you ain't forget a nigga. I need that back."

I was shocked. "C'mon, son. I know you ain't about to bug me for that li'l bit of paper."

"Nigga, I gave you almost thirty grand to get that bitch back. That was my last."

"Damn, son. You a foul nigga. You know I'm broke right now."

"A'ight. Check this out, B. I'mma give you twenty-five hundred and keep the rest, and you can consider the debt cleared."

"You a grimy nigga, son. That's why you ain't want Rule on the job, huh? You probably had this planned from the beginning. The least you could've did was tell me from the jump. Here. You can have all this shit, son. Drop me off at my crib."

I felt robbed.

"Don't worry about it. I got plenty more spots lined up, B. Everybody is gonna get paid. Trust me. This is just the beginning."

Dro wasn't wrong for asking for his money back. He was wrong for the way he did it. Sometimes that nigga was too slick for his own good. After Paula crossed me, I was watching everybody closely.

"Yo, y'all niggaz need to take a cab. I ain't trying to drive y'all all the way back to Kingston this late at night, three deep."

Rule and I decided to go to McDonald's and eat before we went home. We sat there in silence for almost thirty minutes. I was tight. By the time the cab came, I already knew what I was gonna do.

The white gray-haired driver spoke as we got in the cab. "Where to?"

"We headed to Kingston," Rule replied.

"Kingston? That's thirty dollars. I'mma need that upfront if you don't mind."

"Upfront? Nigga, is you stupid? I bet you if we was two mothafuckin' crackers, you wouldn't ask us for it. You'll get your money when we get there." I was pissed.

The cabdriver's face turned beet red. "If you guys can't pay upfront, then you'll have to get out of my cab, or I'll call the police."

Rule handed the cabdriver a ten and a twenty. "Here. Chill, duke.

We don't want no problems."

We rode in silence for the entire ride. My blood was boiling. I was so mad that my lips were twitching and my hands were shaking. Looking back at it, I wasn't that mad at Dro. I guess it was just a culmination of everything from the last couple of months. When we got a few blocks from our apartment, I told the cabdriver to make a left instead of making a right.

"Yo, Ski, we going the wrong—"

I cut Rule off before he could continue. I whispered to Rule, "Chill, son. I got this. Just be easy."

I directed the cab deep into the woods by a retirement home. There was a hill behind it that led straight to my complex.

I spoke to the driver. "Pull over right here."

The driver stopped the cab in front of the retirement home and put the car in park. "Alright, guys. Thank you. Have a good night."

I pulled out my .38 and put it in the back of the cabdriver's head. "Turn the ignition off."

I don't know who was surprised more, Rule or the driver. Rule was looking at me like I had gone crazy. The cabdriver turned the ignition off. "Jesus Christ Please, man, I have kids."

"Shut the fuck up, nigga, and put the car in park."

"The car is already in park," the cabdriver said, putting his hands in the air. "I turned the ignition off."

"A'ight, nigga, now gimme the keys and pull out ya CB radio and hand them to me," I yelled.

He did as he was told. The cabdriver was visibly shook. I could tell that I wasn't gonna get much resistance from him.

I continued to yell, "A'ight, you bitch ass nigga, now gimme the money—every fucking penny of it before I shoot ya white ass."

The cabdriver handed me all of his money in a ball. I gun butted him in the back of his head splitting it open. "Nigga, didn't I tell you everything? Pennies, nickels, dimes and all, mothafucka."

After he passed me a Ziploc bag with dollars and lose change, I put the CB radio in my hoody pocket along with the money, then Rule and

I ran out the car to the back of the retirement home and down the hill to my apartment complex.

I made seven hundred and forty-seven dollars and sixty-five cents. I was addicted to robbery. Not only did I love the fast money, I loved the power that it gave me over people's lives. Nothing and nobody was safe.

By the time June 1999 rolled around, it was going on two years since Natalie's death. Even though Snoop still blamed himself and visited her grave once a week, he was relatively happy. He had a full-time job at the Department of Sanitation making six hundred and change a week. He moved into his first apartment—a one-bedroom tenement in Hempstead. He had all the clothes he wanted, jewelry and a car. He wasn't getting money like Dro, Boota and Ski, but when they all went out to the club, he bagged just as many bitches and popped just as many bottles. He looked, dressed and acted like a hustler, but he was working for his money. Boota always wanted Snoop to be his partner, but Snoop just wasn't a hustler. He didn't have the patience for it.

Snoop hopped off the back of the garbage truck, dumped two garbage cans and moved to the next house. He repeated this process until they were almost done with that particular section of the route. When Snoop tried to hop on the back of the garbage truck after he had finished the route, the truck inched up a few feet. He tried to board the truck again, but something happened.

Snoop calmly walked to the front of the truck. "Yo, Tone. Stop playing with me, son. I ain't in the mood today."

Tone was dying laughing. "C'mon, Snoop. Lemme see if you still got that athleticism you used to have."

Snoop was serious. "Tone, stop playing with me. I don't even like you. If I fall off this truck, I'm telling you I'mma beat yo' ass."

Tone used to go to high school with Snoop. He was a grade higher than him. Tone was light skin with freckles and fat. He always envied Snoop in high school because Snoop was so popular and admired for his athletic ability, whereas Tone was barely known. Now that he was in a higher position than Snoop at something, he used the opportunity to belittle him.

Tone spoke to Snoop from the driver's side of the truck. "C'mon, Snoop, you gotta learn to have fun."

Tone stopped the garbage truck, waited for Snoop to grab the handrail and drove to the next route. When they finished their last route, Tone accidentally pulled off while Snoop was halfway on the back of the truck sending Snoop flying into the middle of the street.

Snoop was heated. He scraped both of his hands and knees. Snoop got up, walked to the driver's side of the truck and pulled Tone out by his jacket. Tone fell and hit his head hard on the step rail. On the way down he busted his head wide open.

Snoop kicked Tone in the mouth repeatedly with his size twelve Timberlands, knocking out his teeth. Snoop then got on top of Tone and punched him in the face until his knuckles were bleeding and Tone was no longer conscious. The other garbagemen wanted to stop it but were too scared to try and break it up. Snoop continued to beat Tone after he was unconscious for nearly ten minutes. Snoop stood over Tone kicking him in the ribs. "You always think shit is a joke, huh, you bitch-ass nigga? I'mma kill you."

One of the neighbors called the cops, and when they arrived, Snoop continued beating Tone like they weren't even there. They arrested Snoop and charged him with first-degree assault. Tone left in an ambulance.

Snoop sat in the back of the police car knowing that he had fucked up. Not only was he going to jail, but he was also going to lose his job as well.

"Alright. Listen up, guys, and come into the living room. I got a lot of information to tell y'all," Danielle said excitedly as she walked into the house that she and Dro shared. Anxious to hear her plan, we all followed into the living room.

Dro took a seat next to Danielle. "What's up, baby? Did you remember to look for all the shit I told you to look for?"

"Yes, baby, I remembered everything. Listen up. There are three employees—two females and one male. The older female with the gray hair appears to be the manager. The brunette is a salesclerk. Her display cases are all the way in the back of the store. In her display cases, she has two trays of engagement rings, one tray of fourteen-karat women's chains and some other unimportant antique bullshit—"

Dro cut her off, "What do you mean antique bullshit?"

"Bullshit that you guys are not gonna waste time taking, like pearl necklaces and antique vases. The male salesclerk has nothing but watches in his case. Twenty-five Rolexes and twelve Cartiers. When you walk in the store, they're in the first display case to your left."

"How many cameras?" Dro inquired.

"Oh yeah. I almost forgot. There are three cameras—one behind each salesclerk and one overlooking the whole store. The two behind the salesclerks stay still, but the one at the entrance moves. That doesn't matter because you guys are gonna wear masks, right?"

"Danielle, did you check to see if they had electric deadbolt doors?" Dro asked, completely ignoring Danielle's question.

Danielle pulled out a sketch of the jewelry store that she had drawn. "Of course I did, baby. No electronic doors and no security guard. This store is ripe for the picking. I drew up a diagram so you can understand the layout better, baby."

I had to give it to Dro. He had his girl trained. While Danielle explained the layout of the jewelry store, I stared at her in shock. Danielle was perfect to case the spots because of how she looked. She was Puerto Rican, but could easily pass for being white with her pale olive complexion. She was medium height and real thin with short black hair. She was a pretty girl, but she had the face of an innocent.

"So what y'all think about it?" Dro asked as Danielle got up from her chair and walked upstairs to their bedroom.

Rule rubbed his hands together. "The shit sounds sweet. Only question I got is when we gonna hit it?"

I smiled, giving Dro dap. "Yo, I can't front. That shit do sound sweet. Dro, you're the illest nigga. You even got Danielle on some other type of shit."

"So we on then?"

Rule and I nodded.

"A'ight. I'mma case the spot for two more weeks and put a plan together. Matter of fact, come on. I'mma show y'all the spot right now."

Dro was feeling real confident about this shit too.

"Yo, should I bring my gun?" Rule asked.

Dro smiled. "Nah, B, leave ya guns here. Y'all niggaz starting to go a little hard."

☐☐☐

The next month, Dro, Rule and I were in a stolen Chrysler Lebaron across the street from Pioneer's Jewelry store. We'd been coming to the spot every day for nearly three weeks to jux it, but each time, Dro said it wasn't the right time. Rule and I were starving. We were damn near broke. We were so hungry to make a buck that we started robbing broke-ass hustling niggaz on the block. Dro, on the other hand, was good. He was still sitting on that twenty grand we made off Blockbuster, so he was in no rush. Rule and I had decided that the next time we went to look at the spot we were gonna pop it off with or without Dro.

"Yo, B, tonight isn't right." Dro wasn't feeling the spot again.

"Here we go again," I shouted with my hands in the air dramatically.

"Dro, what's the problem this time, son?" Rule was getting frustrated too.

"I don't like that car in front of the post office. They've been staring at us for like five minutes."

"Nigga, fuck that car and whoever is in it. You've been bullshitting for almost a month now," I shouted from the backseat. "What the fuck, nigga? Is you scared or something?"

Dro was annoyed. "How the fuck can you talk about me being scared? Do you know how many juxes I've done, B?"

I yelled back, "I can't tell, son. You look and act like a shook nigga to me."

Rule intervened, "Yo, Dro, look. The car pulled off. Park the car in the Laundromat parking lot and let's get out and walk to the front. If it don't look good, we bounce."

Dro pulled around to the back of the jewelry store and parked in the Laundromat parking lot adjacent to the jewelry store. We got out and walked around the corner to the front of the post office, which was next to the jewelry store.

We were all dressed up in suits and ties to blend in with the people coming home from work.

"Yo, Dro, how many more minutes 'til the cops make their rounds?" Rule asked.

Dro looked at his watch before answering, "About seven minutes."

Rule turned to me. "Yo, Ski, you ready?"

I was. "You know it."

Rule looked at Dro. "Dro, what about you?"

Dro shouted, pulling his ski mask on, "Fuck it. Let's go."

Once again the plan was simple. I was to enter the store first and announce it was a robbery and lay down everyone in the store. Dro and Rule were to enter the store behind me and go to their designated display cases to smash and grab. Dro was responsible for the watches. Rule was responsible for the engagement rings, and I was responsible for our overall safety. After forty seconds, we were to run down the alley and go through a hole in the fence Dro had cut and run to our getaway car in the Laundromat parking lot. From the Laundromat, all we had to do was make two rights and we'd be on the highway on our way to Dro's crib, which was only ten minutes away.

I brandished my chrome .45. "Everybody, put ya mothafuckin' hands in the air. This is a robbery. Don't move or you'll be killed. If you try and be a hero, I'll make you a victim."

The store had only three employees who worked there inside, and four customers were there as well—two men, one woman and a little girl. I took my position in the middle of the store where I could see everything and had them all lay down on their stomachs with their hands on their heads. Dro and Rule came in and wasted no time getting to business.

The only sound that could be heard was glass breaking from the display cases that Rule and Dro smashed with mallets. The little girl cried and held her mother's hand. Glass was flying everywhere. Time seemed like it was moving in slow motion. All of the nervousness and anxiety I felt outside in the car was gone as soon as I stepped into the spot.

Rule couldn't break the display case all the way, so instead of using the mallet, he broke it with his open fist. He was the first one done emptying his display case. This was his first heist, but he was moving like a professional.

"Let's go, y'all. The clock is ticking. Move fast," I shouted, not taking my eyes off the people I had lain down.

When I glanced to my right, I saw Dro snatching up watches and putting them in a plastic shopping bag. Only problem was there was a hole in his bag. Every time he threw a watch in, it fell straight to the floor.

I called out to Dro, "Yo, ya bag gotta hole in it, son."

Rule ran over to Dro and put his ripped plastic bag in his and picked all the watches up and threw them in the bag. After that, he helped Dro pull the remaining watches out of the display case.

Rule yelled out to me, "Yo, fam, we done. Let's roll out."

Dro and Rule stuck their heads out the door to check for police and saw none. Dro yelled, "It's clear. On three, we out. One…two…three."

Dro and Rule ran out the store, and I followed them, leaving out with my back to the door, gun pointed at the employees and customers. "Thank you and have a nice day."

We ran down the alley, went under the fence and ran across to the stolen Chrysler in the Laundromat parking lot. Dro hopped in the driver's seat. Rule jumped in on the passenger side and I lay down on the backseat floor. Rule pushed his seat all the way back and laid down as well to give the appearance that Dro was in the car by himself as Dro calmly pulled out of the lot like he had just finished washing clothes.

Dro whispered, "Oh shit, B, there's a cop right next to me at the light."

Rule and I responded in unison, "What? Damn."

Dro spoke softly, "Calm done, B. He doesn't know the jewelry store just got hit yet."

Right before the light turned green, the cop put his sirens on and made a U-turn heading toward the jewelry store. Dro made a slow right turn onto the highway. "I told y'all! He must've gotten the call.

He's headed back to the spot."

Once we got on the highway, we knew we were home free. We were hollering and screaming like we had just won the NBA Championship.

We made it to Dro's crib a little bit after eight at night. We went into the living room and emptied all of the jewelry onto the dining room table.

"Damn, son. Look at that watch," Rule exclaimed.

"Ayo, check this out, y'all. What do you niggaz wanna do with the jewelry? I got a jeweler on Jamaica Avenue we could sell all of this shit to wholesale."

I was quick to respond, "Yo, fuck all of that. Let's just go around in a circle picking one at a time. I'll fence my own jewelry."

We went in a circle picking watches and rings for half an hour. Me personally, I didn't know the first thing about watches or rings and Rule didn't either. Dro was the only one who knew what he was picking. He had been studying and reading up on the jewelry for months. The only thing that helped Rule and me were the price tags. If it wasn't for them, I'm sure we would've picked out all of the cheap shit.

After we finished dividing the jewelry, Dro had Danielle drive Rule and me back to my apartment in Kingston. When Rule and I got inside my apartment, we immediately pulled out calculators and added up the price tags in the jewelry. Rule's totaled up to two hundred and ten grand and mine was one hundred and ninety-five grand. I was excited. "Yo, Rule, we did it, son. We got damn near half a mil between us."

Rule looked like he was about to pass out. He sat down on the couch and put his hands over his eyes. "I can't believe this shit. We rich. Good look, my nigga. Since we've met, you kept it nothing but real wit' me. I love you, nigga." Rule was emotional and gave me some dap.

"Nah, nigga, you earned this. You was the MVP tonight. We wouldn't have made it without you."

"There should be no reason why we ain't millionaires by this time next year, son. This is when we gotta get focused." Rule sounded ready for the next robbery.

I was daydreaming of different things I was gonna buy. "This shit is crazy. I'm only nineteen years old and I got more money than old mothafuckas. It's a wrap. I'mma show niggaz how to floss."

That night I could barely sleep. I woke up every hour and counted my jewelry. I was rich—well, at least I thought I was.

When Rule and I went to sell our jewelry in the Diamond District in Manhattan, reality hit us like a freight train. Not only did we not make half of the money we added up from the price tags, we didn't make a fourth of it. We got just under half the price tag amount for the watches, but we didn't get a tenth of the price for the rings. It turned out that most rings in display cases of jewelry stores have cubic zirconiums in them instead of diamonds. The price on the tag is what the ring would cost if it had the specific diamond cut in it. So, for a five-thousand-dollar gold engagement ring, we were only getting two hundred dollars, because all the jeweler could do with it was melt the gold down. Rule, Dro and I still each made out with roughly twenty grand apiece. I couldn't be mad because it was free money, plus it was only forty seconds of work. I kept one gold presidential Rolex for myself, put twenty-inch chrome wheels on my GS, copped five pounds of weed, and traded in my old chain and pendant for a white-gold iced-out Cuban and customized iced-out pendant that read, GO HARD. Dro and Rule spent their money just as frivolously. Dro copped a brand-new Lincoln Navigator. He tinted the windows, put twenty-two inch chrome wheels on it, and had four TVs and a DVD player installed. Dro spent every penny he had made from the two heists on that truck. Rule spent most of his money on jewelry and clothes for him and his pregnant girlfriend, Tiesha.

I also moved out of my one-bedroom condo and into a four-bedroom house with Rule and Tiesha. We didn't need four bedrooms. We just got it because we could. The rent upstate was cheap. All we were paying was twelve hundred dollars a month. I felt like I was on top of the world.

Dro, Rule, Snoop, Boota, Wise and I were in the basement of Boota's house smoking, drinking and talking.

Boota passed the blunt to Wise and looked at me. "So, Ski, you got nerve to put a white-gold chain around that long neck of yours. If I was you, I wouldn't wanna draw no extra attention to that go-go gadget neck of yours." Everybody started dying laughing.

"Nigga, I know you ain't trying to snap, you garage nose, African warrior–lookin' mothafucka."

Everyone continued to laugh.

"Yo, Snoop, what's so funny, nigga? Yo, the other day this nigga put a peppermint ball in his mouth, and the shit evaporated in like thirty seconds. Word to my kids: Snoop's breath smelled like old grease." Boota made the whole room erupt once again into laughter.

Snoop shot back, "Rule, I know you ain't laughing, you ol' Damon Wayans in the face ass nigga. Oh shit, Rule looks like Damon and Boota looks like Keenan. Funny face-ass niggaz always wanna tell jokes."

"Damn, Wise, how long you gonna pull on that Dutch?" Dro shouted, slurring his words. "Puff, puff pass, nigga. Go get a drink of water or something. Ya face needs some oxygen, B." Dro said, referring to how Wises face got red when he was twisted.

Wise smiled as he passed the blunt to Dro. "If my face needs oxygen, what the fuck does ya head need, you helium head–ass nigga. You the only nigga I know who gotta order fitted hats through the mail."

It felt like old times. It was rare for all of us to get up and just chill, smoke blunts and crack jokes. I loved my niggaz. There was nobody like us. We were one of a kind.

"Yo, Snoop, what happened wit' that case at your job? They gonna give you time for that?" Dro asked.

"Nah," Snoop replied. "My lawyer said I'm looking at five years probation."

"So what about ya job?" I asked.

"They fired me."

"Word? Damn, son. What the fuck you gonna do now?" I asked with concern.

Snoop took a sip from his cup of Hennessy. "I don't know, son. I'm fucked up right now. Wise and me both lost our jobs."

Dro looked at Wise. "Wise, you lost your job too? Y'all niggaz is buggin', B. How the fuck did you do that? I thought ya shorty was ya boss."

Wise explained, "I got caught fuckin' a bitch in the mop closet on my break."

"So what's the big deal?" Rule asked nonchalantly.

"I got caught by my supervisor who happened to be my live-in girl-friend," Wise said as the whole room broke out in laughter again.

I was laughing hysterically. "Damn, son. You fucked that up. Shorty was trickin' on you crazy. You was living the life just off her."

Wise shook his head as if the memory of it still upset him. "Yo, the shit gets even crazier, son. When I went to leave, my car was sitting on cylinder blocks. They totaled my Benz. Some bitch left a note cursing me out."

"Rachel did that?" I asked.

"Nah, it couldn't have been her. She ain't have enough time. The fucked-up shit is that I've been dissing so many bitches, I can't even narrow it down."

Boota was on the floor dying from laughter.

Snoop looked annoyed at Boota. "What's so funny, nigga?"

"I'm laughing because we all broke, and Dro and Ski is shining on us. Two bird-ass niggaz. I put my last bricks in Dog and them niggaz' crib, and they let some bitch come in and rob them."

I looked over at Boota. "Word? I know you killed them niggaz."

"Nah, I just beat the shit out of them and pissed on them," Boota announced casually as we continued in laughter.

"Damn, B, all y'all niggaz is broke?" Dro asked. "Y'all niggaz might as well fuck with Ski, Rule and me and start going hard."

Rule agreed, "Yeah. Y'all niggaz might as well. It's easy money."

Snoop was curious. "Jewelry stores? I don't know about that shit. What if we get caught?"

Rule clarified the situation. "We'll never get caught, Snoop. Dro be having the whole shit mapped out to the smallest details."

"I'm wit' it. Fuck it. It don't take much more than looking at these niggaz' jewelry to convince me," Wise said emphatically.

"Yo, Boota. What up, son? You fuckin' wit' us or what?" I asked.

"Nah, I ain't fuckin' wit' y'all niggaz. I'mma keep selling my drugs. Robberies?" Boota said, shaking his head. "They ain't my style."

The Go Hard Crew now had five members. The more people we had, the bigger the jobs we could do. And with the bigger jobs came more money. No place of business was safe.

The following night we were all high and drunk, we went to the strip club and paid the six baddest strippers to come to the hotel for a private party. We got two suites next door to each other and freaked off all night. We switched girls, ran trains, had ménages and watched them eat each other out. The only thing missing was my video camera.

□□□

Dro, Rule, Wise, Snoop and I were in Albany, New York, in two stolen vans outside a fur coat store at seven-thirty in the morning. The store was in a secluded spot to the right of the New York State Thruway. It was run down and owned by a Jewish family named the Schwartz's. On Mondays, which is the day we were there, an old

Jewish woman opened up and worked the store all by herself until twelve in the afternoon. The only problem was that the store had doors that only open by an electronic buzzer. Since we knew the Jewish lady wouldn't buzz any of us in because of the way we looked, Dro got Danielle to come pose as a customer. Everything was easy to rob upstate because robberies weren't that common up there. Therefore most places were behind the times when it came to security. Upstate people actually slept with theirs doors unlocked at night.

The plan was as uncomplicated as a plan could be. Danielle was to ring the bell posing as a customer. After she was buzzed in, Rule and I were to run inside and tie the old lady up while Dro and Wise backed the vans close to the entrance. After that task was completed, Snoop, Wise and I were to get out and form an assemblyline from the inside of the store to the back of the van. In five minutes the whole store would be empty and we'd be on the thruway.

Danielle rang the bell, and just as expected, the old Jewish lady smiled and buzzed her in. Surprisingly, when Rule and me ran inside, the old lady pulled a .22 out on us.

She pointed the gun at us and shouted, "Get back. Get back. I'll kill you. I'm warning you."

Rule and I stopped in our tracks and put our hands up. Danielle, who held the door open for us, got scared and ran out the store leaving us locked inside.

The old lady reached for the phone. "Now stay still. Don't' make me shoot you, 'cause I will. I'm calling the police."

As soon as she took her eyes off us for one second to reach for the phone, Rule lunged at her and hit her with an overhand right to the jaw sending her stumbling back, dropping the gun. Rule hit the old woman again with a two-piece to the face and she ate it. She didn't even take a step back.

The old lady looked at Rule. "You hit like a bitch."

As much as I wanted to laugh Rule and the old lady continued to shoot the fair one, and time was ticking, so I blindsided her in the temple and knocked her out.

I was focused, and there was money to make, but I couldn't stop laughing. Tears ran down my face as I pressed the buzzer to let Snoop, Wise and Dro inside. I tied the old lady up and put her in the bathroom. We emptied the store and were on the thruway in six minutes. Another plan perfectly executed.

Still crying from laughter from the passenger seat, I told Dro about what happened to Rule inside. "Yo, y'all niggaz should've seen that shit, son. That old lady was eating all of Rule's blows. After he hit her with a two-piece she told him 'you hit like a bitch'."

"I don't know if she said all that," Rule stated, lying because he was embarrassed, "but that bitch could take a punch. She got a boxer's chin," Rule said, rubbing his knuckles.

"Then how the fuck did Ski knock her out, B?" Dro asked, "Just face it. You hit like a bitch."

We all burst out laughing.

Rule retorted in defense, "If it wasn't for me, we would've got knocked. When she pulled out that .22, Ski was shook. I was the MVP again today."

Dro smiled. "Nah, B, Ski was the MVP today because if he didn't knock her out, she would've knocked ya ass out. You would have lost ya street cred."

From the fur spot, we drove straight to a U-Haul Storage center where Dro rented two storage rooms and put the furs inside. From there, we dumped the stolen vans in a nearby town and hopped in our own cars.

We sold the furs wholesale to a Russian dude from Delancy Street in Manhattan. Everybody kept a couple for themselves. I kept two Sable minks and gave both of them to my mother. Wise kept four coats. He was walking around Long Island like he was the Mack. The job was a small one, but it put money in everybody's pocket, and when money was in everybody's pocket, everybody was happy. The good times were definitely rolling, and I was planning on riding that robbery shit until the wheels fell off.

"Yo, I need some money, Dro," Roach said. "Lemme hold something."

"Damn, B, I just spent two G's on you at the mall. You ain't never satisfied."

"I'm talking about real money—house and Navigator type money. I want the same type of money you gettin' nigga, then I'll be satisfied."

Dro spoke coolly, "Calm down, B. Everybody is gonna get their turn."

Roach snapped, raising his voice, "Get my turn? What? Dro, you got me fucked up. I don't gotta wait for nothin'. I don't need you, nigga. Are you forgetting who put you on to this robbery shit?"

"Nah, B, I ain't forget that. I also ain't forget how ya careless ass almost got me knocked wit' ya dumb ass for some petty shit. I stepped up the game, B. We pullin' heists now, B. Every move gotta be thought and plotted out. There's enough spots to run in and money to make for all of us."

"Yeah, whatever. Yo, pull over at the next corner."

Dro and Roach were driving down Sunrise Highway in Massapequa,

Long Island, on a windy November afternoon in Dro's Navigator. Roach had just come home from Sing Sing the week before after doing a little bit over a year and a half for burglary—again.

Dro pulled over at the next corner, directly in front of Dime Savings Bank. "Since you ain't trying to look out for ya boy, I'mma have to withdraw some money out my old lady's account. Park across the street. I'll be out in a minute," Roach said as he hopped out of the truck.

Roach was dressed in a blue Polo sweater, light blue Polo jeans and a dark blue Nautica windbreaker, topped off with a dark blue Yankees fitted hat lowered to his eyes. He didn't stand out in the least bit from the other afternoon customers waiting in line at the bank. When he made it to the teller's window he smiled at the female teller and slid a note to her.

I got a gun. Don't do anything stupid. Empty out ya register and put the money in a plastic bag. I want all unmarked bills, and don't try to put no dye pack in there.

The female teller read the note and looked at Roach with shock and horror. Roach nodded his head at her calmly and showed her the bulge in his jacket to give her the hint. The teller's eyes widened to the size of quarters, and she proceeded to empty out the register into a plastic Dime Savings bag as Roach requested. After she was finished, she passed Roach the money and he exited the store as if he was a regular customer.

"Damn, B, what the fuck was you doing, robbing the bank?" Dro asked sarcastically.

"Actually, yes. Pull off slow. We don't wanna draw any attention to the truck," Roach spoke coolly, looking in the rearview mirror.

Dro didn't believe Roach could be so stupid. "Yeah, right."

Roach shouted at Dro, showing him the bag full of money, "No bullshit, nigga. Drive."

Dro screamed as he pulled off quickly, "What the fuck is wrong wit' you? What if someone saw my license plate? Did you think of that shit? Huh?"

"Didn't I just ask you to loan me some money, Dro? If you would've saved up some paper for me to come home to, I wouldn't have had to rob a bank. But no, you wanna be Puff mothafuckin' Daddy, spending all ya money on whips, gear and jewelry."

"What? Are you serious, B? You can't be fucking serious, B. If you ain't have us on that bullshit-ass jux, you would've never got knocked in the first place. Don't blame me because you fucked up, B. You know who's the only nigga you should be mad at?" Dro asked, pausing for a dramatic effect, "You, nigga."

"Fuck you," Roach shouted

"Fuck you," Dro shouted back.

Dro and Roach drove in silence for ten minutes. They had been best friends since high school. They were the perfect combination, a thinker and a live wire. They balanced each other out. After ten minutes, Dro burst out laughing.

"What the fuck is so funny?" Roach asked, confused.

"I'm laughing at you. You the craziest nigga in the world, B," Dro replied, still laughing.

Roach joined in the laughter. "You should've saw ya face when I showed you the bag. You was shook, nigga."

"Yo, how much money did we make?"

"We? What the fuck you mean *we*? I don't speak French, nigga."

"Getaway drivers always get a cut, especially a getaway driver of my caliber and skill. Just give me a third and you can keep the rest."

Roach laughed. "You greedy, son of a bitch."

❑❑❑

Club Jamroc was packed. Girls were walking around half naked, bottles of Cristal and Moet were getting popped, trees were in the air, and the music was knocking. I never was a partying type dude, but on that night I felt like I was a celebrity. Girls were walking up to me practically handing me their panties. Some I went to school with who never gave me the time of day were smiling and breaking their necks every time I walked by.

We all had decided to party at Jamroc to celebrate Roach's release. It was rare that we all were together, especially partying. Weed, liquor, bitches, haters, plus the seven of us always equaled drama. It wasn't if it was gonna pop off, it was when was it gonna pop off.

"Yo, Ski, come here, son. Look at ya man Rule. This nigga is buggin'." Snoop put his arm around my shoulder and walked me to the middle of the dance floor.

At first I didn't see him because of the crowd of bitches around him. Then I saw him. Rule was in the middle of the dance floor doing the robot. He had the sleeves of his Coogi sweater rolled up, two iced-out gold Yach masters on his wrist and two iced-out bracelets. Every dance move he made was to floss his wrist wear. Girls were loving him. If he didn't have jewelry on and he was doing the robot, they wouldn't have given him the time of day. When you got money, you can do anything.

I yelled out to Rule with tears in my eyes from laughing so hard, "Easy on him, son. You're killing 'em."

Rule smiled and continued doing the robot, moving his arm up and down to floss his ice. Rule was a funny dude for real, especially when he was drunk.

Later that night, I was in the VIP talking to Wise when I heard someone screaming my government name across the room.

My high school sweetheart Kim staggered toward me. "Isaiah! Isaiah! Is that you?"

Wise looked at me. "Yo, Ski, look who's coming our way. It's Kim, and she looks drunk as hell. Is this shit déjà vu or what?"

Kim grabbed a hold of my Go Hard pendant on my chain. "Hey, Isaiah, I figured that was you. I couldn't really tell from across the room because ya ice was blinding me."

"Damn, Kim, is Ski the only one you see standing here?" Wise asked with a fake attitude.

"Oh, I'm sorry. Hi, Wise. Isaiah, who wit' you tonight? You don't have a girlfriend, do you? You my man tonight. You in here shining. I heard you was getting money now, but I didn't believe it. You should've started getting money a long time ago, maybe we'd still be together," Kim said, still staring at my jewelry.

Kim was brown skin, medium height with shoulder-length hair. She had a nice set of C- cup titties, a cute face and a small waist with a fat ass, she sort of resembled Keisha Knight Pulliam who played Rudy on *The Cosby Show*. I spent many sleepless nights agonizing over her in school. Three years ago I saw her at the club after a playoff game with the cat she left me for, and she was trying to play me. Kim was a gold digger. When I was playing ball, going to school and trying to do the right thing, she didn't want me. Now that I was getting money, she was all on my dick.

"Isaiah, you're looking good tonight. Come to the bar and buy me a bottle," Kim said with dollar signs in her eyes.

"Yo, you look like you had too much to drink already," I replied. "I don't know how you still walking in them heels."

Kim whispered in my ear, putting her hands down my pants, "Trust me, Isaiah, I can take a lot of wet stuff down my throat, if you know what I mean. I can handle a lot. C'mon, Isaiah, take me home tonight. You've been dying to get this pussy for years." She started kissing me hard and unbuttoning my jeans right there in VIP. "Where should we go? I'm horny and I wanna fuck now. I don't have any panties on." Kim began sucking on my neck.

I put my hand underneath her skirt and felt nothing but wetness. I had to fuck her. She had my dick hard as a rock. "A'ight, look, go sit down and order us a bottle of Moet. I'mma holla at the bouncer and see if I can find somewhere for us to go in private." I smacked Kim on the ass playfully, and she walked away.

"Yo, Ski, Kim is drunk as hell tonight. She's all over you, son. You gonna fuck her tonight or what?" Wise asked, looking at Kim's ass as she walked to the bar.

I gave Wise dap. "Yeah, I'mma fuck her, but I'mma do her dirty. Watch this shit, my nigga."

I hollered at one of the bouncers who I knew from my high school basketball playing days, and he found me a dark room in the back of the VIP to freak off in. I went to the VIP and found Kim at the table guzzling Moet straight from the bottle.

I pulled Kim up by the hand. "C'mon. You can take the bottle wit' you."

The storage room was about the size of a jail cell. Brown cardboard boxes and broken barstools were everywhere. As soon as we shut the door behind us, Kim was all over me. She was wearing a strapless black mini dress with no panties and some sexy porn star five-inch heels, showing off her freshly pedicured feet. Kim was tongue kissing me and jerking me off at the same time. I ran my hands over her body and almost couldn't believe that Kim was such a freak.

"Sit down on the stool," Kim ordered.

I sat down on the stool, and Kim dropped to her knees and started licking around my dick with her tongue ring. She lifted my dick up and licked my balls one by one and started deep throating me. As her head was bobbing up and down on my dick, I pulled her dress over the top of her head, leaving her completely naked. I got up, bent Kim over a stool in a doggy style position and began fucking her roughly.

Kim screamed in pain, "Slow down. Isaiah…you're hurting me."

I pulled on her hair. "Take this dick, bitch. Take it."

Kim screamed out with pleasure, "Ohhh! Ohhh! Yes, daddy. Yes. Fuck me like that."

Kim's pussy was so wet and tight, that I came in about five minutes. When I was about to come, I pulled out of her and jerked my dick off, nutting all over her face and hair. I screamed as the last drop of cum dripped out of me. "Yeah. Take that, you nasty bitch. You like that, don't you?"

Kim lay out on the dirty and cold storage room floor naked with nut all over her face and hair. "Why are you treating me like this, Isaiah?

What did I ever do to you?"

I poured the remainder of the bottle of Moet on her hair. "Bitch, you got me twisted. You think I'm some lame-ass nigga? I treat bitches according to how they deserve to be treated, and you're a slut, so I'm treating you like one."

I peeled off a hundred dollar bill, threw it at her, picked up her dress and left. Twenty-five minutes later, Kim walked through the VIP ass naked. Girls were laughing and pointing at her, and guys started throwing singles at her like she was a stripper. I was laughing so hard I was crying. I knew Kim was embarrassed. As she walked by our table, I threw her dress at her.

Kim yelled as she put her dress on, "Fuck you, Isaiah. You gonna get yours."

I threw a five-dollar bill at her as the whole table erupted in laughter. "Bitch, I just got mine back. Get ya five-dollar-ass out of here."

It was some foul shit to do, but she was a foul ass trick. She deserved it. Karma was a mothafucker. Tupac said it best, *"Revenge is like the sweetest joy ...."* And that night my joy was definitely sweet and the pussy was even sweeter! After Paula, I didn't trust a bitch farther than I could throw her. To me, bitches were hoes and tricks— nothing more.

An hour later, the club was shutting down and we were all pissy drunk and high. We were in the parking lot pimping when a Jamaican cat walked by grilling us like he was a killer. The only reason we were looking his way in the first place was because he had a big-ass iced-out cross. We let it slide and he went to his car with his girl and drove by us grilling again.

Snoop looked at the Jamaican from the passenger side of my Lex. "Yo, what the fuck is he looking at? He acting like he trying to die tonight."

Wise looked at the Jamaican. "Yo, isn't that the same dude who just walked by us with the chain?"

Snoop looked at Wise. "Yeah, that's the same one."

"Ayo, Ski, follow that nigga. Let's yap him for his chain," Wise suggested from the backseat.

Snoop, Wise and I were in my Lex, and Dro and Boota were in Dro's Navigator. I pulled alongside Dro. "Yo, we gonna meet y'all at White Castle."

Snoop yelled out, "We about to go yap this Bob Marley–ass nigga. Y'all comin'?"

"Nah," Dro said, "Fuck that shit. We'll meet y'all at White Castle. Y'all dawgz is wilding, B."

We followed the Jamaican cat all the way to Jamaica, Queens. He must've been drunk, because he didn't notice that we were following him. Finally, he stopped at 133rd and Linden and parked in front of a house. Snoop, Wise and I didn't have masks on us, so we tied our durags around our faces and put fitted caps on.

Wise had two cousins who lived nearby, and he knew the neighborhood better than either of us, so we decided he should be the getaway driver.

Snoop and I hopped out the car with our guns out and ran to the car. I knocked on the window of the Jamaican's car with my .45 and signaled for him to roll down the window.

"Where the fuck is the chain, nigga? Run that," I hollered, cocking back the .45 as soon as the window rolled down.

"Mi nah haf nuh jewels, star. Whatcha ah talk 'bout?" he said in a thick Jamaican accent.

"A'ight, you wanna play dumb? Get the fuck out the car, you bitchass," I demanded.

As soon as he had both feet to the ground, I smacked him in the temple with the butt of the gun, splitting his shit wide open. Snoop had his girl laid out on her stomach in the grass.

"Strip, nigga. Take all ya shit off right now," I shouted.

The Jamaican dude took all his clothes off and stood there in the freezing cold, ass naked. I checked all of his clothes and all of his pockets and couldn't find a thing except for five hundred dollars.

"I got it," Snoop called out.

"Where was it?" I asked.

"In his girl's pocket," Snoop answered.

I gun butted him to the floor.

The Jamaican begged for mercy. "Please, player. Please."

"Stop the blood clot crying," I said with a fake Jamaican accent, dying laughing. "Yo, Snoop, I always wanted to say that shit. Remember the movie *Marked for Death*?" I asked, still laughing.

Snoop and I were so drunk that we just stood there after we had the chain for a minute laughing. I smacked him in the face with the burner one more time and we ran back to the car. When we pulled off, Snoop and I were still laughing.

That was one hell of a night.

When the clock struck midnight on New Year's 2000 and the world didn't end, it was on and popping. I turned twenty two days after Christmas, and if everything went according to plan, I was gonna be filthy rich before I turned twenty-one. As a matter of fact, we all were gonna be rich. We had more than fifteen juxes lined up for the year.

Rule and I were in Canarsie, Brooklyn, across the street from the Domino's pizza spot we were about to hit. This jux was the sweetest one yet. The manager of the store was the older brother of this Puerto Rican girl Rule was fucking named Gloria who was the cashier. Her older brother Javier was the manager of the Domino's pizza on Flatlands Avenue, on the border of Canarsie and East New York. One day Rule went to pick up Gloria from work and he saw her brother Javier counting stacks of money. Somehow or another, Rule convinced Javier to let us run up in the spot. The thing I didn't like about it was that we had to split the paper down the middle with Javier, but Rule assured me that Javier wasn't gonna get a penny.

Every Friday night at about eleven, Javier had to count and wrap up all the money that the store made for the week and drop it in a lock box at the bank. We chose to rob the spot the week after Super Bowl Sunday because we figured that was when they would have the most money. We were expecting no less than twenty-five to thirty grand apiece.

The store had a bulletproof window and a door that required some-one to buzz you in, so the only way to get into the back was to follow one of the delivery boys inside and rush the door. Javier was down with us, so we didn't have to worry about him calling the police or triggering the silent alarm. Besides Javier and the delivery guy, the only other employee who would be in the shop was Gloria. We didn't want it to look like an inside job, so Javier agreed to let us beat him up a little bit to make it look real. The getaway was just as sweet. After we robbed the spot, we were gonna walk out calmly, dump our black hoodies, jeans, masks and gloves in a Dumpster, then take the L train two stops down to Rockaway Boulevard where I had my Lex parked in a shopping center parking lot. I hated using my car as a getaway, but we needed the money. We were damn near broke again. We were running through money like it was water.

"Yo, Rule, I think that's the nigga right there, son. Let's cross the street," I said as the delivery boy chained his bike up.

"Hold up. Lemme see…Yeah, that's him, son. Let's move," Rule responded as we jogged across the street to cut the delivery guy off.

We made it through the entrance just in time. We walked in right as Gloria was unlocking the door to let the delivery boy in the back. "Hurry up and open this door, bitch, before I put his brains on the glass," I shouted, putting my gun to the delivery guy's head.

As soon as Gloria opened the door, Rule pushed her on the floor and gun butted Javier in the nose making blood come gushing out.

Javier yelled, rolling around on the floor, "You stupid mothafucka. You broke my nose. You broke my nose."

Rule kicked Javier in the ribs and the face repeatedly until he was almost unconscious.

Rule shouted standing over Javier, "Where's the money, faggot? I ain't gonna ask you again."

Javier looked confused. His face was covered in blood and he could barely breathe. He was scared for his life.

While Rule was busy beating the shit out of Javier, I was tying and gagging Gloria and the delivery boy in the bathroom. When I finished tying the two of them up and came out of the bathroom, Rule was still beating on Javier.

I threw Rule my Jansport book bag, "That's enough, son. Chill. You gonna kill him. Start getting the money, and I'll tie him up."

By the time I came back to the front of the store, Rule had already filled the bag up.

"Yo, you got all the paper?" I asked.

"Yeah. You got everybody tied up tight?"

"Yeah. Let's roll."

Just as we were leaving the bell on the door sounded, which meant people had just walked in. We looked at the security camera and saw two customers at the door, a male and a female. They looked like they were a couple.

"Follow my lead," Rule said, pulling both of our masks off.

"Yes, lemme get a cheesy bread to go please," the man ordered.

"No problem, sir," Rule answered, throwing some bread in the oven.

"How the fuck do you know how to cook Domino's?" I whispered to Rule.

"Don't worry about it. Go back there and ask Gloria where the video is," Rule whispered back.

I didn't have to ask Gloria where the tape was. When I pushed the door open to Javier's office, I saw the VCR on the shelf. I took the tape out and put it in the book bag along with the money and walked back to the front window. When I saw all the customers waiting on line, my heart nearly dropped out of my chest. There had to be at least ten people waiting to place orders. Rule had the Domino's hat on and was flipping pizza dough on his hand like he was a professional. The customers were applauding, leaving him tips. After we served the last customer, we stayed there an extra ten minutes making pizza for ourselves.

"Yo, where the fuck did you learn how to cook pizza and all that shit?" I asked while we were on the L train.

"I told you, Ski. I do it all, son. I wish you would've took the tape out right before we left. Niggaz ain't never gonna believe this one," Rule responded, laughing, eating a slice of pizza.

The robbery lasted almost an hour, but it was time well invested. We came off with almost thirty grand apiece. Of course, Javier didn't smell a penny of it either.

□□□

"This is a robbery. Nobody moves. Nobody gets hurt. Everyone lay on the floor on your stomachs and put ya hands behind ya head," Wise announced, brandishing two Glock nines.

Wise, Roach and Dro were robbing a jewelry store in a town named Schnectady in Upstate New York, about thirty-five minutes from Kingston. Dro preferred pulling heists upstate because the security systems were so far behind the jewelry stores in New York City. Jewelry stores upstate rarely had security guards, silent alarms or electric bolt lock doors. Small towns also had small police departments, which meant that police patrols were farther apart. Dro found all the jewelry stores by calling the central office of Rolex and asking them for the nearest locations where Rolexes were being sold. Not only did the Rolex operators give Dro the addresses to the jewelry stores, they also supplied directions.

Dro and Roach snatched up every ring and watch in the store. When Wise announced they still had ten seconds left, they busted open the bracelet display case and stole two trays of tennis bracelets they didn't plan on taking.

"Ten seconds is up. Let's move. Let's move," Wise yelled, looking at his digital watch.

Dro and Roach ran to the getaway car—a stolen Honda Accord—that was parked across the street and watched as Wise calmly walked out with his back to the door and his two hammers aimed at the employees and customers.

"Hurry up, nigga. Get in," Dro said impatiently, unlocking the back door to the Honda.

Wise jumped in the backseat, and Dro drove ten minutes across town to another jewelry store. As they drove down Main Street they saw police cars flying toward the spot they had just robbed. Dro's plan was to hit the next jewelry store while all the police were at the first spot finding out what happened. In Schnectady, robberies were so rare that the whole police department would get dispatched to the scene of the crime.

While the police were investigating, Dro, Wise and Roach would be running in the next spot ten minutes away making a new crime scene. By the time the police made it there, they'd be long gone.

"Yo, Wise, don't let us stay in here more than thirty-five seconds. We gotta do this on the clock. I don't give a fuck how many watches we got. After thirty-five seconds, pull us out. Stay calm, B. Keep ya eyes open. It's a big score. If anybody makes a move, don't hesitate to shoot them," Dro said, pulling his mask down.

"I got you, son," Wise answered.

Dro parked directly in front of the store and they got out. Since Wise was the gunman, he was the first inside.

"This is a robbery. Everybody come to the middle of the store wit' ya hands up and ya mouths closed. We'll be gone in thirty-five seconds. Just chill out and stay still. If you attempt to make a move I won't just shoot you, I'll kill you," Wise announced.

The second jewelry store name was Cothren's. It was on Main Street a block away from the police department. Cothren's was the biggest jewelry store they had ever attempted to rob. The store was one hundred square feet. On one side was a bank, and on the other side was a gas station. The store had six employees—four males and two females. All the display cases were connected around the store in a square. Cothren's sold Rolex, Movado and Cartier watches. Each watch

had its own designated section in the store. Danielle had counted fifteen to twenty watches in each section, so if they emptied all three
display cases, they were gonna make a lot of money. Dro was responsible for the Rolex display case and Roach was responsible for the
Movados and Cartiers.

Wise had the six employees and seven customers in the middle of
the store on their knees, with their hands on top of their heads.

Dro and Roach were in their allotted sections snatching watches at
a dizzying pace. By the time Wise's watch got to thirty-five seconds,
Dro and Roach had emptied all three display cases.

"Thirty-five seconds, y'all. Time to move. Let's go," Wise called
out.

Dro and Roach ran out the store, into the stolen Honda Accord and
waited for Wise to join them. Wise backed out the store slowly with his
two guns raised, making sure no one called the cops or got close enough
to the front of the store to get a description of the getaway car.

After Wise jumped in, Dro pulled off and headed to a Key Food
parking lot a few blocks away where Danielle was waiting in a Nissan
Maxima and Dro's Navigator was parked. Dro, Roach and Wise hopped
out, took off their hoodies, masks and gloves and threw them in a nearby
trashcan. They all had regular clothes on underneath. Dro took all the
jewelry and guns, and hopped in the Maxima with Danielle, and Wise
and Roach hopped in the truck. They split up so that just in case they
got pulled over, they wouldn't look suspicious. Since the robbery had
three people involved, Dro figured the police would be pulling over every car in sight, especially cars with black people. Any three black
people in a car would be suspects. With innocent-looking Danielle driving, chances were null and void they'd search the car. Nobody could
ever look at Danielle and think she would be a part of any robbery.
Wise and Roach were also in the clear. There were only two of them,
and even if they got pulled over and searched, they didn't have anything
on them.

Both cars made it through the checkpoint without incident, and they cruised on Route 87 all the way to Dro and Danielle's house in Poughkeepsie.

In total, they made out with sixty-five watches and six trays of genuine diamond bracelets. After Dro fenced all the jewelry, they made almost two hundred and fifty grand to split. Dro and Roach took a hundred apiece and they gave Wise fifty grand. Wise didn't mind though because he had more money than he'd ever had in his life, and he knew there were plenty more jobs to do.

*I*t was April 2000 when the phone rang one day.

"Who the fuck is this," Roach answered.

"It's ya momma, nigga," Boota yelled back.

"Boota, what do you want now?"

"Who you talking to like that?"

"You, nigga. Listen, B, I'm busy. What do you want? Or should I say, how much do you want?"

"How you know I want something?" Boota asked.

"Yo, Boota, I'm busy right now. Tell me what you want before I hang up this phone on you," Roach said, frustrated.

"I need seventy-five hundred."

"Seventy-five hundred? What the fuck you need seventy-five hundred for? Nah, son. You bugging. What I look like to you, an ATM? What the fuck did you do wit' the three grand that I gave you last month?" Roach inquired.

"I told you that was for my car note."

"So what do you need seventy-five hundred for?"

"The bank is about to foreclose my house next week. If I don't come up with that seventy-five hundred, they gonna take my crib, son. I don't want this money, bro. I need this money. If it was just me, I wouldn't care, but, I can't lose my crib, son. I got family," Boota explained.

Boota was at his lowest point in the game since he started. Everything he spent his money so frivolously on when he had it he was losing, slowly but surely. Boota sold all of his jewelry, his dirt bikes, and took a second mortgage on his house in the past six months to make ends meet. Boota would've lost his Lexus if Roach didn't give him money the month before for his car note. Every time he copped work, he'd flip it a couple times and end up blowing the money. Boota wasn't focused at all. Times got so bad that Shamika had to get a job.

Roach, on the other hand, was the complete opposite of Boota. He was focused. Roach wasn't flashy and into material things like his younger brother. The only jewelry Roach owned was a Rolex that he kept from a jux, and he rarely ever wore that. Roach didn't party or even go to strip clubs. All the money he made, he stacked and bought a three-bedroom house in Pennsylvania and a brand-new ride for his girlfriend and two kids. Since the New Year, Roach had pulled four heists and was sitting on a couple of hundred thousand dollars. Even though he had the money to give Boota without hurting him, he hated giving money to his brother. He hated that Boota wouldn't pull juxes himself, but would ask him for money that he made off them. To Roach, there was no excuse for anybody to ever be broke, especially when they owned a gun.

"Yo, when you said you need that by?" Roach asked Boota.

"Next week."

"I ain't giving you shit. You gonna have to earn ya money the same way I earn mine. I got just the spot for us."

"Roach, c'mon, son, I told you that robbery shit ain't my style."

"Boota, you ain't in no position to bargain with me. You about to lose ya crib. You better make this ya style. Get some rest. I'll be over in the morning," Roach said then hung up the phone.

"Roach? Roach?" Boota yelled into the phone as it went dead.

☐☐☐

"So is y'all niggaz down or what?" Dro asked.

"I ain't feeling it," I responded to Dro.

Dro tried to explain, "It's not as complicated as it seems, B. It's a sweet job."

I crossed my arms over my chest. "It ain't the plan I ain't feeling, it's the split."

"C'mon, B. I'm giving y'all fifteen apiece. How much do you want?"

"Nigga, I want the same amount you gettin'. If the pie ain't evenly sliced, I ain't wit' it," I said, pounding fist to hand for emphasis.

"Listen, B, it's my spot, my plan, and my getaway car. I've been watching the spot for a month. Why would y'all get the same cut as me?" Dro responded calmly.

Rule chimed in, "Yo, Ski, he's right, son, and we could use the money."

Rule, Dro and I were eating dinner at a diner in upstate Kingston. It was almost two in the morning, and we were the only customers inside. Dro showed up at our door at one in the morning asking us to pull a jux with him on short notice. The plan seemed sweet, but I didn't like the fact that we weren't splitting the take down the middle. Rule and I hadn't pulled a jux since Domino's, and that money was almost gone. I needed the money, but I wasn't trying to take no shorts. I hadn't worked for anybody but myself since I got in the game, and I didn't have any intention on starting. To me, Dro was getting greedy.

I stood up out of my seat and looked at Dro. "You know why we should get the same cut as you? Because we risking our lives the same as you risking yours. If we get knocked, we gettin' the same amount of time."

"Ski, let's do it, son," Rule pleaded. "We ain't got no paper coming from nowhere else. Na'mean?"

"Yo, son, you ain't seeing the big picture. The nigga said that there's thirty Rolexes, twenty Cartiers and ten Movados. That's sixty watches.

If we only get a G for each watch—and you know we gonna get more than a G—that's sixty grand. We probably gonna take a hundred grand worth of shit, and we only get fifteen apiece. C'mon, son, that don't even sound right. Dro, we good, son. We ain't fuckin' wit' it."

"Speak for yaself, son. I'm riding. I need some paper, and it's easy money—too easy to pass up. I never been the type to turn down free money," Rule stated, giving Dro dap.

Dro looked over to me. "Ski, c'mon, B. I'll give you twenty. I need you."

"Nah. Y'all go ahead. I'm good," I said, getting back up and walking away from the table.

I don't know who I was tighter with that day, Dro for trying to give me shorts or Rule for selling me out. Rule was my man. I brought him into the clique. He was never supposed to go against me, especially when I was right. And Dro was just as bad if not worse. I knew this nigga since I was eleven years old, and he was pulling some sheisty shit like that. I couldn't believe it. Dro had been acting funny ever since Roach had come home. Roach was Dro's right hand man and I knew it was him who was putting all that bullshit in Dro's ear. Roach was greedy and as grimy as they came, and it seemed like he was rubbing off on Dro. At that point, I'd been in the game two years. I didn't need to kiss anybody's ass to get money. My problem wasn't making money. It was keeping it.

Boota's stomach was in knots. He was sweating profusely and his palms were dripping sweat. All he could think about was getting shot or getting caught in the spot—or both. Boota wasn't a stickup kid at all—he was a hustler. If he didn't need the money for his mortgage, he never would have agreed to run in the jewelry store.

꠸꠸꠸

Boota, Snoop and Rule were outside Butler's Diamonds in a stolen black van. Dro and Roach were across the street in Dro's Navigator in a Sleepy's mattress store parking lot watching everything. Butler's Diamonds was also the only jewelry store the crew ever tried to rob with a security guard. The spot was risky, but it had more than sixty watches in it, so instead of doing it themselves, they got Boota, Snoop and Rule to do it for fifteen grand apiece. Dro and Roach figured they could get one hundred grand for all the watches after they paid Snoop, Boota and Rule, and they would still bring home twenty-five apiece. And the best part about it was that they didn't have to do anything to get it.

Boota was the gunman and Snoop and Rule were the smashers and grabbers.

Rule pulled his mask down. "Yo, Boota, you ready?"

Boota was nervous. "Gimme a couple more minutes."

Rule opened the van door. "We gotta go now. The guard just walked to the middle of the store."

Boota and Snoop hopped out the van and pulled their masks down and walked into the store. When Boota entered, the security guard had his back turned toward the door and didn't see them come in. Boota gun butted the security guard in the back of the head with his Desert Eagle, knocking him down instantly.

"Don't nobody move. This is a robbery," Boota announced.

Snoop and Rule immediately pulled their mallets out of their waist and started breaking the display cases. But to everyone's surprise, when they broke the glass, a loud alarm sounded.

"Oh shit! Y'all hear that? Let's bounce," Boota screamed, panicking.

"Just chill, son. Twenty more seconds," Rule said calmly as he put watches into his bag.

Snoop and Rule ignored the alarm and Boota and continued snatching up watches. Snoop turned to look at Boota and saw the security guard reaching for his gun.

Snoop screamed out, "Boota! Look out, son."

Boota turned around and shot the security guard two times in the chest and kicked his gun away from him. The security guard slumped to the floor with his hands covering his chest.

"I'm out. Y'all niggas can stay here if you want, but I'm out," Boota declared, running out of the store, leaving Snoop and Rule with no protection.

When Boota ran out of the store, two female customers ran out screaming behind him.

Snoop shouted to Rule, "C'mon, son. Let's be out. Fuck it."

Rule didn't bother to look at Snoop as he snatched up watches from the display case and continued throwing them in the bag. "There are only a few watches left. We might as well get 'em. We got time, son. Don't panic, we a'ight."

"We don't even got no ratchet, son. We could get popped in here. I'm out," Snoop responded and jogged out the door.

When Snoop left, the three remaining employees tried to follow him. Rule ran in the middle of the store and picked up the security guard's Glock. "Don't y'all even try it. Matter of fact, come here. I want y'all three to put the rest of those watches in this bag," Rule demanded, handing one of the female employees his bag. The three employees stood in place with their hands up.

Rule fired three shots in the air. "Next time I won't miss. Now hurry the fuck up and get the rest of them watches."

The three employees smashed and grabbed like professionals. They emptied the display case in seconds. Rule had all three employees lay on the floor on their stomachs and walked out the store backward with his gun pointed at them.

When Rule made it outside, it was complete chaos. Sirens could be heard in the distance, the alarm was blaring, people were staring and Boota was honking the horn in the van.

"What the fuck you doin', nigga? You could've got us knocked. We've been waiting on you for sixty seconds," Snoop shouted.

"Never again. Never again," Boota shouted. "What's wrong wit' you, nigga? Get in the car and close the door."

Rule was oblivious to Snoop and Boota' previous comments. "I got everything, y'all. I got everything."

Across the street, Dro and Roach watched the whole thing go on through binoculars. As the van pulled off, Dro put his binoculars down and took a deep breath. "These niggaz are crazy, B. The Feds could be after us after this one."

"Fuck it. What's important is that they made it up out of there," Roach responded.

"We would've been better off doing this ourselves," Dro added.

"Don't speak too soon. They ain't get away yet. That spot was dangerous. Better them than us." Roach sighed.

"Lemme hold three grand until next week, son," I asked Rule one day in June.

"Three grand? For what?" Rule asked.

"Does it matter? I said I'd hit you back next week," I responded.

"Yeah, it matters. It's my money you asking for, ain't it?"

"Lemme find out you on some petty shit. My moms just called me and told me she got laid off. She's two months behind on her mortgage."

Rule raised his voice, "So how the fuck you gonna pay me back next week?"

"'Cause I just re-upped, that's how."

"You ain't makin' three grand a week pushing them couple of ounces. Nah, son. I can't do it. You ain't gonna be able to pay me back."

"Petty-ass nigga. You probably don't even got three grand left."

"Call me what you want, just don't call me asking for money. If you would've got up off ya ass and pulled that last jux wit' me, you wouldn't be having no problem right now. You too good to pull a job for fifteen grand, but you ain't too good to ask me for some of my money. You a funny style nigga, Ski!"

Rule, his pregnant girlfriend Tiesha and me were all in the living room of our house. After all that shit I had done for that nigga, I couldn't believe he was acting the way he was. I was so tight that I felt like hookin' off on him.

I pointed my finger in Rule's face. "Who you callin' funny style, nigga? You got nerve, son. You get a li'l bit of paper and start acting up, huh? I'm glad ya showed ya true colors. Don't ever ask me for shit."

Tiesha tried to defuse the situation. "Ski, Rule's only playing. You know he's gonna give you the money."

"I ain't giving him shit. Fuck that. Get the money after you flip ya li'l work."

Tiesha became upset. "Rule, stop it. What is wrong with you? Why are you acting like that toward, Ski?"

I looked over at Tiesha. "Don't worry, T. He can keep his money. He probably don't even got three grand left."

Rule shouted over to me like he wanted to do something. "Don't talk to my girl, talk to me, nigga."

I balled up my fist and walked toward him. "Son, I know you ain't getting on no gangsta shit."

Rule swung a wild left at me. I weaved it and hit him with a two piece, a right cross and left hook that connected right in his eye. Rule stumbled back, and I rushed him and slammed him into the floor. I pinned his arms down with my knees. "You bitch-ass nigga. You lucky I got love for you. Don't ever jump out there with me again. Next time I'm really gonna punish you," I said, pointing my finger in his face.

"I'mma kill you, nigga. I'mma kill you," Rule shouted.

"You ain't gonna kill nuffin'," I said, getting off him.

I stuck out my hand to help him up, and as soon as he got up, he threw another wild overhand left. I weaved it and hit him with a right cross to the nose, knocking him out.

Tiesha yelled kneeled down over Rule. "Ski, what did you do? You might have killed him."

"He ain't dead. He'll be a'ight," I stated, walking out the door rubbing my fists.

I felt bad about beating Rule's ass in front of his girl, but he deserved it. He swung first. Rule had been acting shady toward me ever since I turned down the jux. For some reason, he felt superior over me because he had more money than me. I don't know how or why he felt like that because all I ever did since I met him was look out for him. I treated Rule like he was family. Anything he ever asked me for or needed, I gave it to him with no questions asked. Now here he was talking to me greasy and stunting on me for a lousy three grand. It was then that I realized for the first time that money brings out the worst in people. I was cursing myself for even letting Rule get so close to me. I'd been best friends with Wise, Dro, Boota and Snoop since junior high. Although we had many arguments and disagreements, none of us ever came to blows because regardless of anything we were brothers. I felt the same way about Rule, but that night I found out he didn't feel the same way about me.

I hopped in my Lex and took a drive to clear my head. I had to figure out how I was gonna come up with the money for my mother's mortgage. After I came up with that money, I was still gonna need paper to re-up with. The more I thought about it, I didn't even wanna live in the same crib with Rule anymore, but I definitely ain't have enough cake to put down on my own spot. Something had to give. I needed a break.

I ended up driving to a bar named McKennas, right off of Broadway in Kingston. I needed something to take my mind off my problems, and a drink seemed like the quickest solution.

McKennas had a mostly white crowd. Other than the female bartender, there wasn't a bad bitch in the whole spot, black or white. I sat at the end of the bar and ordered three shots of Henny. After I downed them, I happened to glance in the back of the bar and saw a Puerto Rican cat I knew named Raphael.

Raphael was the older brother of a girl I was fucking with at the time named Candy. She wasn't my girl, but she was my main broad. Raphael was about six feet tall and real thin. He was in his thirties, but looked like he was still in high school. He had curly hair and sharp facial features. In the face, he looked just like Richard Hamilton from the Detroit Pistons. We weren't cool, but we were cordial. Raphael was supposed to be some big-time drug dealer, but I never saw him on the block. He wasn't selling weight, and he definitely didn't have a spot. I always thought of him as lame.

I watched Raphael dance with white girl after white girl. He was pissy drunk. I couldn't figure out why he came to McKennas if he wanted to party.

McKennas was dead. I observed two cats around the same age as me sitting on the opposite side of the bar staring at Raphael also, but the way they were looking at him was different, like they were plotting on him. I recognized the look in their eyes. They had to be stickup kids.

I hopped off the barstool and walked over to Raphael in the back of the bar.

"Oh shit! Ski, what the fuck you doing in here, pai? Come sit down and have a drink with me. Where's Candy?" Raphael asked.

"I think Candy is at the crib," I answered.

"Yo, sit down, Ski. Stop being so uptight and hang out with me for a while."

"A'ight, but only for a minute. I want to put you on to something anyways."

"What you drinking, kid?"

"Henny."

"Bartender, get me a bottle of Hennessy. Yo, Ski, I've been meaning to holla at you, but I never got the chance. I like ya style. You a fly-ass nigga, pai. You remind me of myself. I want you to marry my sister." Raphael blew smoke from his Newport in my face.

"Raphael, you buggin', son. I know you drunk now. Forget all that for now though. Yo, you see them two cats sitting at the end of the bar near the jukebox?"

"Which ones?"

"The two young ones—the dark skin cat and the Spanish-looking kid. You know them?"

"Never seen them before in my life."

"Well, they've been staring at you all night. You need to let me drive you to the crib. You need to go home. You pissy right now. I think them niggaz might be trying to get you."

"Who? Them? Nah, pai. You buggin'. Niggaz around here know better than to try me. Is that what you came over to tell me?" Raphael said, smiling.

"Yo, Raph, I'm telling you, son. You need to go home. You ain't on point right now."

"Trust me, pai, I'm good. Thanks for your concern though. Now relax and have a couple of drinks with me."

I stayed at the table with Raphael for more than an hour. Every time I looked up, I saw the two cats at the bar turn their heads away from us. They were definitely up to something.

"Ski, I'm a grown man, pai. You ain't gotta baby sit me. I'm good. I know you have to leave. You ain't even finish ya first drink yet. Call my sister up. I know she would love to see you."

"I don't want to leave you in here by yaself. I'd feel fucked up if something happened to you."

"Go ahead, pai. Go check my sister. I'mma make a phone call, and I'm right behind you."

"You sure?" I asked.

"Yeah, pai. Go ahead, Dalé." Raphael answered.

When I made it to my car, I heard my phone ringing, but I couldn't find it.

After the eighth ring, I finally found it under the seat. "Hello?"

"Hola, papi. You miss me?" It was Candy.

"What up, ma? Yeah I miss you. You miss me? Me and ya brother was just talking about you."

"I know. He just called me and told me. So, am I gonna see you tonight?"

"It depends."

"Depends on what?" Candy asked in her sexy Puerto Rican accent.

"It depends on how bad you wanna see me."

"Papi, I'm laying here playing with myself right now thinking about you. I wanna feel you. Don't you wanna fuck me, papi?"

Candy was getting my dick hard the way she was talking to me. "I'll be there in five minutes. Leave the door open and take everything off. Keep playing with yaself too." I hung up the phone.

Right when I was about to pull off, I saw Raphael walking out the door of the bar through my rearview mirror. Just as I suspected, the cats from the bar were right behind him. Raphael was so drunk, he didn't even notice. I decided to sit in the car and wait to see what was gonna happen. Raphael was sitting in his 745i BMW rolling a blunt when the two kids ran up on the car with their pistols out.

The Spanish kid spoke, "Where's the work, Raph? We want everything—the jewelry, the drugs and the money."

"You can have my jewelry, but I ain't got no drugs or money," Raphael said, but I knew he was lying.

The two cats gun butted Raphael in the face and pulled him out of his car and onto the parking lot pavement. The bar was on a one-way street, so I decided to ride around the block and catch them off guard.

I turned my headlights off and drove slow down the block. As I approached McKennas parking lot, I saw the cats stomping Raphael. I took my .45 out my stash box, checked the clip and cocked the hammer. I rolled the passenger window down and let off.

My first two shots hit the Spanish kid in the shoulder, knocking him to the ground. My next three hit the black kid in the chest, killin' him instantly. When he fell to the pavement, it looked like all of his insides fell out. I hopped out the whip and shot the Spanish kid one more time at point-blank range in the head, spilling his brains across the parking lot.

"Yo, Raph? You a'ight? C'mon, son, we gotta bounce. I'll meet you at your sister's crib."

I helped Raphael to his feet.

"Holy shit, pai. You're fucking crazy. You saved my life," Raphael said, hugging me.

"Thank me later, son. We gotta bounce," I said, hopping into my whip.

I peeled off in my Lex and he pulled off in his BMW. We made it to Candy's apartment in close to five minutes. When Candy laid eyes on her brother, she almost fainted. Raphael's left eye was swollen completely shut, his lip was busted, he had three knots on the back of his head, and the whole right side of his face was skinned from the two cats dragging him in the lot.

"Oh my God, Raphael. Who did this to you?" Candy asked, applying ice to Raphael's face.

"Don't worry, *hermana*. We took care of it. Ya boyfriend saved my life."

Candy looked back at me and smiled. The thing that I didn't like was how he kept calling me Candy's boyfriend. It was like he was pushing her on me. Candy was a bad chick, but she was far from wifey material. She had fucked every hustler in Kingston at one time or another. Candy was five feet two inches tall and about one hundred and thirty pounds. She had olive skin, light brown eyes, big titties and a fat ass. She was real hood too. She could cook coke, bag up and sometimes even pump on the block. If she didn't have such a bad reputation, I might have made her my girl. She wanted badly to be my girl too. She was playing the good girl role to a T.

"Candy. Dalé. I'm fine. You need to take care of ya boyfriend, You didn't offer to feed him or anything. C'mon, Candy, you was taught better than that. What kind of way is that to treat ya man?" Raphael stated.

Candy turned to me with her hands on her hips. "Oh, I'm sorry, papi. Are you hungry? What do you want to eat?"

"Nah, ma. I'm good. No thanks. Yo, Raphael, you really should go to the hospital, son. That cut under ya eye looks bad. It might need stitches."

"I'm fine, Ski. You're just as bad as my sister. I'm outta here. Ski, good looking, pai. I owe you big time. If you ever need something, don't hesitate to ask. You family now," Raphael said, giving me dap while looking me square in the eyes.

"That was nuffin', son," I stated.

"Yo, Ski. You staying here for the night?" Raphael asked.

"Yeah. He's staying here tonight," Candy answered for me.

"A'ight then. I'll see y'all tomorrow. Gook look, Ski. I owe you," Raphael said as he walked out the door.

That night, Candy fucked me so good that I almost thought about making her my girl.

I didn't know why I blacked out and killed those two cats like that. I still couldn't believe I'd done it myself. The first time I had to body somebody, I was apprehensive, but this time I did it without thought. Things that I was doing started to surprise me. Life was going too fast. As I lay in Candy's bed that night, I started questioning if I had made the right decision. I didn't even know Raphael. I finally decided that it was done and there was no going back, so I closed my eyes and fell asleep. If I knew then what I know now, I would've slept real good that night because I had just made the biggest connection of my life.

I woke up early the next morning and hit the block. Normally I would work off my pager because the block was hot, but I needed it fast. I was in by any means necessary mode. If someone on the block was making more sales than me, I was gonna yap him.

The block was slow. It looked like a ghost town. I'd been on the block for almost three hours and hadn't even made five hundred dollars. At a little bit after noon, a white 745i BMW pulled up across the street.

Raphael called out from the window of his whip, "Ayo, Ski, come here, pai. What are you doing out here?"

I had an attitude. "What does it look like I'm doin', nigga? I'm getting money."

"Ah, man, you're bugging out. Don't you know the Feds are swarming around here? You must wanna get knocked."

"Fuck the Feds. I gotta get this paper, and I gotta get it now. I got bills to pay and mouths to feed, B. I gotta look out for my mother and my sister."

"Please tell me you ain't out here slinging rocks."

"Yeah. And?"

Raphael hit the automatic door unlock button on his steering wheel. "Yo, Ski, get in, pai. Hurry up. Lemme holla at you for a minute."

I got in his whip, and Raphael drove six blocks up Broadway and got on Interstate 87.

I was anxious at this point. "Where you going, son? I can't be taking no trips. I gotta go back on the block and get this paper."

Raphael spoke coolly, "Suave, pai. Suave."

After a short while, Raphael came out and asked me, "Why you out here selling hard? I thought you were smarter than that."

"I don't know what you mean. I'm a hustler, son. I'mma sell whatever makes the fastest money."

"Did anyone ever tell you that all money ain't good money?"

"Nah. And if they did, I would look at them like they was crazy. All money is good money."

"Listen, pai, what makes you think crack money is the fastest money?"

"'Cause I know."

Raphael reached in his pocket and pulled out two knots full of hundreds. They had to be at least ten stacks apiece.

Raphael looked me square in the eyes. "You think this is crack money?"

"It can't be."

"Why?"

"Because I never seen you on the block or heard of you selling weight, and I know you ain't got no spot—well, at least around here you don't."

"Listen, pai, the best money up here is coke money. Grams go for a hundred a pop. The clientele is a better class of people, and it's less risk. That's what I was trying to explain to you earlier. The money you are getting is bad money. There's no longevity in standing on the corner selling crack. The object is to make money and still have your freedom."

I nodded in agreement and asked, "Grams go for a buck? Damn. Where you been knocking that off at?"

Raphael looked at me with a smirk. "Right at the bar."

"McKennas?"

"Yeah, pai, right at McKennas. What did you think I was doing in there? Partying?"

"I ain't know what the fuck you was doing there. I was trying to figure that out." I had to ask him again to be certain. "You made all that paper in McKennas?"

"Yeah, and I'mma show you how to make money in these bars just like I do."

"Where we goin'?"

"I'm taking you to my connect's crib so you can get some of that raw."

"I ain't got no paper right now to be re-ing up, B."

"How much work you got?"

"I'm fucked up right now. All I got is two Os"."

"How much you suppose to make off all that?"

"Like five grand."

"I'mma give you five grand and you give me ya work when we come back. A'ight?"

"Bet."

Raphael took me to Manhattan, introduced me to his connect and bought me a quarter of a kilo of raw powder. He even paid the money to the transport girl to bring my work back upstate on the bus. Nobody ever looked out for me like Raph did.

Later on that night after my work arrived, he showed me how he bagged up—no cut and nothing but grams. Raphael said that off that quarter of a brick, I should make twenty grand, and that I would be finished in two weeks at the most. After we finished bagging up, he drove me to a bar named Scrupples and introduced me to the bartender and a six-foot-eight fiend by the name of Tone.

The bar was completely different than the one Raphael pumped out of. Raphael's bar was upscale and occupied by mostly middle-class white people, whereas my bar was hood and occupied by lower-class white people, crack heads and people my age.

"Yo, what's good? Why are we at this bar instead of McKennas?" I had to ask.

"McKennas is my spot. This is gonna be your spot, pai. Don't sell nothing hand to hand. Let Tone make all the sales and break him off a few grams at the end of the night. If you need something, page me," Raphael said, smiling at me as he walked out the bar.

The night started off slow, but picked up gradually. I almost couldn't believe that fiends were paying a hundred a gram. Coke heads were completely different than crack heads. They rarely ever came with shorts. At the end of my first night, I went home with twenty-five hundred dollars. That was the easiest money I had ever made off drugs in my life. All I had to do was sit down at a table, watch sports and drink. I loved it. By the time I finished hustling out of this bar, I figured I'd probably own it.

ho the fuck is that constantly paging you? That's the fifth fucking time ya pager went off and you ain't answer it. Who is it? I know that's a bitch. I swear to God, if I catch you, I'mma kill you both," Candy shouted.

"Keep talking that gangsta shit. You starting to turn me on. You look sexy when you're mad. Come here," I said, standing behind her and kissing her on the neck.

"Get off me. Don't touch me," Candy screamed, starting to cry.

"What's wrong wit' you? You spazzing for nuffin'," I spoke calmly.

"You think I'm stupid? I'm not stupid. Every time ya pager goes off or ya cell phone rings, you always leave the room. I hear you whispering, mothafucka. Besides, all that, all of my friends tell me you cheating on me. I hate you," Candy yelled with tears rolling down her cheeks.

"Ya friends is lying 'cause they jealous, and they ain't got nobody. Who you gonna believe? Me or them?"

Candy and I were eating dinner in the dining room of my new four-bedroom house. I had been hustling in the bar for only two months and I was already re-ing with a brick and a half. The house I was renting was off the hook—four bedrooms, a living room, two dens, an outdoor swimming pool, a Jacuzzi in the master bedroom, a large kitchen, a finished basement and a two-car garage. Candy decorated the crib and bought the finest and most expensive shit. We had Italian leather furniture, fifty-two-inch big screen televisions all over the house with a surround sound system. I called it the mini mansion. I also leased a brand-new 2000 red 600 Benz in Candy's name. I upgraded all of my jewelry from white gold to platinum and paid the mortgage on my mother's house for six months. Things were going so good that I finally gave in to Raphael's urging and made Candy my girl and moved her in with me. And the truth be told, Candy was starting to grow on me. The only problem I had with her was that she was so insecure and jealous. Every time my pager went off, my cell phone rang, or I left the house, I was getting accused of cheating on her. Not that I didn't want to or plan to, but I was so focused on getting money that I didn't have time to fuck anyone else.

Candy continued shouting, "I'm not stupid, Ski. You think I don't know what's going on?"

"Calm down and stop yelling. Let's talk like adults."

Candy threw a plate at me. "I don't wanna talk about nothing. Is this how you repay me? I've been good to you. If it wasn't for me and my brother, you wouldn't be making all of this money, you no good son of a bitch."

The plate missed my head by inches. I got up, grabbed Candy by the shoulders and shook the shit out of her. I could tell by her reaction that she was scared. Up until then she had never seen me get mad.

I yelled as I pinned her against the wall, shaking her, "What the fuck is wrong with you? I ain't fucking nobody but you. You hear me? If you want me to fuck other bitches, I will. Is that what you want? Huh? Answer me."

Candy fought to get me off her. "Get ya hands off me. You're hurting me."

I let her go. "What the fuck do you want from me?"

"Lemme call back all the numbers on ya pager and cell phone."

"What? Are you crazy? For what?"

"I knew it. You must got something to hide then," Candy stated, crossing her arms.

"A'ight, bet. You wanna play games? We can play games. I'll let you call every number on my pager, but after you find out there ain't no other females, it's over. You gotta pack your shit and leave."

"What do I get if you are cheating?" Candy asked.

"I'll give you my Lex."

"Bet," Candy said with her hand out waiting for me to hand her my cell phone and pager.

"A'ight. Remember, after this there ain't no coming back," I said, handing her the phone and pager.

Candy was like a little kid at Christmas. She called every single number I had in both my pager and phone. A few of them were from my little sister, a couple was from Snoop and Boota, and the five pages that I received at dinner were all from her brother Raphael, paging me from the bar. After she made the last call, her eyes immediately welled up, and she came running over to me in tears.

Candy pleaded with me sitting on my lap, kissing me on my neck. "I'm sorry, papi. I should've believed you. Are you mad at me? You know I love you, right?"

I pushed Candy off me and got up off the couch. "Well? What are you waiting for?"

Candy looked at me confused. "What do you mean?"

"Pack ya shit and get the fuck out of my house. That's what I mean."

Candy cried out, falling to her knees in front of me, "Papi, no. Please. I love you."

"Pack ya shit and get the fuck out, Candy. It's over. I'm going to the bar now. When I come home, make sure all of your shit is gone." I walked out the house slamming the door behind me.

That night I went straight to the bar and told Raphael what happened. He said he understood my decision and he didn't wanna get involved in our relationship.

Raphael ran out of work, so he let me get all of the sales at his bar. Between his bar and mine, I made ten grand. I was so happy and so drunk that I didn't even remember what happened with Candy earlier. When I stepped through the front door of my house and turned the light on, I sobered up immediately. Candy had trashed the entire house. She cut up the living room furniture, broke the screens on all the televisions and put holes in my walls. I was so tight that I felt like killing that bitch. She was gonna have to pay for that one.

□□□

"Yo," Dro answered the phone.

"Dro, what's good, my nigga?" Rule responded.

"Who's this?"

"It's me, nigga. Rule."

"Oh, my bad, B. What's up?"

"That's what I'm trying to find out. I ain't heard from none of y'all niggaz in a minute. You ain't get my pages? I've been paging you every day for the last week."

"Word? That was you? I ain't know who that was."

"Yeah, son. I need some paper. I need a job. You ain't got nothing coming up?" Rule asked.

"Nah, son. We chillin' right now. Yo, hold on for a minute. Somebody's calling me on the other line." Dro placed Rule on hold.

Dro was on top of the world. In the last four months, he had made two hundred grand. Dro, Wise, Roach and Snoop were robbing everything. Dro put down on a house in Poughkeepsie for him and Danielle and another house in Long Island to hang out and party at.

At the time, Dro was at his house in Poughkeepsie he shared with Danielle. Dro had every toy he had ever dreamed of. He had a 2000 white 745i BMW, a 2000 drop-top candy apple red Porsche and three dirt bikes. He also copped a Lexus truck for Danielle. Dro's jewelry was ridiculous. He was so iced out that he could light up a dark room. His jewelry was better than most rappers. Dro had plenty of juxes lined up, but after he found out that Ski and Rule weren't cool anymore, he started playing Rule to the left. Dro barely knew Rule. The only reason he ever dealt with him in the first place was because he was Ski's man.

Dro answered the other line, "Hello."

A male voice spoke. "Yeah. Can I speak to Danielle?"

"What? Who the fuck is this?"

"Dro? What up, yo? It's me, Jamal."

"I'm on the phone," Dro stated angrily switching the line back to Rule.

Jamal was Danielle's best friend. Dro couldn't stand him or the fact that he was spending so much time with his girl. It wasn't that he didn't trust Danielle, he just didn't like anyone around his girl, especially another guy.

Dro switched back to Rule. "Yo."

"Yeah, son, like I was saying, I need a job. I'm fucked up. Since Ski moved out, I gotta pay all my bills by myself, son. That shit ain't easy, fam. I'm fucked up right now. Tiesha is about to drop the baby any minute and I'm dead broke," Rule explained.

"Damn, B. I feel for you. I wish I could help, but I'm fucked up myself. We ain't pulling no more juxes till this winter. Shit is too hot right now, B," Dro lied.

"Damn, son, you think I could borrow a G until I get on my feet?" Rule asked.

"I wish I could, B, but like I told you already, I'm fucked up too. I ain't got a pot to piss in."

"A'ight, fam. Just keep me in mind. I'm trying to eat."

"Just be patient, B. Holla at me next month." Dro hung up the phone.

Dro shouted from the bottom of the stairs, "Danielle. Danielle."

Danielle was in the bathroom. "What's up, babe?"

Dro was tight, and his blood was boiling. Dro had told Danielle a couple of times that he didn't want Jamal calling the house anymore. He stormed up the steps and went into the smoking hot bathroom where Danielle was taking a shower.

Dro sat down on the toilet. "Jamal just called here."

"Oh, he did? Where's the phone?"

"It's on the mothafuckin' charger. Didn't I tell you I didn't want this fucking clown to call my house anymore?" Dro said with attitude.

"He's only calling because we're supposed to go to dinner tonight to celebrate his birthday. It was last Tuesday."

"What the fuck are you going out to dinner with this bitch-ass pussy for?"

"DaShaun, it's only Jamal. He's my only friend. I need someone to hang out with while you're gone. It's boring sitting in the house all day. You don't spend time with me anymore. I barely see you."

"I'm out making money for us. How you think you pushing that truck and living in this fly-ass crib?"

"I know you have to work, babe, but I miss you. What's the point of having this big-ass house and all these nice things if I can't enjoy them with you? If I wasn't going to dinner tonight, I'd be in the house alone. Aren't you going to Long Island again tonight?"

"Yeah, but I'll…" Dro tried to explain, but got cut off midsentence.

"You don't trust me anymore? I don't ever question you or accuse you of doing anything because I know better. And you should know better, DaShaun. I love you. I'd never cheat on you with anyone. Jamal is my friend. You're my soul mate," Danielle explained.

Dro knew Danielle was right. He was just accusing Danielle of cheating because he was feeling guilty because he was doing dirt. Ever since Dro started making a lot of money, he stopped spending time with Danielle and started hanging out and club hopping every night with Wise. Dro was far from a womanizer—in fact that summer was the first time that he ever cheated on Danielle. Now Dro was fucking a different woman every night. That night he was going to Long Island to get up with a Korean chick he'd met a week earlier.

"Babe, listen, it's not that I don't trust you because I do. Do you think I like not spending time with you? It's driving me crazy. When I'm in Long Island, I be lonely too. I promise when I get back that we'll go somewhere real nice, just the two of us," Dro said sincerely.

Danielle's eyes lit up like a Christmas tree. "You promise?"

"I promise."

Danielle got out the shower with only a towel on. "Babe, you don't have nothing to worry about. Nobody can replace you."

Danielle sat on Dro's lap and began kissing him and unbuttoned his pants at the same time. She pulled her towel off, grabbed Dro's throbbing, rock-hard dick and slid it inside of her. As Danielle started riding Dro, he thought he should start spending more time at home. To him, there was no pussy better than Danielle's.

◻◻◻

It was a warm Saturday night in the middle of September 2000, the night of Raphael's birthday bash. Intuitions was the hottest and biggest club in that section of upstate New York. Raphael rented out the club for the night and paid Kid Capri to deejay and The Lox to perform. Everybody and their mother was gonna be there. I invited the whole clique up for the weekend to party and stunt, but mostly to show off my crib, my new jewels and my whip. When I told Raphael what his sister did, he paid for all the damages and made Candy call and apologize. Deep down, I think he thought we'd end up back together, but that was the farthest thing from my mind. I was fucking everything in a skirt. At times, my crib looked like the Playboy mansion. Boota, Snoop, Dro and Wise came up to chill for the weekend. When we pulled up outside of Intuitions, all eyes were on us. We rolled up to the club five deep in five different whips. Dro brought out his Porsche 911, Wise drove his brand-new CLK, Boota had his Lex, Snoop had his Escalade and I had my 600 Benz. All of us were dressed fly as hell and our ice had us looking like strobe lights. When we passed by the girls who were waiting on line, they did everything but take their panties off and hand them to us. There wasn't a chick out there that wouldn't have left with us right at that moment.

The speakers blared the summer anthem "Best of Me" remix with Mya and Jay-Z as we walked in.

Inside was standing room only. There was hardly enough room to dance without bumping into someone or stepping on someone's feet. I bought the bar out, and we took two bottles of Cristal apiece and joined Raphael in the VIP section.

I gave Raphael dap and put a bottle of Cristal in front of him. "What up, old man? Happy born day, my nigga."

Raphael passed me a Cuban cigar. "I ain't old yet. Thirty-five is still young, pai.

"Ayo, these are my niggaz. The big head one with all the ice is my man Dro. The black-ass one right there with the big lips that look like an African is my man Boota. The light skin kid who look like a fake-ass Al B. Sure is my man Wise, and my man with the permanent ice grill is Snoop," I introduced jokingly.

"What's good?" they all spoke in unison, giving Raphael dap one at a time.

"Ski talks about y'all all the time. I feel like I know y'all already," Raphael replied.

"We heard about you too. We heard you out here getting that paper," Boota stated.

"Yeah, we tryin' to do our thing out here. Ya man Ski is doing very good for himself. He's a fast learner. He got more money than me now," Raphael joked.

"Shit! You know that's a lie," I responded.

Someone came in the middle of our conversation and whispered something in Raphael's ear, and as soon as they left, Raphael spoke. "Ayo, y'all enjoy yaselves. I'll get up with y'all a li'l bit later. I gotta go play the host role and make sure they ain't stealing money. Excuse me." Raphael left the table.

"Damn, Raph, you even thinking about money on ya day off," I shouted.

Raphael turned around and shouted before he left the VIP section, "Ain't no such thing as a day off, pai. Enjoy yaselves."

"Yo, so that's who put you on?" Wise asked.

"Yeah, that's him. Raph is mad cool," I replied.

"You hustling for that bird-ass nigga?" Snoop asked in disbelief.

"I ain't never hustled for nobody. Raphael is just the one who showed me how to hustle right," I explained between sips of Cristal.

"He's a bird-ass nigga. I don't like him," Snoop answered back.

"Damn, son, you don't even know him." I looked over at Snoop.

"How much money do you think dude be making a week? We could run up his spot. I know that'll be an easy payday, B," Dro said seriously.

"Damn! Y'all niggaz need to chill the fuck out. None of us ain't gotta like him. All I know is he's looking out for Ski, and Ski is making a lot of paper. For that, he's a'ight with me. Now I don't know about y'all meatball-ass niggaz, but I came here to party. I'm going to bag some bitches," Boota stated, getting up from the table.

We each grabbed our bottles of Cristal and headed to the dance floor. The party was jumping. The ratio of girls to guys was at least ten to one. It was bad chicks of all shapes, sizes and flavors, and they were all on our dicks. No group was shining more than us that night, including The Lox and Kid Capri.

Wise and Boota scooped up three bad strippers and were doing everything but fucking inside the club. Dro grabbed a chick that was half Korean and black and was pollying with her all night. Snoop met a dimed-out Dominican girl and they were either dancing or talking all night. On the other hand, I was in heaven. I lucked up and bagged two bad-ass redbone lipstick lesbos. I was in the middle of the dance floor sandwiched between them kissing, fingering, humping and everything else that came to mind. Candy stayed no more than ten feet from me all night. She was all dressed and made up, trying to do anything to draw my attention. I caught glimpses of her dancing dirty with someone here and there trying to make me jealous, but I couldn't give two shits what she was doing. All I was concerned with was my two lesbos.

One of the girls whispered in my ear, "Ski, c'mon. Take us home with you. We're ready to fuck. I haven't had dick in more than two years."

The other girl put her hand underneath her skirt. "Yes, baby, let's leave. My pussy is throbbing. Feel it."

Those two lesbos had me going. Just the thought of me fucking with them had me pre-ejaculating. My dick had been rock hard for almost an hour straight. The Lox were my favorite group and they were set to perform in ten minutes, so I decided to wait and leave after the performance. I had no reason to rush. I was gonna have those two all night long.

"Just chill. We got all night and all morning, y'all. Lemme just see the first ten minutes of The Lox and then we can skate," I advised.

Just then, Candy came walking up to us and stood in front of me with her hands on her hips. "Did he tell y'all he's a married man? Ski is my husband and baby's father."

I said to Candy for what seemed like the millionth time, "Candy, don't start no shit. Why you gonna come over here and embarrass yaself like this? I ain't ya baby's father, and I definitely ain't ya husband. How many times do I gotta tell you that it's over?"

Candy shouted, completely ignoring my last statement and pushing one of the girls off me, "Get y'all hands off of him. He's my man."

I yelled out, "Candy, chill. You making a scene."

My words were of no use. Candy swung and hit one of the girls in the temple, grabbed a handful of her hair and threw her to the ground. The other lesbo swung at Candy and missed, but still managed to wrestle Candy to the ground. When the two girls started to really get out on Candy, I broke it up, but not before she got what she deserved. The entire party stopped. Candy's skirt was torn in the back exposing her thong, and one of the lesbo's shirt was torn off exposing her titties. Just as the men started whistling and making slick remarks, Raphael and two security guards ran over.

"Candy, what happened to you?"

"These bitches jumped me. I want them out right now. Get them out," Candy shouted at the top of her lungs.

Security escorted the two lesbos outside, and I stayed behind to explain to Raphael what really happened.

"My bad, pai. I shouldn't have even let Candy come to the party. I knew something like this was gonna happen. My bad. I hope she ain't fuck up ya night. You look like you had a good thing going over there," Raphael said, apologizing.

"Don't worry about it, son. I'm good. I'mma leave now though. I ain't trying to miss out on this ménage a trois," I responded, giving Raphael dap.

I found the fellas and told them I was going to the crib. They all said they'd be there after the party. I was still feeling good. Nothing could possibly ruin my night. I was drunk, high and young with money. I had two lesbians waiting for me in the 600 too. Life couldn't get any better.

When I got in the car and sat in the driver's seat, it seemed like the party had gotten started without me. The lesbians were in my backseat freaking off. One was eating the other one out.

One of them screamed out as I closed the door, "Yes! Right there, baby. Suck that clit. I'm about to come."

"Damn! Y'all started without me?" I asked, starting the car.

One of the girls hopped into the front seat, unbuttoned my pants and started giving me some of the best head I ever had in my life. While one was sucking me off, the other one was rubbing my chest and licking my ears from the backseat. I could barely drive. I was swerving lane to lane. We were on Interstate 87 when I saw lights in my rearview mirror. It was the state troopers. I pulled over to the side of the road, put the car in park and pulled my pants up.

Suddenly, three more state trooper cars showed up and boxed me in. I ain't know what the fuck was going on.

A demand came from the loudspeaker of one of the cop cars: "Take your keys out the ignition and put them on top of the car." Once I had done what he'd asked, the cop continued, Good. Now everybody put your hands out the window."

Millions of thoughts were racing through my head. From the way they had their guns drawn on us, it had to be more than a routine stop. And if it was more than a routine stop, what did they have on me? Robbery? Drugs? I was doing too much dirt to narrow it down. All I could think was, *Not now*. Everything was going too good. Every dog had its day, and it must've been mine.

By September, Rule was pissy drunk and fuming mad. He was broke, two months late on his rent and his girlfriend Tiesha had just given birth to their first child a week ago. When it was time to bring the baby home, Tiesha had to bring the baby to her mother's house because their apartment had no electricity. Rule felt like half a man. Here it was, he just brought a new life to the world and he couldn't even provide a home for his child. Rule didn't even have enough money to buy formula or diapers. He blamed no one but Ski, and he wanted to make Ski pay. Rule heard that Ski was hustling coke in Scrupples, so he decided to confront him once and for all. Rule felt like Ski told Dro not to let him eat with him anymore.

Rule stumbled into the bar and looked around. He didn't see Ski. There were only two people in the entire bar, an old drunk and the bartender. *That bitch-ass nigga must be hiding from me. I know he's in here,* Rule thought, not knowing that Ski never went to the bar at two o'clock in the afternoon.

"Ski, I know you're in here, mothafucka. Don't try and hide. Come out and fight like a man," Rule shouted.

Rule stumbled over to the bar and asked the bartender who was really the owner if he knew where Ski was.

"I'm sorry, man. There isn't a Ski who works here. I think you got the wrong place," the bartender replied.

Rule was swaying back and forth and slurring his words, "Don't lie, mothafucka. I know you know Ski! How much does he pay you to say all that shit? Tell Ski to come out and fight me like a real man."

The bartender remained calm. "I told you, sir. I don't know the person you're looking for. You're too loud. Now, if you're not gonna buy a drink and calm down, I'm gonna have to ask you to leave."

"Stop lying to me, you no-good cracker. Don't make me tear this shit up," Rule threatened.

'Sir, please leave. I don't want any problems. Don't force me to call the cops because I will," the bartender said.

"Do you know who I am? Huh? You think I give a fuck about the police? Go ahead and call 'em," Rule shouted.

"I told you I don't know the person you're asking for, buddy. Please leave."

"You gonna lie to my face like that? A'ight. Watch this."

Rule picked up a stool and threw it straight into the bar, shattering several bottles of liquor that were on the mantel. He continued throwing stools over the bar until he shattered the large mirror behind it and broke almost every single liquor bottle.

"I'm warning you. Tell me where Ski is. I'm gonna fuck up this whole spot and then I'mma start to beat yo' ass," Rule threatened.

"Hold on, buddy. Hold on. I haven't seen Ski in a couple of days. He usually only shows up at night," the bartender pleaded, balled up underneath the bar.

"I knew it, you no-good cracker. I should kill you. Fuck this. Tell Ski if I can't get no money, then neither can he."

Rule walked over to a table, picked up a chair and threw it into the jukebox, shattering glass everywhere. From there, Rule broke the screens of every video game and mirrors in the entire bar. He also broke every stool, chair and table. Rule was on a rampage. He took a razor and sliced all the pool tables from top to bottom and turned them over. By the time Rule finished, the bar was completely totaled. It looked like a hurricane had just passed through.

"Tell Ski that Rule said if I can't eat, then he can't eat either, and if he don't like it to come see me. He knows where I'm at," Rule stated as he walked out the door.

"Hey, you, freeze. Put your hands in the air," two policemen shouted, pointing their guns at Rule.

Rule knew the procedure all too well. He put his hands in the air, and the police officers pushed him against the wall, patted him down and cuffed him. Rule was so drunk he didn't even care. He laughed himself to sleep all the way to the police station.

□□□

I was heated and my blood was boiling. I spent two days at the county jail for stealing my own car. Apparently Candy had reported the car stolen that night I kicked her out of the house. I knew I shouldn't have put my car in her name in the first place. I was kicking myself in the ass for making such a stupid mistake. Candy was the most spiteful, vindictive bitch I had ever encountered. I felt like I was Michael Douglas in the movie *Fatal Attraction*. Everywhere I turned, Candy was always right there. I had a feeling in my gut that she was gonna end up being the death of me. I called Raphael from the county and explained the situation to him. Of course Raphael forced Candy to drop the charges, but I still had to spend the weekend in county because of the DWI charge, and I wouldn't be able to see a judge until that following Monday.

Earlier that morning, I pleaded guilty to driving while intoxicated, and the judge suspended my license for six months and ordered me to serve ten hours in a drug and alcohol treatment class.

Not only did Candy fuck up my ménage a trois, she fucked up my entire weekend. I didn't even get a chance to party with the fellas before they went back to Long Island. As soon as I got released, I took a cab home, jumped in my Lex and drove straight to Candy and Raphael's apartment without taking a shower or brushing my teeth. I sat in the car for ten minutes to calm myself down so that I wouldn't do anything crazy. Candy was becoming a big problem in my life, and I had to resolve our issues some way or another. I wasn't gonna be able to beat Candy physically and get away with it, so I decided to try and beat her with my mind. I took a deep breath, got out the car, walked to her apartment door and rang the doorbell.

Candy looked through the peephole, saw me and opened the door. She had nothing on but a wife beater and panties.

"Ski! Oh my God! Are you all right, papi? I was worried sick about you. Come in," Candy said, hugging me like she wasn't the reason I was locked up.

That was the moment that I realized Candy was truly crazy. How could she act so concerned when she was the one who had me locked up in the first place?

"Nah, I ain't trying to come in. I just came to talk."

"Come on, papi. Let me fix you something to eat. I know you're hungry," Candy pleaded, trying to get me in the apartment.

I pushed Candy's hand off mine. "I'm good. I don't want nothing but your attention right now."

"Okay, papi. I'm listening."

"Look, I know we done had our little drama and shit, but I wanna put that in the past. You might not believe me, but I do care about you. I'd never wanna see nuffin' happen to you," I explained before Candy cut me off in the middle of my speech.

"I don't wanna fight anymore either. I knew you loved me," Candy responded then proceeded to stick her tongue in my mouth.

I gently pushed her away from me. "Candy, what are you doing?" I asked, shocked.

"Come inside, papi. I wanna feel you inside of me. You don't know how much I missed you. I haven't fucked anyone since you," Candy said, putting her finger in her panties.

"Candy, you're buggin'. I ain't come here to fuck you or get back with you. I came here to try and squash our beef."

"Just come inside. Come inside," Candy pleaded, grabbing and pulling my arm.

"What the fuck is wrong wit' you? You just got me locked the fuck up. I could've had work or a hammer in the car with me. I could've got some real time because of your stupid ass. And now you're trying to get me to fuck you? Are you crazy? Next thing I know, you'll be calling the police saying I raped you. First you trashed my house and then you get me arrested. What's next?"

"I only did it because I love you. I couldn't stand to see you with anyone else. We can still make it work. It's not over," Candy replied as her eyes began to water.

"Candy, it's over. There will never be a me and you again. It's a wrap."

"Then why the fuck are you here?"

"Because I'm trying to dead this beef that you seem to have with me."

"Fuck you. I swear to God that you're gonna regret this. Nobody uses me and gets away with it."

"I ain't use you."

"Please, before you got wit' me, you didn't have shit. All that shit you got is from me and my brother. I made you," Candy shouted, pointing her finger in my face.

"Lemme get the fuck outta here before I do something I regret," I said, turning around to leave.

"Don't talk about it, be about it. If you feel like doing something, do it."

"Candy, get out of my face, yo, for real. You better ask your brother about me. He knows my work."

"Ski, when I'm done wit' you, you gonna wish you had me. You ain't gonna have shit after I tell Raphael to stop fucking wit' you."

"You think Raphael is gonna listen to ya nasty ass? Now I know you really seven thirty," I said, walking to my car.

"You'll see. You gonna regret this. Nobody uses me," I heard Candy shout before I drove off.

Going to Candy's apartment was a stupid decision. And in the game that I was playing in, mistakes were costly. That mistake turned out to be the biggest of my life.

I drove home, checked my messages, took a shower, ordered some Domino's pizza and fell asleep watching *Jerry Springer*. The sound of the phone woke me up.

"Hello," I answered half asleep.

"Yo, Ski, you dead, pai. You cut off. Only reason I'm not gonna murder ya ass is because I owe you. Consider yaself lucky," a male voice said angrily.

"What? Who's this?" I answered, disoriented.

"It's me, pai…Raphael."

"Raph, what up? What the fuck is you talking about? Stop scream-ing, yo."

"You know what the fuck I'm talking about. Don't play stupid. I just came from the house. I saw Candy. I saw her eye. You lucky I don't kill you for that, pai. Her eye is the size of a baseball."

Raphael was Candy's brother, but he was more like a father to her. Since their mom died almost fifteen years prior, Raphael had to support himself and Candy. There was nothing that Raphael loved more than his kid sister. She was all the family he had.

"Yo, Raph, word on everything I love. I don't know what you are talking about. I've been in the crib all day."

"Ski, you're starting to piss me off, pai. I know you were here this morning. My neighbor heard the two of you arguing and saw you this morning."

"I didn't say I wasn't over there this morning. What I said is I don't know what the fuck you're talking about."

"Why would you go over there anyways? Didn't I tell you that I was gonna take care of everything? You had no right to put your hands on my sister, bro. You're lucky, pai. You're really lucky."

"I ain't touch Candy. I went over there to try and talk shit out with her, and she started spazzing out, so I—"

"So you hit her? You no-good son of a bitch. I told you that I wouldn't get involved in y'all's relationship. All I asked was for you to never put your hands on her. I had a lot of love for you, pai. Normally, you'd be dead by now, but I told you I'mma spare you. The nerve of you to hit my kid sis. And just because she wouldn't sleep with you."

"Raph, I told you I didn't hit her. She's lying. You know how she is. Don't let her trick you, son."

"Then how the fuck did her eye get swollen shut? Huh? Ski. You're starting to dig yaself in a hole that you ain't gonna be able to get out of. Quit while you're ahead, pai."

"Yo, Raph, lemme call you back. I'mma go to the house and handle everything."

"Stay away from Candy and stay the fuck away from me. Don't try to see the connect or hustle in the bars. You're dead, and you're lucky you ain't in the fucking ground."

"Yo, Raph, stop fucking threatening me. You of all people know how I get down."

"Yeah. That's what you told my sister today after you hit her, didn't you? She told me. But check this out, pai, your gun isn't the only one that busts. Remember that," Raphael stated and then hung up on me.

I sat on the couch in disbelief. For a minute I thought I was dreaming. Candy wasn't lying when she said she was gonna fuck up my life. What I couldn't figure out is how Candy's eye was swollen shut. Raphael believed her, and I knew there was nothing I could do to change his mind, but I still had to do something.

The longer I sat there and thought about it, the tighter I got. Since Candy lied and said I hit her, I figured I might as well really beat her ass. Raphael was talking all that gangsta shit on the phone, like he was a killer. I was mad at myself for letting him get away with talking to me like that.

I got up, grabbed my nine and drove to Candy and Raphael's place. I knew I was making a mistake by going over there because most likely Candy was gonna call the police as soon as she saw me. I weighed out the pros and cons and decided that beating Candy's ass once and for all was worth the jail time.

I pulled up to their crib and parked across the street. I jogged to the front door and rang the doorbell, then I stepped to the side of the door so that when Candy looked through the peephole, she wouldn't see anyone. Candy opened the door, stuck her head out and looked around. I punched her in the forehead, knocking her into the house. I walked behind her and locked the door behind me.

Candy lay on the floor on her back crying, holding her face.

"Don't cry now, bitch," I shouted, standing over her.

"Ski, please stop. Lemme explain. Don't hurt me. Please," Candy cried out, folding her body into a ball.

"It's too late, bitch. Everything was going fine until you had to come along and fuck it up. I asked you—no, I begged you to let bygones be bygones—but ya stupid ass wouldn't listen. I didn't wanna have to do this. You forced me to do this," I screamed, walking around her body, pacing with my nine in my hand.

I dragged Candy into her bedroom by her hair and went into her dresser drawer.

"Where are ya handcuffs? I know you got some handcuffs, you freak bitch. Where are they?"

"I don't have any handcuffs," Candy answered, still crying.

"Then where the fuck is the duct tape?"

"In the kitchen drawer. What do you need duct tape for?"

I dragged Candy from her bedroom to the kitchen by her hair and grabbed the duct tape out of the drawer. I then made Candy sit on one of the dining room chairs, and I proceeded to tape her feet and arms to the chair.

Candy spit in my face. "Raphael's gonna kill you for this one, *puto*."

I punched her in the nose with a right, and blood came streaming down her face. Candy was unconscious. I sat in the house for more than three hours waiting for Raphael to come home. I made myself at home. By the time Raphael pulled up outside, I had hamburgers on the stove and French fries in the deep fryer. I knew Raphael knew I was inside because I watched him park his car from the living room window, and he parked right next to my Lexus. I turned off the TV and all the lights, and stood by the door with my nine out.

I watched carefully as the locks to the door opened slowly.

"Candy! Candy," Raphael screamed, pushing the door open.

I gun butted Raphael in the back of his head, knocking him out instantly. He never saw it coming. I dragged him into the kitchen by his arms and duct taped him in a chair right next to Candy. After I was sure Raphael was secure, I turned off my hamburgers and fries, made a plate, got some Kool-Aid and watched a rerun of *Martin*. The show was going off when Raphael began to wake up.

"Raph, what's good, pai? You had a good nap?" I asked imitating his accent, getting up from the couch, walking over to him.

Raphael looked around as if he was in a daze.

"Ski, what are you doing this for, man? Why are you even here? You couldn't just let shit be?"

I gunbutted him with my nine in the mouth. "Shut the fuck up, nigga. What happened to all that killer shit you was talking on the phone? It's too late to cop out now."

Raphael looked from left to right and left to right again and saw Candy laid out on the floor sideways, taped to the chair.

"Oh God! What did you do to Candy? You killed her? Oh my God," Raphael cried out.

"Stop crying, you bitch-ass nigga. She ain't dead, but I can arrange it if you'd like. Candy had a smart ass mouth, so Candy had to take a nap for a while."

"What do you want, Ski? I don't have cash here. All I have is what's on me and you're welcome to it. Just don't kill or hurt my sister anymore," Raphael pleaded.

I smacked him with the nine in his mouth again, knocking two of his teeth out.

Raphael cried out in pain, spitting out blood.

"Nigga, do you think I'm stupid? I've been waiting for ya punk ass in this house for three hours. You think I ain't find ya safe?"

"I don't got no safe."

I cocked back my hand to smack him with the gun again, but before I could he quickly changed his tune.

"A'ight! A'ight! Please. No more. I'll open the safe."

"Nigga, please. You won't open shit. I'll open it. What the fuck is the combo?"

"Eleven, eight, twenty-three."

I walked to Raphael's bedroom, stood on top of his bed, slid over the portrait of Raphael and Candy, and opened the safe. This nigga had a revolver, a passport and fifty grand inside it. That must've been his emergency stash money because he was making way more than that. I was disappointed. I was expecting hundreds of thousands of dollars. I went into Raphael's closet, snatched up a plastic bag from Foot Locker and emptied all the money out the safe. I came back into the kitchen and began beating Raphael like he stole something from me. The real reason I beat him so bad was because I was mad that he only had fifty grand in his safe.

I kicked him in the ribs, punched him in the face repeatedly, stomped him and everything else that came to mind. I was beating him for so long that I had to take a break. Raphael looked up at me like I was the grim reaper. He was bleeding from everywhere. I stood over Candy and smacked her in the face to wake her up.

"Get up, bitch. Get up. I got a surprise for you," I shouted, standing over her.

It took a while, but Candy finally came to. I pulled my dick out and pissed all over her face. A year earlier, I heard Boota tell a story about pissing on the Three Stooges and I always wanted to do it to someone myself. To me, that was the ultimate humiliation.

"Y'all two oughta consider yaselves lucky. The only reason I ain't gonna kill y'all is because my car is outside, and one of y'all's nosy neighbors might recognize it. If y'all was smart, y'all would get the fuck out of Kingston, 'cause I'm coming back. And when I come back, I'm coming to kill you. Raph, I hate to do this to you, man. You was good to me. You just fell into ya sister's trap. Get the fuck out of town, and don't make me have to kill you because I will. See you later, pai," I stated, smacking him in the face with my hand and walking out the door.

I knew I made a mistake by not killing Raphael, but it wasn't the right place or the right time. I didn't feel like I would've gotten away with it. To me, Raphael was a pussy, but he had money, and that gave him power. So I knew I was gonna have to see him again down the line.

*I*t was ten o'clock on a boring Tuesday night in November. I was smoking weed, watching *Belly* on DVD in my living room. It had been two months since I robbed Raphael, but I was still paranoid. Word was that Raphael and Candy moved to another town upstate named Middletown. Nobody had seen or heard from either of them in weeks. I knew that Raphael was soft, but I also knew that I wasn't supposed to leave him or Candy alive.

The doorbell damn near made me jump out of my seat. *Who the fuck could be coming to my house this late at night unannounced,* I thought.

I felt underneath the couch, grabbed my .357, cocked it back and cut off all the lights I had on in the house.

The bell rang again.

"Who is it?" I asked, not hearing an answer.

"Who the fuck is that?" I asked again, still not hearing anything.

It had to be a setup, but luckily I had the home-court advantage. If niggaz came to kill me, I was going out banging, and somebody was going with me. I unlocked the door and swung it open fast with my gun raised.

Rule's wifey Tiesha screamed at the top of her lungs when she saw the gun pointed at her.

"T, what the fuck are you playing games for? You know what type of life I'm living. I could've killed ya stupid ass," I shouted, lowering my gun.

"I'm sorry. I got nervous when I got to your door. I didn't know how you'd react to me showing up at ya house like this," Tiesha explained.

I hadn't seen her since I got my shit out of the house that we shared with Rule. Tiesha was brown skin with hair down to her shoulders and dark brown eyes. She had a fat ass, a small waist and small titties. In the face she resembled Pam from the sitcom *Martin*. Tiesha and me always got along well. Tiesha was a go hard chick for real. When Rule met her, she was in her senior year in high school at Kingston High. She was an honor student on her way to college to study criminal justice. After Rule got his hands on her, she was selling weed in school, cutting class and was now an eighteen-year-old mother. Her college dreams were over. I always felt bad for her because I felt like Rule fucked her life up. But the thing I liked about T was that she was about getting money. She wasn't one of those prissy bitches out spending her man's money. She was the type of girl who was always thinking about a way to make more money. Rule didn't know what he had. If I ever had a wifey like Tiesha, I would've been a millionaire.

"So, what's good? What you want?" I asked.

"Damn, Ski, lemme find out it's like that! You ain't got love for me no more?" Tiesha asked, looking at me with her hands on her hips.

"My bad, T. You know you still peoples. My mind is just twisted right now. I'm going through it. Pardon me. What can I do for you?"

"Well first, you can invite me in."

"Damn. My bad. Come on in."

"Damn, Ski, what's good? Lemme find out you ain't got no electricity."

"C'mon, T, you tryin' to play me? I turned the lights off when I heard the doorbell. I ain't know who the fuck you was."

I turned the kitchen light on, and that's when I noticed what Tiesha was wearing for the first time. She had on a pair of booty-hugging jean shorts and a halter top exposing her navel. Tiesha was looking right. That baby did her body justice. She gained weight in all the right places. Her titties looked like they got a cup bigger and her ass was even fatter than I last remembered. Her stomach was washboard flat and stretch mark free. Her skin was flawless. You couldn't even tell that just two months earlier she had given birth.

Normally, I wouldn't pay any attention to what she was wearing, but it bugged me out how she came to my house at ten o'clock at night with half of her ass hanging out.

"Yo, T, where the fuck you coming from, a Luke video?" I joked.

"Oh, you got jokes? If you don't like it, then don't look, Ski. This house is off the hook. You doing it. I wish Rule was as business minded as you," Tiesha said, completely changing the subject.

I walked Tiesha into the living room, turned the light and TV on, and sat down on the sofa. Tiesha sat right next to me.

"So, how you been?"

"Yo, T, cut the bullshit, yo. You ain't come here to ask me how I've been. Beating around the bush ain't for us. What's good?"

"Ski, you know what happened to Rule? He's been locked up for almost two months now. Since he got locked up, I lost the house and everything. The baby and I are staying at my mom's house. I got a job at Wal-Mart to try and make ends meet, but it ain't enough. I'm fucked up, Ski. A baby is expensive. I can't do it by myself. I need Rule."

"A'ight. And?"

"Well, like I said, I'm sure you heard how Rule got arrested."

"Yeah. I heard about that stupid shit he did."

"Rule's public defender said that Rule won't do prison time if he could come up with the money for all the damages."

"How much time is he looking at?"

"Five years," Tiesha answered.

"Damn. Five years? That's a long mothafuckin' time to be getting for trashing a bar. How much is the damages?"

"Fifty thousand dollars."

"Fifty thousand dollars? Got damn! That's a lot of mothafuckin' money. Hold up. I know he ain't send you to ask me for fifty stacks."

"Yeah, but it's not like…" Tiesha tried to explain, but I cut her off.

"This nigga got the nerve to send you over here to ask for fifty grand when he fronted on me for three thousand dollars? And after all that shit he was talking at the bar about killing me? That nigga got nerve. I wouldn't piss on that nigga if he was on fire. Tell Rule that I said to eat a dick," I said, raising my voice.

"Ski, I know how it sounds. Don't get mad at me. I'm just trying to get some help. I can't take care of the baby by myself for five years. I can barely take care of myself, Ski. If he wasn't my baby's father, I would leave him. I know he's a fuck up and all, but please help me. He was drunk when he did that. He's really sorry. He knows he was wrong."

"Yo, T, you speaking to dead ears right now. I know y'all ain't think that I was gonna come off fifty grand. You know me better than that."

"No. I knew you were gonna say no. I don't have a dollar to my name. Please help me. You're the only person I could come to. I understand that you don't wanna pay the money to get Rule out, but could you please help me a little bit so that I can get on my feet? You know my mom's a crack head. I can't raise my baby around all that smoke and shit. I'll work for you if you want. Gimme a job. I'll earn mine. You know how I get down," Tiesha said to me with tears in her eyes, looking like she meant every word.

"A'ight, listen. Call me tomorrow, and I'll see what I can do."

"Thank you, Ski. Thank you so much. I promise I'll pay you back every penny you give me. That's my word."

Tiesha hugged me.

"C'mon, T, chill. Stop crying. You making me feel bad."

"Ski, I wish you would've hollered at me that night at the fair instead of Rule. If I had your baby, I know I wouldn't be struggling like this."

Tiesha hugged me tighter.

I felt Tiesha's warm tears leaking into my shirt. Tiesha started rubbing my waves with her hand and kissing me on the neck. I was in a trance. I knew what we were doing was wrong, but it felt so good. Tiesha looked me in the eyes, and we started kissing and fondling each other hard.

"I've always wanted you, couldn't you tell? Let me spend the night with you. One night. No strings," Tiesha suggested, breathing hard on my neck with her hot breath.

I had Tiesha in her panties when I finally realized what I was doing. True, Rule and me had our little beef, but I still had love for him. He was loyal to me, and here I was about to fuck his baby's mother while he was in jail. I got up off Tiesha and lit a cigarette.

"What's wrong?" Tiesha asked.

"This whole thing is wrong. I can't do this, T. This is foul."

"Ski, come on. It's too late now. We'll keep it between us, just one time. Do you know how many times I've fantasized about this?"

I got up off the couch and picked up Tiesha's clothes and threw them at her.

"Get dressed. I'm taking you home."

"Why?"

"Because I fucking said so. Get dressed. Call me tomorrow. I'm gonna get Rule out of jail first thing in the morning. Don't forget to call and wake me up early, a'ight?"

"You gonna pay the whole fifty thousand?"

"Yeah. Fuck it. I ain't gonna let this nigga miss five years of his son's life when I can prevent it. Y'all need him."

Tiesha jumped on me and started kissing me on the cheek.

"Thank you so much. Thank you, Ski. I can't believe this," Tiesha exclaimed.

I put Tiesha down on the couch. "Enough with the kisses and hugs. That's what got us in trouble the first time. C'mon. Hurry up and put ya clothes on so I can drive you home before it gets late. We got a long day ahead of us."

After I dropped Tiesha at her mother's house, I parked in the driveway of my crib and lit up a clip of a L that I had in my ashtray. I felt guilty for letting things get as far as they did with Tiesha. As I smoked, I asked myself over and over if I was making the right decision by paying the money to get Rule out. Every time I thought about changing my mind, I remembered that night that Rule shot Thirsty when we were making a sale. If Rule wasn't there, I'd have probably gotten shot or killed. He practically saved my life. I had to get him out. Before I yapped Raphael for fifty grand, I had a little bit over forty grand in the stash and half a brick of coke. After the drama, Raphael must've instructed the connect to stop fucking with me because he wasn't answering my phone calls or pages. When I went into McKennas or Scrupples to hustle, both owners threatened to call the police if I didn't leave. Raphael deaded me for real. All I had left was a few loyal customers, and they weren't copping more than an eight ball at a time. I still hadn't moved my half brick, and it had been more than two months. My coke-selling days were finished. Fifty grand was more than half my stash, but to me loyalty was everything. I could easily make another fifty grand, but I could never give Rule back those five years of his life.

I made up my mind. I was gonna get Rule out of jail first thing in the morning.

"So Rule, what you been doing for money?" Dro asked one December day.

"Shit, I've been living off Ski this last month. Why? What's up? You got something lined up?" Rule asked.

"Yeah. I got a nice spot for us. It's an easy come up. I need you and Ski."

"Yo, Dro, how many times did I tell you I ain't fucking wit' you when it comes to these juxes?"

"C'mon, B. I need you. It's not even a jewelry store," Dro shot back.

"Dro, you my man and all, but you and me don't click right when it comes to business."

Dro, Rule and I were in the basement of my crib the night of Rule's son Kato's christening. I had a small get together at my house to celebrate—mostly Tiesha's family and friends. Dro was there because Rule made me and him godparents. Getting Rule out of jail wasn't easy or as cheap as I thought it would be. Rule was charged with malicious mischief and vandalism. Both charges were misdemeanors, but the DA moved them up to statutory felonies because of the large amount of damages. The problem was the owner of the bar had already contacted the insurance company, so I had to hire a lawyer for five grand just to deal with the insurance company to get them to drop the criminal charges. The company agreed to drop the charges for the fifty grand, but the state would've picked up the case, so I had to pay the lawyer another five grand to make sure they wouldn't. I knew it was bullshit, but I figured it would be better to be safe than sorry because I didn't wanna end up paying the insurance company and still have Rule brought up on charges. That would've defeated the purpose. The total cost of getting Rule out of jail was sixty grand. It was a lot of money, but it was worth it. Rule would've done the same for me...well I hope he would've.

"Ski, do you want something to drink?" Tiesha asked, bending over in front of me to pick up a plastic cup.

"No thank you."

"A'ight. I'll be in the kitchen. Holla if you need something." Tiesha walked away, switching her hips.

"Damn, baby, is Ski the only one you see down here?" Rule asked.

Tiesha stopped, turned around, sucked her teeth and kept walking up the stairs.

"Fuck you too!" Rule shouted.

Rule and Tiesha lost their house, so I let them and the baby move in with me until Rule got on his feet. Ever since the night she and I almost fucked, Tiesha was playing me real close, even in front of Rule. It made me uncomfortable. I knew Rule noticed, but I wondered if he thought anything of it.

"Yo, Dro, you see how my girl treats me when I ain't making no paper. She's been acting like that since I came home," Rule replied.

"It ain't nuffin', son. She probably just tight 'cause y'all staying here with me and not in y'all's own crib. When you get back on, she'll be a'ight. You know she loves you," I said, trying to smooth things out.

"Yeah. I know, son. I'm frustrated too. I need a come-up, and I need one fast. Christmas is only a week away. I need some paper, B," Rule stated.

"And you gonna get some, too, if you can convince Ski to ride with us," Dro chimed in.

"Yo, on some real shit, after all Ski done did for me, I can't ask him for nuffin', yo."

"I can. That nigga didn't do nuffin' for me. Yo, Ski, lemme find out you lost ya heart," Dro said.

"Nigga, is you stupid? Matter of fact, I am scared. You ain't gonna get me with that reverse psychology shit," I answered.

"Yo, Ski, for real, B. How come you don't wanna get money wit' me no more?" Dro asked seriously.

"C'mon, Dro, don't play dumb. You know why I don't fuck wit' you. You be jay jerking people. I ain't doing no juxes with anybody if we ain't splitting the money evenly. Yo, I ain't never said nuffin' before, but that's some foul shit you and Roach doin'. You jay jerking family, son."

"C'mon, B. Miss me wit' that bullshit. I'm the nigga making sure everyone in the family is eating. When you was selling ya coke, I ain't see you putting anybody on. I'm putting money in niggaz' pockets, B. Look at Wise. He's chillin'. He just copped a CLK, got mad jewelry, clothes and paper in the stash," Dro said in a defensive tone.

"Yeah, but how much money did you make off Wise, son? If Wise made CLK money, you made house money, and that's foul."

"Listen, B, why does it matter how much I'm getting? What's important is that everybody's eating. These juxes is feeding families, B. If it wasn't for me, who knows what they would be doing, B."

"You take advantage of niggaz being hungry, son. We suppose to be family. That shit is foul."

"Yo, whatever, B. Let's talk about money. How much is it gonna cost me to get you on this jux?" Dro asked.

"It ain't about the paper. It's about the principle. My paper is straight now."

"My paper is straighter than yours, B, trust me. I'm doing this for peeps like Rule," Dro responded.

"It never stopped you before, you greedy ass," I said, smiling.

"C'mon, Ski, it's the holiday season. Don't you wanna help ya man make some paper?"

"What you trying to run up in?"

"Toys 'R' Us. I know it sounds crazy, B, but Toys 'R' Us be having money this time of year, especially the day I'm trying to go up in there."

"When's that?" Rule asked.

"Christmas Eve," Dro answered, looking directly in Rule's and my eyes.

Rule and me started dying laughing. Dro came up with the craziest shit you could imagine. He always had a plan. He was like Hannibal from the *A-Team*.

"How much paper you talking about?" Rule inquired.

"One hundred and twenty five grand at the least, B."

"He don't mean that. He means his cut," I replied sarcastically.

"It's a four-man job, so I'd say about…matter of fact, we could split it four ways down the middle. How about that, Ski?"

"Yo, why you trying so hard to get me on this jux? What's really good?"

I had a hard time trusting Dro. He had to have an ulterior motive.

"Nah, B, it's not like that. It's just that it's a four-man job, and I only got three," Dro explained.

"So why don't you go with them?" I asked.

"I am. Roach is out of town and Wise is visiting family. You're my last hope. Without you, this shit ain't going down, B."

"What about Boota?"

"C'mon, B. You know Boota ain't pulling no more juxes. Boota ain't built for this shit. He's a drug dealer. He ain't no robber, B. Besides, thirty grand won't hurt. You can always use more money, B. C'mon, son. Take one for the team," Dro said, trying his best to persuade me.

Dro was right. Thirty grand definitely wouldn't hurt. Besides, I wanted Rule to make some money so him and Tiesha could move out of my house. Ever since that night, she was pratically throwing pussy at me.

"A'ight. I'm wit' it, son. What's the plan?"

"Yeah, Ski, that's what I'm talking 'bout. We back, son. It's like old times again," Rule shouted, giving me dap.

"A'ight, listen up. The plan is sweet, B. Y'all gonna love this shit. The Toys 'R' Us is in Massapequa, right off Sunrise Highway. We gonna wear…" Dro went off explaining.

*I*t was a snowy December night, fifteen minutes to midnight on Christmas Eve. Late shopping parents scrambled in and out of Toys "R" Us with hopes of finding the item that their child coveted the entire year.

"Ho, ho, ho! Merry Christmas," Dro shouted, standing in front of Toys "R" Us jingling a bell in a Santa Claus suit.

"Hey, ho. Hey, ho. Yeah, you ho. Lemme holla at you for a minute," Rule said to a dark-skin woman who walked passed him and into the store.

"Yo, Rule. Chill, B. This is business, not joke time," Dro whispered to Rule.

"My bad, son. But yo, that honey had a fatty. You ain't see that?" Rule asked.

"You crazy, B. Pull up ya beard. Too much of ya face is showing," Dro replied, smiling.

"Ho, ho, ho," Dro and Rule said in unison as a couple entered the store.

Dro and Rule were standing in front of Toys "R" Us posing as

Santa Clauses from the Salvation Army. The real purpose of them being outside was to keep their eyes on the security truck that was patrolling the shopping center. At midnight when the shift changed and the security guards switched, we were gonna make our move. Snoop and I were in a stolen minivan freezing our asses off, parked in the lot across from the entrance.

"Look at them, son. Dro is crazy as hell. He comes up with the craziest shit," I said shaking my head.

"Look at them! Shit, look at us. We're sitting up in a stolen van in Santa Claus outfits freezing our asses off on Christmas Eve, getting ready to rob Toys 'R' Us. Dro ain't the only crazy one, son. We all crazy," Snoop said, looking at me.

We both started cracking up because it was the truth.

"Good look on coming through tonight, son. Dro told me you ain't really wanna do it. I need this money bad, son. If it wasn't for you, we couldn't have done it. Dro said we needed four to pull this off," Snoop said sincerely.

"You ain't gotta thank me for coming, son. I'm getting paid for this shit like you."

"Yeah, I know, but you don't really need it."

"Are you buggin'? I always need more money. You don't even sound right," I responded loudly.

Snoop started laughing.

"What the fuck is so funny, son?"

"You funny. Sometimes you be talking and I think about how you used to be back in the day, wearing bootleg clothes, pimples all on ya face, scared to talk to girls. Now all of a sudden, you think you Tony 'Mothafuckin'' Montana," Snoop said, referring to the _Scarface_ character, then he started laughing again.

"Yeah, I came up fast. All I need is another six-month run, and I'll be straight for a little while."

"For a little while? Damn, son, what, you gonna do this shit forever?"

"Why not? I don't see you doin' nothing great wit' yo' life."

"Yo, you ever think about how we turned out to be who we are?"

"What type of shit you on tonight, son? You buggin'. You don't even sound like yaself."

"Yo, do you know I still think about Natalie every day—every fucking day, son. I can still hear her voice. I can still smell her scent, and see her face. It's all my fault she's gone. All this time since she passed away, I've just been walking around in a daze with no purpose. I don't wanna do this shit no more, son. I wanna do something that would make Nat proud of me. I don't want her death to be in vain. I'm tired of this shit. Shit is getting stale."

"So what you gonna do, get a job, son? I ain't wit' that nine-to-five shit."

"I'm going back to school to play ball. That was always my dream, son. Nat wanted me to go to college too. After this jux, I'mma take my thirty Gs, put it in the bank, and start training to get back in shape. I'mma make it, son. You never think about how ya life would've turned out if you kept balling?"

"Nope."

"Damn. That's a shame, son. Back in the day, all you ever wanted to do was play ball. Now look at you. You was nice, Ski. You could've made it. You could still make it. We still young, Ski. Why don't you start training wit' me and go back to school?"

"Yo, if that's what you want to do, I'm wit' you, but that's not what I wanna do. That basketball shit is a dream. I'm about to be twenty-one in a couple of days. I gotta deal wit' reality, son. I ain't got no time for dreams. I gotta get this paper."

"Son, this don't even sound like you. Who the fuck do you really think you is? You ain't no gangsta. This shit ain't you, man," Snoop said, beginning to get aggravated.

Just then I heard Dro calling us on the walkie-talkie. "Showtime, niggaz. Let's roll. We waiting on y'all, over and out."

I cocked back the hammer on my .357. "Yo, let's bounce. I'mma show you how gangsta I am, nigga."

Snoop and I put on our Santa beards and hopped out the van. The more I thought about what Snoop said, the more tight I got. Nobody could tell me I wasn't a gangsta. In the short time that I'd been in the game, I'd put major work in. I was so mad that I almost broke the promise to Dro that I'd never tell anyone about what happened to Thirsty and Paula. Snoop was bugging. I had never heard him talk like that before. As he was talking, I couldn't help but think that he was going crazy.

We walked to the front of the store and met up with Rule and Dro.

"A'ight. Let's make this shit quick. Everybody know the plan?" Dro asked.

We all nodded.

"Let's go," Dro shouted.

When we walked into the store, I almost forgot what time it was. Toys 'R' Us was flooded. It looked like a zoo inside. People were running from aisle to aisle and arguing about who was gonna get the last of a particular toy. Every checkout line had a dozen people deep or better waiting.

"Ho, ho, ho," we all said in unison as we walked through the store.

People smiled and some of them even put money in our Salvation Army donation cans.

The loud speaker blared the popular Christmas song, "Here Comes Santa Claus."

I couldn't help but laugh to myself as we made our way to the back of the store. This was the craziest shit that I had ever been a part of.

The counting room was located in the back of the store next to the manager's office. Inside the counting room, there were three female employees counting and wrapping money from the cash registers up front and placing them in a safe. Next door, in the manager's office, the manager sat behind a small desk, watching video monitors and doing paperwork. The employee's lounge was a little farther down the hall, next to the customer's bathroom. The amount of people inside the employee lounge varied. It could be one person or it could be five. Dro and

Rule were to go to the counting room, tie up the three female employees, and empty the safe. My job was to run in the manager's office and handcuff and gag him. After I was sure the manager was secured, I was to join Snoop in the employee lounge and help him hold down however many people were inside and wait for Dro and Rule to finish in the counting room.

I walked into the manager's office. "Ho, ho, ho. Merry Christmas."

The manager smiled at me, sitting upright in his chair. "Well, Merry Christmas to you, buddy. What can I do to help you, sir?"

I calmly brandished my .357. "Nah. You can't help me. I think I'll help myself. Don't move, nigga. I got six bullets wit' ya name on them."

"Please don't shoot. Please. The money isn't in here. Please. I have family, man. Please don't kill me," the manager said.

I responded by punching him in the mouth. "Shut the fuck up. Don't say shit."

The manager fell out his chair and onto the floor. I stomped him in the back, kicked him in his ribs and then handcuffed both of his wrists to the legs of his desk. I couldn't find anything to gag him with, so I kicked him in the back of his head and knocked him unconscious. After I made sure that the handcuffs were secure, I took out the videotape and walked down the hall to the employee lounge. When I walked in, Snoop had a blond-headed white girl around the same age as us on her knees with her hands on top of her head. Snoop must've heard my footsteps because he turned around quick with his gun pointed at me.

I shouted, "It's just me, son. Chill."

Snoop spun around to keep an eye on the girl. "You lucky, nigga. You was a second away from a slug. You handled everything there?"

"Of course. I'm a professional. Yo, how come you ain't tie her up?" I asked.

"I was waiting for you. I ain't wanna have my back to the door. Hold me down, son."

Snoop pulled a rope out of his pocket. A couple of seconds after Snoop finished tying up the girl, I heard Dro calling me on the walkie-talkie.

"Ayo, how we lookin' over there?" Dro asked.

"We waiting on y'all. What's the holdup?" I asked

"Ya boy is tying up the last bitch now. How's our exit looking?" Dro asked.

I stuck my head out the door and didn't see a person in sight. "Exit looks great."

"A'ight then, let's roll out," Dro ordered.

Snoop and I came out of the employee lounge and went down the hallway where we met up with Dro and Rule who were walking out the counting room with Santa Claus bags filled with money.

"This shit here was easy money. It don't get sweeter than this," Rule exclaimed.

We were almost at the end of the aisle when I heard footsteps in the distance running in the opposite direction. I looked back and saw the white girl from the employee lounge tearing ass down the aisle.

"Oh shit. That's the bitch from the lounge," Snoop yelled out.

"What? How the fuck did she get untied?" I asked, dumbfounded.

"Damn. I forgot to tie up her feet. Damn. I was rushing," Snoop explained.

"What the fuck do we do now?" Rule asked.

"C'mon, we just gonna walk out the exit. Ain't nobody gonna pay attention to us. We in Santa Claus outfits. Keep ya hands on ya hammers and ya eyes open. Ain't no security in here, but let's be safe," Dro said, pulling out his gun from his waist.

We all pulled out our weapons and walked the rest of the way down the aisle into the front of the store.

"Help! Help! The guys in the Santa suits just robbed the store. Stop them," the white girl from the employee lounge screamed at the top of her lungs with rope still tied around her body, drawing attention from the whole store.

We stepped up our pace and went down the closed checkout line and headed toward the exit.

"Get them. Stop them. They're getting away," the white girl continued to shout.

The whole scene was surreal. I couldn't take my eyes off the white girl screaming and hollering. I was almost out the door when Snoop snapped me out of my daze.

"Ski, look out, son," Snoop yelled, jumping in front of me and pushing me onto the floor.

An off duty cop who was in line shot four bullets in our direction, hitting Snoop three times in the chest. Dro and Rule returned fire.

People screamed and ducked for cover, enabling me to get Snoop to his feet and help him out the store.

As we were putting Snoop in the minivan, the cop ran out the store pursuing us. Rule let off seven shots in his direction, sending the cop running back inside the store to retreat. Dro and I laid Snoop down on the first row of seats in the minivan, and I jumped in and sat behind him on the second row of seats. Dro got in on the driver's side and Rule got in on the passenger side. As we were pulling out the parking lot, sirens could be heard in the distance.

The cop shot out the back window of the minivan, sending glass everywhere. After we made it to a nearby back street, I looked down at Snoop for the first time and saw how badly he'd been hit. His Santa Claus beard was the same color as his suit. Snoop looked up at me with glassy eyes and said, "I'm dying,"

"Don't talk like that, son. You ain't dying. You gonna be out the hospital smoking weed and spending this money we took tomorrow," I told him matter of factly.

I hopped over the seat and sat down with Snoop, placing his head in my lap. Snoop was fading in and out of consciousness. His eyes were rolling around in the back of his head.

"Yo, Dro, fuck making the switch to the other car. Get us to a hospital. Snoop is hit bad, son," I yelled

"We can't take him to the hospital. We'll all get knocked," Dro answered nervously, turning his head back and forth to look at Snoop lying on my lap.

"So what the fuck are we gonna do, let him die? Fuck all that shit, nigga. Drive to the mothafuckin' hospital now," I demanded, pointing my .357 at the back of Dro's head.

Snoop's breaths were getting farther and farther apart. Blood was leaking out of his mouth, nose and ears.

"C'mon, Snoop. Keep ya eyes open. We almost at the hospital. Just hold on, nigga. Keep ya eyes open," I said, rocking his head back and forth nervously.

"Ski, I ain't gonna make it, son. Tell Dro to drive to the getaway car. It's no use, son," Snoop whispered, looking up at me with glassy eyes.

"Stop saying that, son. You gonna make it. Stop trying to talk," I insisted.

"Yo, Ski, do you think I'mma get to see Natalie and my pops? I wanna be wit' them, son. I'm ready to go. Let me go, son. I'm ready," Snoop said, forcing a smile.

"Shhh! Stop talking."

Snoop grabbed me by the collar forcefully. "Yo, Ski, I want you to promise me something."

"Anything, my nigga. Just name it."

"This life ain't for you. Promise me you'll go back to school and play ball. Promise me that. Do it for me, son. Make it for us. You hear me?" Snoop said so low that I almost couldn't hear him.

Tears started rolling down my face. I wanted to answer him, but I couldn't open my mouth to speak.

"Promise me, son. Promise me right now. I always looked at you like my li'l brother. I love you, nigga. Get out the game and make ya dreams come true. Promise me, nigga…Say it. Say it right now," Snoop demanded, pulling me with all the strength he could muster.

Crying, I looked down at Snoop. "I promise son. I promise. Just stop talking, a'ight? We almost there."

Snoop started laughing and choking on his own blood.

"What's so funny?" I asked.

"Look at you crying like a li'l bitch. I told you, you wasn't no mothafuckin' gangsta," Snoop said with a weak smile.

Snoop swallowed two times, blinked and shut his eyes for the last time. Snoop was gone. I kissed him on the forehead and wiped my eyes. "Yo, Dro, drive to the getaway car. Snoop is gone."

Snoop died in my arms. I couldn't believe it. It was all like a bad dream that I couldn't wake up from. I'd known Snoop since I was nine years old. He was my best friend. He died saving my life. As we drove, I looked out the window and thought about all the times we shared. I couldn't stop myself from crying. Snoop lost his life for thirty grand. If it wasn't for Snoop, it would've been me laying dead on that seat.

Snoop was right all along. This life wasn't for me. I didn't even know who I was anymore.

We drove to the getaway car and drove to the projects. We stripped Snoop's body down to his boxers and T-shirt and left him in the parking lot. Snoop was gone forever.

I was slow, uncoordinated and out of shape. My lungs felt like they were going to collapse, and my heart felt like it was beating so fast, it was going to jump out of my chest any minute. My mind knew the right moves to make, but my body couldn't react in time. Cats were stealing the ball from me, blocking my shots and scoring on me at will. At one time in my life, a basketball court was the only place I felt comfortable. Now here it was February 2001, a few short years later, and I was more comfortable with a gun and a mask on than I was with a basketball.

"Hey, Ski, lemme speak to you in my office," Coach Wilkins said to me after practice. Coach Wilkins was the new head coach at Ulster. He was six feet, seven inches tall with a wide chest and broad shoulders. He was brown skin and baldheaded. His face had a lot of wrinkles, which always made him appear like he was deep in thought or angry.

I followed Coach Wilkins into his office and sat down in the chair across from his desk.

"Ski, I'm gonna be honest with you. You looked like you didn't have a clue out there today. I heard from the A.D. that you used to be a pretty good player when you came out of high school, but as of now, I don't think you're good enough to play at this level anymore. I hate to be so blunt, but I didn't wanna waste your time or mine. I'm not gonna offer you a scholarship," Coach Wilkins explained honestly and sternly.

"Coach, I had a bad practice. I'm better than what I showed you. It's just that I haven't played in a while," I pleaded.

"I can tell. You look like you haven't played in years. Basketball isn't something you can do halfheartedly. You have to be dedicated. You gotta want it. If I were you, I'd apply for financial aid and hit the books. Education is more important than basketball. If you'd like to continue playing ball here, I'll be more than happy to put you on the practice team."

"The practice team?"

"Yeah, the practice team. And I'm being generous offering you that. Good day, Thompson," Coach Wilkins said, shaking my hand and walking me to the door.

I was at Ulster Community College trying out for the basketball team, hoping to earn my scholarship back. I played like shit. I was crushed. Not only did I disappoint myself, I felt like I disappointed Snoop.

After Snoop passed away, I decided to get out of the street life, go back to school and play basketball. I gave Snoop my word as he took his last breath on my lap, and that was a promise I couldn't break. Snoop gave up his life for mine, so I felt it was only right to try and do something productive, so that his death wouldn't be in vain. All of our crew was affected in different ways, but none as much as me. The few times we got up and chilled felt awkward without Snoop there. It didn't feel right to be having a good time anymore, so I stayed to myself in my crib upstate and rarely visited Long Island.

After practice, I sat in my car in the parking lot for almost an hour thinking of my next move. I didn't have enough money to pay for school on my own. After the Toys "R" Us robbery, I had almost seventy grand in the stash, but I felt so guilty that I gave Snoop's mother fifty grand and my mother fifteen grand in case she ever encountered rough times and couldn't pay her mortgage. All I had was five grand to my name. I gave all my money up because I thought I'd be able to get my scholarship back. The tuition from my last semester was four thousand five hundred dollars, and the tuition for the upcoming semester was the same. I needed nine thousand give or take just to get back in school. I could've asked Rule for the money, but him, Tiesha and the baby had just moved out of my house and into their own. Rule needed every penny he had. Boota was doing good for himself selling coke, but I doubted he had five grand just to give away like that either. Wise was saving up his money for a recording studio, and although I knew Dro had the money to spare, for some reason I couldn't bring myself to ask him for it.

I was still trying to figure out what to do when someone knocked on my car door.

"Hey. What's up, stranger? I was wondering if that was you. What are you doing sitting in here looking like you just lost your best friend?" Michelle asked.

Michelle was a girl I used to deal with when I first came upstate to go to school. Since I got in the game and quit school, I stopped seeing her. She was a good girl, but she wasn't my type. She was five feet two inches with a honey-bronze complexion, light brown eyes and shoulder-length hair. She had huge thirty-six double D breasts that made her appear heavier than what she really was, and she had thick thighs. She was cute in the face with a beautiful gap-toothed smile, but she wasn't the type of girl who you'd turn around to do a double take when she walked by. She wasn't into designer clothes and partying. She was more of a homebody. A real plain Jane.

"Hey. What up?" I asked, unenthused.

"I haven't seen you in all these years, and that's the response I get? I guess you didn't miss me, huh?"

"Nah. It ain't like that. My bad, ma. I'm just going thorough it right now. I'm sorry."

"You and me both. Most days I don't even have enough strength to leave the house."

"I feel you on that one. I be feeling the same way. Yo, what you doing up here anyways? This is a two-year school. You should've been graduated by now."

"I had to take off for a while. I had a baby two years ago and my father passed away in the summer. It's been a rough couple of years, but I'm still breathing," Michelle explained.

"Damn. I'm sorry to hear that."

"Which one? My dad or my son?"

"I'm sorry to hear about your dad. But I'd be sorry to hear about ya son, too, if his father is still around."

"No. Fortunately for us, he's a deadbeat. But what do you care anyways? All you ever wanted from me was sex. My child has nothing to do wit' that," Michelle said defensively.

"Damn. Look at you. Here it is we ain't seen each other in years, and five minutes into the conversation you're already talking about re-lationships."

"Well, you haven't changed either. You're still good at ducking a question."

"So what are you doing out here anyway?"

"I'm waiting for the bus."

"For what?"

"Ski, you ain't offering me no ride wit' ya fancy ass car. What is this, a Benz? How you get a nice car like this?" Michelle asked.

"This is a Lexus, for your information. And how I got this car is none of your business. Now get ya question-asking ass in this car be-fore I bounce on you," I joked.

Michelle hopped in, and we went to my house to catch up with each other. Since Snoop passed away, I rarely invited anyone over to my house. Being alone was when I was the happiest. I had a lot on my mind, and the girls I dealt with were so shallow that I couldn't have a conversation with them without talking about clubs or rap videos. I had a lot on my mind, and it felt good having someone to talk to about anything.

"Losing my father was the hardest thing I've ever been through in my life. He was so disappointed in me when I quit school because I was pregnant. He worked eighteen-hour shifts at the factory to put me through college. Even though I'm struggling being a single parent right now, I registered for school this semester. I had to do it, not only for him, but for me. Ya know?"

"Damn. I feel you on that. I know exactly how you feel."

"Okay, I answered all of ya questions, now it's my turn. This house is beautiful. How can you afford this?" Michelle asked, looking around.

I don't know how or why, but I answered her questions truthfully. Before Michelle, I never told anyone about how I made a living pulling heists. She poured her heart out to me, and I poured my heart out to her. I never felt as comfortable talking to a female as I did with Michelle. I told her almost everything, from the first jux to selling coke in the bar with Raphael, to the Toys "R" Us jux where Snoop lost his life. Talking about everything like that for the first time had me feeling emotional. Michelle listened intently and never took her eyes off me. After I finished talking, neither one of us said a word for a couple of minutes. I was beginning to regret telling her what I did. I couldn't imagine what was going through Michelle's head. Michelle finally broke the silence.

"So how much is it for you to get back in school?"

"A lot of money. Probably close to ten thousand dollars. Why you ask me that?"

Michelle got up off the couch, grabbed her pocketbook and pulled out her checkbook.

"What are you doing?" I asked.

Michelle didn't answer me. A few seconds later, she handed me a check for ten thousand dollars.

"What is this?"

"What does it look like? It's your tuition money," Michelle replied, smiling brightly.

"Yo, you buggin' out. Where did you get ten thousand dollars from?"

"I got it from my father's life insurance policy. He left me twenty thousand dollars. Before tonight, I couldn't figure out what to do with it, but after hearing your story, I know it's the right thing to do."

"Michelle, I appreciate the offer, but I can't take this from you. Ya pops left you money for you and your son."

Michelle slid over on the couch closer to me, held my hand and said, "Isaiah, please take it. I want you to have it. I don't want you to go back to dealing drugs and robbing people. You're so much better than that. You can do anything you put your mind to. My father believed in me more than I believed in myself. He sacrificed his whole life for me to be able to go to college, and Isaiah, I believe in you. My father would want me to do this, Isaiah. Please take it. I don't know what I'd do if something happened to you out there on the streets," Michelle pleaded with tears rolling down her cheeks.

"Michelle, calm down. Listen to me for a minute," I interjected.

"No! You listen to me, Isaiah. I'm not taking no for an answer. I love you," Michelle shouted.

When Michelle told me she loved me, it took me by surprise. Before her, only two other women ever told me they loved me, and none of them were more convincing than her. Looking at Michelle sitting in my den, I realized that everything I ever wanted in a woman was sitting under my nose the whole time. I was just too shallow to see it.

"What did you say?" I asked not because I didn't hear her but because I wanted her to say it again.

"You heard me."

"Nah, I ain't hear you, and even if I did, what's the big deal? You ashamed of loving me?"

"I'm not ashamed of anything. I love you. I've loved you ever since the first time I laid eyes on you. You know that."

"Damn, girl, since the first day you laid eyes on me? What was I wearing? I must've been fly as a mothafucka that day," I said jokingly.

"See, that's why I never told you. All you wanna do is make fun of me," Michelle said, crossing her arms and pouting.

I don't know what it was, but that day Michelle looked better to me than she ever did before.

"Come here," I said, holding my arms out.

Michelle came across the sofa and sat on my lap.

"It's crazy how I let the best thing that ever happened to me slide out of my grip."

"And what's that?"

I answered after kissing her passionately, "You."

Michelle and I sat in the den of my house, kissed and touched each other for almost ten minutes. It was like time was standing still and nothing else mattered.

I picked Michelle up and carried her up the stairs into my bedroom. After we were in the bedroom, I put on my Carl Thomas CD and undressed Michelle slowly, kissing every inch of her body. When I got Michelle down to her bra and panties, I took off all my clothes and got on top of her naked, kissing and fondling her. When I removed her panties, they were soaking wet.

"Damn, girl, that thing is wet. Can I taste it?" I whispered, sliding down on the bed between her legs.

I spread her pussy lips apart and began licking her clit in a slow, circular motion.

"Ohhh, baby. What are you doing to me? Ohhh! Oh my God," Michelle screamed out in ecstasy as she climaxed.

I licked and sucked Michelle's pussy for a half hour, sending her to three orgasms. Her pussy was literally sopping wet. I straddled Michelle and sucked her neck as I rubbed my rock-hard dick on her clit.

"Put it in, baby. Put it in. I wanna feel you. Put it in," Michelle begged, squirming around on the bed trying to guide me inside of her.

I entered Michelle slowly from the missionary position. Our bodies were grinding together in a steady rhythm. It was as if we were one. Michelle was biting my neck, licking my ears, digging her nails in my back and grinding her hips with perfect timing to meet my deep, long strokes.

"Promise me you'll never leave me again. Promise me," Michelle said, throwing it even harder.

"I'm all yours, baby," I responded, not believing the words were coming out of my mouth.

"I love you."

"I love you too," I answered truthfully.

When I said that Michelle's whole body shook and started convulsing, and her pussy kept getting even wetter. I couldn't hold it back anymore. Michelle and I came together.

As I lay on my back with Michelle asleep on my chest, I was happier than I'd been in a long time. I fucked lots of women, but this was the first time that I had ever made love. It was ironic that the night I decided to get in the game I was with Michelle, and the night I decided to get out of the game, I was with Michelle again.

As I reflected on my run-in on the street, I realized that none of the superficial shit was important anymore. I no longer cared about wearing the flyest clothes, driving the hottest whips and fucking the baddest bitches. I was content going to school, playing basketball and being with Michelle. I knew it wasn't gonna be easy to become the basketball player I once was, but to me anything was possible with the right focus and drive...and a strong woman behind me.

27

"Ski, I must admit I was thoroughly impressed with your game. Not only were you the best player in the game tonight, you were the best player in the entire tournament. You really made me put my foot in my mouth. You've worked extremely hard these past few months, and it's paying off. The A.D. told me that you had a 3.0 grade average this past semester and that you enrolled in summer courses to become academically eligible. I don't know if you're still interested in playing here at Ulster, but we'd love to have you. It would be an honor for me to coach you. Not only am I offering you a scholarship, I'm also offering you a starting position. As you already know, I have a lot of connections, and I know a lot of people. I guarantee if you play for me and keep your grades up, you'll play for a major division one school. So what do you say?" Coach Wilkins said to me from behind his desk.

The words were music to my ears. I was sitting in Coach Wilkins' office after the Mid- Hudson Summer Classic at Ulster that July, in the same seat I had sat in four months ago when he told me I wasn't good enough to play college ball. Now, the shoe was on the other foot. My team won the championship, and I was Most Valuable Player for the entire tournament. Every major school in New York State was there, and I expected letters from each and every one of them. Even though I had no intention on playing anywhere but Ulster, I wanted to make Coach Wilkins sweat a little after all he did to shit on me a few months back. But I was so happy I couldn't even hide it.

"Coach, you don't know how good it feels to hear you say that, man. It would be an honor for me to play for you," I said, shaking Coach Wilkins' hand, grinning from ear to ear.

"Ski, you're a fine young man. You showed discipline, dedication and determination. You're going to go far with basketball. You've got a strong will to succeed—the sky's the limit."

I signed my letter of intent and scholarship papers right there on the spot. It was a dream come true. I knew Snoop was looking down on me smiling. As I drove home, I reflected on the past four months of my life. I was happier than I'd ever been, and I was broke. Michelle gave me her father's insurance policy money to go to school and her and her two-year-old son moved in with me. Michelle put her life on hold for me. In addition to being a full-time student like myself, she also worked full time at Kingston Hospital as a phlebotomist and part time at the college bookstore. She was paying all the bills, including the rent. Michelle jogged with me five miles every morning to help me get back in shape. She came to the gym to pass me the ball and helped me study. She was my driving force. She believed in me so much that it made me work harder not to let her down. I was truly in love for the first time in my life. Michelle taught me that life wasn't all about material things. Most of the time we barely had a dollar between us, but we were happy as hell.

I was a few minutes away from home when my cell phone rang. "Hello."

"Where the fuck you been at, B?" Dro shouted into the phone. "I've been calling you down for hours. You ain't get my messages?"

"I had a game tonight."

"Nigga, you still living out them hoop dreams? Give it up already, B.

You're washed up. Ya career is over. Twenty-one is too old to be going back to college and playing ball. You're supposed to be out of college by twenty-one, ain't you? You bugging out, B."

"Never say never. I just finished bussing major ass in this big tournament. I got offered a full scholarship to play at Ulster," I said proudly.

"Big deal, son. I just put twenty carats in my watch and Sprewells on my coupe. I don't know how you're doing it. What are you doing for money? What you gonna do when shorty leaves you 'cause you ain't got no paper?"

"My girl ain't going nowhere, son. She ain't on no materialistic shit. We got that real love."

"Oh yeah? Well, love don't pay the bills, and you definitely can't eat love. You a funny nigga, B. All of a sudden, you wanna be a family man now, playing stepdaddy and shit," Dro replied, dying laughing.

"Yeah. Whatever, son. I know you didn't call to tell me all this bullshit. What up? What can I do for you?"

Ever since I got out of the game, everybody always had something negative to say about it. It's crazy how those who were doing the wrong thing kept criticizing me for trying to do the right thing.

"Yo, remember a couple of years back when me and you took care of Paula's situation?" Dro asked, sounding serious.

"Yeah. Why? What up?"

"Remember how I was there for you, no questions asked?"

"Yeah."

"Well, now I need you."

"Anything, son. What up? You got beef?"

"Nah, B, nuffin' like that. I need you for this job coming up."

"C'mon, son. I told y'all I'm done wit' the streets. What part of that shit didn't you understand?"

"I ain't tell you that when you needed me, did I? I need you, Ski, one more time. After this, we all gonna be straight. You ain't gonna want for nuffin', B. This is big money, B. I'm talking three hundred stacks apiece."

"Damn, three hundred grand? That's a lot of paper. But I still don't understand. What you need me for?"

"It's a five-man job, and I only got four."

"Who you got?"

"Me, Roach, Wise and Boota."

"Boota? Say word? Boota is going on a jux again? I thought he said he'd never do one again?"

"Money talks, B. Three hundred grand is a lot of cash. That would hold you and shorty down for a minute. You can play ball and go to school until you thirty years old with that kind of money." Dro replied sarcastically.

Dro was right. Three hundred grand was a lot of money. I hated Michelle working so hard, and she did deserve to live good for once in her life. One more jux wouldn't hurt. Dro was a master manipulator. Ever since I picked up the phone, he was trying his best to get me in. Knowing Dro, he probably had everything he was gonna say planned out ahead of time.

"Why you need me?" I asked curiously.

"Rule is fucked up, B. That nigga is using coke now. He's on some other shit. I can't trust that man with my life."

"Word? No wonder why I ain't seen him in so long."

"Yeah. I went to see him the other day, and his nose was red like Rudolph the mothafuckin' reindeer. Dude was rubbing his nose every second. So what's good, B? You ridin' wit' ya boy or what?"

When Dro asked me if I was riding with him, I got the chills. Last time he tried to convince me to go on a jux, Snoop lost his life. When I closed my eyes, I could still see Snoop on my lap, bleeding profusely and choking on his own blood. I could still hear his voice pleading with me to promise that I was gonna get out of the game. Last time Snoop ended up in a coffin. Who would it be this time? Boota? Wise? Roach? Dro? Me? What if we got caught? How would I be able to look Michelle in the face after all the sacrifices she had made for me? I felt terrible telling Dro no, but I'd feel even worse if my decision cost somebody his life. I wasn't prepared to give up everything I had worked so hard to reclaim.

"I can't do it, son. I'm sorry. I can't risk this right now. I promised Snoop, son. I can't do it. I'm sorry, yo," I tried to explain as best I could.

"Yo, Ski, I can't believe you turning ya back on me like this, B. I really need you. I wouldn't ask you if I didn't. This is the last one. After this, everybody's done, including me. C'mon, B," Dro pleaded.

"Dro, I can't do it, son. I'm sorry."

"Yo, you know what? I knew you was gonna do some sucka shit like this, B. Don't worry about it, B. We gonna get this paper without you," Dro said angrily, hanging up the phone.

When I pulled up to my crib, I sat in the driveway for ten minutes thinking about my conversation with Dro. I felt like calling him back to try and explain, but I changed my mind. I hoped that Dro wouldn't be tight at me for too long. After a while, I started to think about my future with Michelle and playing basketball, and remembered what had transpired earlier. I got out of my car and jogged into the house.

"Michelle! Michelle! Michelle! Where you at? I got good news," I shouted as I walked into the house.

The house was completely dark. Not a light or a TV was on in the whole crib. Michelle had the day off, so she couldn't have been at work. I had the car, so she couldn't have gone out. The more I thought about it, the more I began to panic. It was like déjà vu.

"Michelle! Michelle! Michelle!" I ran up the steps.

I looked everywhere—from the living room to the den to the garage. Michelle and her son were nowhere to be found. All kinds of thoughts ran through my head. If something happened to Michelle or the baby, I wouldn't have been able to handle it. I was sitting on the couch with my hands over my face when the phone rang.

"Hello," I answered frantically.

"Isaiah, come to Kingston Hospital right now. My mother just had a stroke," Michelle replied.

"What? I'll be there in a minute."

I ran out the house, jumped into my Lex and sped off to the hospital. It was terrible hearing about Michelle's mother, but in a way it was a relief. I was thinking that someone had kidnapped Michelle and the baby, trying to get money from me. I already had Snoop's and Kashaun's blood on my conscious, I didn't know if I could handle something happening to anyone else close to me, especially Michelle.

I parked my car in the emergency room parking lot and jogged inside. When I walked through the doors, I didn't even have to look for Michelle, she found me. She ran into my arms and hugged me tighter than she ever had before and began crying hysterically.

"Isaiah, they said that she might not make it. I was just with her yesterday and she was fine. I can't believe this. First my father, and now my mother. I'm cursed. Why do bad things keep happening to me? Why? If I lose my mother, it'll kill me," Michelle sobbed with her voice cracking and tears rolling down her cheeks.

"Baby, calm down. Everything is gonna be a'ight. Your mom is strong. She ain't going nowhere. Stop talking like that. She's gonna make it," I said softly, hugging Michelle and rubbing the back of her head.

When Michelle's son, Trey, saw his mother crying, he started crying and that made Michelle cry even more. I sat down in the emergency room with Trey sitting on my lap and Michelle's head on my shoulder, waiting for the doctor to come out and tell us what the deal was. Michelle never stopped crying the entire time. I was powerless in the situation. It's a helpless feeling when someone you love is hurting and you can't do anything about it.

Almost an hour passed when a pale-faced white doctor finally came out to speak with us.

"Michelle Russell?" the doctor asked, looking around.

"Yes. That's me," Michelle said, standing up and taking a deep breath.

"Does your mother have medical insurance coverage?" the doctor asked.

"No, she doesn't. Not currently."

"Mmm. I see," the doctor replied, looking at his clipboard.

I grabbed the doctor by the collar, throwing him up against the wall, "What the fuck do you mean, you see? What the fuck you keep asking dumb-ass questions for? What does it matter if she has insurance or not? Is she a'ight or what?"

"Isaiah! Stop it. Get off him," Michelle said, stepping between us. "He's sorry, doctor. He didn't mean it. We're all a little high strung now. So, how's my mother?"

"Well, miss, I have bad news for you. Your mother had a stroke. Right now, she's in a coma. We did an MRI and found a brain aneurysm in her cerebellum. Unfortunately, there's nothing we can do, Miss Russell. I'm sorry," the doctor explained.

"What are you saying? My mother isn't gonna make it? Can I see her?" Michelle asked with her eyes tearing up.

"It's too early to tell. She may or may not ever come out of the coma. Right now, she can't breathe without life support. You can see her, but only for five to ten minutes. Visiting hours are over." The doctor walked away quickly.

Something wasn't right about that doctor. For some reason, I felt like he wasn't telling us the truth. When we went inside Michelle's mother's room, Michelle almost passed out when she laid eyes on her mother. It hurt me to see Michelle going through so much pain. Five minutes later, a heavyset black female nurse walked in.

"Excuse me. I know this might not be the right time, and I hate to intrude, but the doctor hasn't been completely honest with you folks."

"No, you're not intruding, please come in," I said.

"Well, normally I don't mind other people's business but I overheard the doctors talking, and it wouldn't sit well in my conscience if I didn't say something."

"Please continue," Michelle said.

"Your mother has a brain aneurysm that can be taken care of by corrective surgery. The procedure is very, very expensive. I overheard

Dr. Campbell talking to another physician, and he said that if the patient didn't have insurance, he was gonna tell the family there was nothing he could do," the nurse explained.

"Son of a bitch! I oughta kill that nigga," I shouted.

"How expensive is the surgery?" Michelle asked.

"Child, don't get me to lying. I'm not quite sure, I'm only the RN, but the surgery has to be in the fifty- to one-hundred-thousand-dollar range, and that's not including aftercare. Now look, please don't mention this to anyone. I can't afford to lose my job. I only said something because I knew it was wrong, and I thought you should know. Please keep this conversation between us," the nurse pleaded.

"No problem. Thank you," I answered.

When the nurse left the room, Michelle fell to her knees and started crying hysterically.

"Where am I gonna get that kind of money from, Isaiah? Oh God, help me. Please don't take my mother away from me," Michelle cried out.

I picked Michelle up off the floor. "Michelle, don't worry about nuffin'. I'mma get the money, I promise. Ya mother is gonna be a'ight. You hear me?" I stormed out the hospital room.

Michelle screamed out as I left, "Where are you going, Isaiah?"

I ignored Michelle's question, walked out the emergency room and went outside to the parking lot so I could get reception on my cell phone.

Dro answered on the third ring. "Yo."

"Yo. What up, it's me. Is that offer still on the table?"

"Of course," Dro responded.

"Count me in," I said and hung up the phone.

"o, Roach, pull off, son. Let's bounce, B. It's a wrap. We can't pop this shit off today. Come on, son. Pull off," I shouted frantically.

"What? Why not? What the fuck are you talking about?" Roach asked.

"You don't see that man staring over here at us? Duke been grilling the whip for the last five minutes. If he ain't call the cops, he definitely got the license plate, maybe both."

"Where? I don't see nobody. Lemme find out you seeing ghosts," Roach replied, taking my observation lightly.

"Don't turn ya head and look, but dude is behind us, in front of that warehouse."

Roach did exactly what I said not to do and turned around in his seat and looked back.

"I know you ain't talking about that old-ass white man. That cracker ain't paying us no mind. That old mothafucka look like he can't even see. Lemme find out you on some shook shit."

"Nigga, is you stupid? Never am I shook. I just ain't stupid. Call Dro and tell him we out. I ain't doing nuffin' today. Fuck that. Y'all ain't gonna get me trapped off."

"Damn, B, you lost ya nerve. I told Dro to get Rule, but he wouldn't listen, then he gonna turn around and put me with you. You soft now, B. Face it."

"Who's soft? Watch ya mouth, son. Ain't nuffin' soft over here."

"I can't tell. You letting some old-ass white man get you shook. Nigga, I do this for real. I don't give a fuck if the police are across the street. I go hard," Roach said, pounding his fist to hand for emphasis.

"That ain't going hard, that's being stupid. You gonna fuck around and get us knocked. Y'all niggaz don't even have this shit planned out right. We've been sitting in front of the spot for hours, making ourselves hot. We all the way out in West Bumbafuck, and ya dumb ass ain't even got us a stolen V. You got us sitting here in ya whip. How stupid can you be? Two black dudes with hoodies on in the summertime sitting across the street from a jewelry store in a Benz wit' New York plates, Ray mothafuckin' Charles could see what we about to do. Fuck this shit. I'm out. Y'all ain't getting me trapped off," I shouted, getting more aggravated by the second.

Roach and I were in Rhode Island, across the street from a large jewelry store named Wears Diamonds. We were all split up into three teams—Roach and me, Wise and Boota, Dro and Danielle. Dro was so thirsty to get this robbery done that he actually had Danielle going in a spot with a burner.

We were all stationed ten miles apart from each other in front of the spots we were assigned to. Each team had a walkie-talkie, and being that all the jobs were to be done simultaneously, we had to wait until the time was right at all three locations. Each store had close to ninety watches, and our objective was to get all of them. To me, this was the worst planned robbery that I'd ever been a part of. I didn't like the plan from the first time I heard it. Dro usually planned everything to the smallest detail, whereas this jux seemed like it wasn't well thought out. The getaways were shaky, and we didn't know how many employees worked in each store, if they had security guards or electric bolt doors. All we knew was the amount of watches each store had and where they were located in the store. We were going in blind. I couldn't understand why Dro was in such a rush to get the jobs done without planning right. Dro was desperate. He had to be, to be having his girl run up in a spot with him.

Before every jux, you always feel nervous and anxious, but I felt different this time. My gut was telling me that if I took part in this, I was gonna end up either dead or in jail. The man behind us, in the front of the warehouse was just the icing on the cake. I was done.

"I knew it. I told Dro, B. I knew you was gonna pull some bullshit. Scared-ass nigga," Roach said loudly.

"Nigga, I ain't never scared. I just got sense. That's why your dumb ass is always in jail. You ain't got no patience. What's the rush?"

"What's the hold up?" Roach shot back.

Our argument was interrupted by Dro calling us on the walkie-talkie.

"Team three, how's it looking over there?"

"Everything is a green light," Roach replied.

"Team two, how's it looking over there?" he asked talking to Wise and Boota.

"Green light," Wise responded.

"A'ight then. Everybody set ya watches. Get back to me in fifteen minutes. Go!"

"Yo, Roach, why the fuck did you tell Dro it's a green light over here?" I asked angrily.

"Because it is, nigga. The white dude is gone. I'm going in there with or without you, so make up ya mind. We on the clock."

I looked in the rearview mirror and the white man who was standing in front of the warehouse was gone.

"What up? You riding or what?" Roach asked impatiently.

I took a deep breath, felt my bulletproof vest underneath my hoody and cocked back my two forty cals.

We hopped out the car, jogged across the street and entered the jewelry store.

"A'ight. I'm sure y'all know what the fuck this is. All we need is forty-five seconds of ya time. Don't start no shit, won't be no shit. Please don't try anything. I'm really not in the mood to kill somebody today. Me and my partner here will be out in a minute," I announced, pacing up and down the middle of the store with my two guns aimed at the employees and the customers who looked on with fright.

Roach broke the display cases that had the watches in them and began emptying them quickly. Roach could be an asshole at times, but when it came to handling his business, he was one of the best. He was the fastest smasher and grabber out of the whole crew. Out of the three teams that we were split into, Roach and I were by far the strongest team.

Inside the store, there were thirteen people—five men and eight women. About six of them were employees. The store was huge.

As Roach was snatching up the watches, he cut his hand on some broken glass.

"Yo, I'm cut, son. I think I might have cut my thumb off," Roach shouted in pain, about to take off his glove.

"Keep ya glove on, son. You don't wanna leave any blood on the scene. Blood is just as good as fingerprints. Keep working. Hurry up. We on the clock."

Roach fought through the pain and continued smashing and grabbing until he had emptied all of the display cases with watches in them.

"I'm ready when you are," Roach said to me, zipping up the duffel bag.

"You got everything?" I asked.

"Yeah. Let's roll."

Roach walked in front of me, and I walked behind him with my back to the door with my two hammers pointed at the employees and customers that I had lay down in the middle of the store. When Roach went to push the door to exit, it didn't move. He tried again and got the same result.

"Yo, we trapped, son. We trapped. They locked the doors on us," Roach yelled.

My heart dropped when those words came out of Roach's mouth. I felt lightheaded, and my knees got weak. I'm surprised that I didn't pass out. I took a deep breath and started to look around for alternative exits. I saw that the front door was the one and only exit. *There's got to be a way out,* I thought. My mind was moving a million miles per minute. I had a feeling that this jux was gonna get me locked up from the very beginning. I thought about everything important to me: my mother, my sister, Michelle, Snoop, my coach, and how disappointed he was going to be in me. *C'mon, Ski. Focus. Focus.*

Roach was frantic, kicking and pushing the door. "What we gonna do, son? What we gonna do?"

"Who's the manager?" I asked.

A gray-haired man with a black suit answered, "That would be me, sir."

"Come here," I demanded

He got up off the floor and walked over to us with his hands on his head.

"Yo. Do you know how to deactivate this door?" I asked, putting both of my guns to his head.

"Sir, I didn't even know we had lock bolt doors," the manager stated nervously.

"He's lying, son. He's lying. Shoot him, B. Shoot him," Roach shouted.

"How the fuck do we get out of here?" I asked.

"Pull the door open," the manager simply stated.

I walked over to the door slowly being careful, still keeping my eye on everyone in the store and pulled the door. It opened.

Roach and I ran out the store and across the street to his Benz.

"You stupid-ass nigga. You ain't think to pull the door? You asshole. You could of got us knocked. We lost mad time because of you. Shook-ass nigga," I said pushing the seat back as Roach pulled off.

"I lost a lot of blood, son. I can't think straight. I felt like I was gonna pass out in there," Roach tried to explain.

"You bitch-ass. And you had the nerve to call me shook. You sounded like a bitch in there."

"Lemme see you lose all the blood I lost and see if you can still think straight."

"Yo, just shut up and drive."

Ten minutes later Roach looked over at me. "Yo, Ski, don't get mad at me, but we're lost. I can't find the parkway, B."

"What? You can't be serious, son? You can't be serious," I said, lifting my head to look out the window.

"What are we gonna do, son? They're lookin' in every car. We about to go down, B."

"Why didn't you get on the I-95?"

"I must've made a wrong turn. We back on the same block as the spot."

I looked out the window and saw that we were headed toward the jewelry store we had just hit. The street was flooded with cops. They had a roadblock set up and were stopping and looking into every car. If any of the people from inside the store saw us get in Roach's Benz, it was a wrap. I had to think, and think fast.

"Take ya hoody off and put it underneath ya seat. Make sure you don't let them see ya hand. Pass them ya license with ya opposite hand. Stay calm. If they stop us and ask questions, let me do all the talking, just follow my lead," I said, taking off my own hoody and shoving it underneath my seat.

Roach took his hoody off and put it underneath his seat, and put on a pair of black leather gloves he found in his glove compartment to hide his hand. I couldn't believe my luck. Out of all the people in the world, I was stuck with Roach's stupid ass. If he wasn't Boota's brother, I would have shot him right there on the spot for his stupidity. We were almost through the roadblock when a policeman motioned for us to stop the car.

"License and registration please," the policeman requested.

Roach passed the policeman his license and registration, and the cop spoke, "You guys are a long way from home. What are you doing all the way out here in Rhode Island?"

We're coming back from the University of Massachusetts' annual summer basketball camp. We got hungry, so we got off the I-95 to get something to eat, sir," I explained calmly, passing him my college ID.

"The University of Massachusetts, huh? You guys play ball? I know the coach there. His name is Jay…uh, Jay…" the cop said, not remembering the coach's name.

"Jay Wright," I answered.

"Yeah. That's it. That's it. Jay Wright," the cop said, getting excited. "You know, I used to play a little ball myself in my time. That sure was a long time ago. Okay, guys, have a safe trip home." The cop handed Roach his license and registration and my ID.

"Hey, officer, could you tell us how to get back on the I-95?" I asked.

"Yeah, sure. Make the first left, go three lights down, and follow the signs."

"Thanks, sir. Have a good day," I said as Roach pulled off.

"Yo, Roach, pull over, son. I'm driving," I said as soon as we got a safe distance from the roadblock.

When we pulled over, Dro called us on the walkie-talkie. "Team three? Where y'all at?" he asked, sounding worried.

"We're on our way home, baby. It was a close one, but we made it. What about y'all and Boota and Wise?"

"Everything is a go. Everybody made it out with everything they were supposed to get. What about y'all? Y'all got everything?"

"Everything is a go, my nigga. We'll see y'all when we hit New York. Drive safe."

"One."

"One."

It was a close call, but we made it out of there. As I drove down I-95, I thought about all the good things that I was gonna be able to do with the money. I was gonna be able to pay for Michelle's mother's corrective surgery and put down on a house of my own for Michelle and me. Renting was becoming too expensive. I also decided that I was going to propose to Michelle. She was my ride-or-die chick, for real. I couldn't see myself with no one but her. Now that we were gonna have some money in the bank, Michelle would be able to quit her two jobs and focus solely on school. For the first time in my life, I was completely happy. I had everything I wanted—a starting position and a scholarship to play college ball, a woman who was down for me and three hundred thousand dollars. Life couldn't be sweeter.

⬜⬜⬜

"Hello," Dro answered after the phone rang.

"Yo. What's up, B?" Roach asked.

"What's really good, B? Where the fuck you at? You a'ight?" Dro asked, genuinely concerned.

"Yeah. I'm good, son. They got me up here at Queens house. All they got me on is driving with a suspended license. I'll be home in a couple of days. I'm just waiting to see the judge."

"Oh. A'ight. That's what's up. The way niggas round here been talking, I was thinking the ATF scooped you up. I've been nervous as hell the last couple of days."

"You know you can't listen to them. They got vivid imaginations. They always exaggerate."

"Yeah, no doubt. Yo, did you have one of them watches on?" Dro asked.

"Yeah, but it ain't nuffin'. They ain't even pay it no mind. They just put it with my property."

"So, what's good? What you need me to do?"

"Just hold my share of the money for me. I gotta go now, son. Make ure you stay in the crib. I'mma call you back. Stay home. Don't go where."

"I ain't going nowhere. I'm waiting for Ski and the crew to come get their money. They was supposed to be here hours ago."

"A'ight. I'll hit you later. One."

"One," Dro said, hanging up the phone.

It had been a week since the Rhode Island robberies. Dro was in his house in Long Island waiting for Ski, Wise and Boota to come pick up their share of the money. Normally, they would split the jewelry up between them and sell it on their own, but it was so much jewelry that none of them had someone to buy that much bulk. Dro had been dealing with a Russian jeweler for a long time, and he arranged to pay one million five hundred thousand for everything. They were supposed to arrive at Dro's crib hours ago, but made a pit stop. Three days prior, Roach went to get something to eat and never came back. Young niggaz who were on the block said that four vans cut Roach's Benz off at the intersection, and police hopped out with their guns drawn, snatched Roach out the car and threw him in one of the vans while another officer jumped in Roach's car and sped off. The whole thing supposedly lasted no longer than a minute. When Dro got that news, he immediately went into survival mode. He took all of his guns, jewelry and money out of both his houses and stayed in a cheap motel in the boondocks. The only reason he was at his house then was to meet up with his crew. Dro was glad that he was home to catch Roach's phone call from jail. He felt relieved after his phone conversation with Roach, but now that they were missing in action, he began to think that they might have got knocked. He knew they wanted their money. Especially Ski.

Dro was pacing up and down the living room when Danielle came in. "Who was that on the phone, DaShaun?"

"That was Roach. They got him in Queens house for driving with a suspended license." Dro replied.

"See. I told you you had nothing to worry about, babe. Why do you still look so nervous?" Danielle asked.

"Because Ski and them ain't here yet. Something had to happen to them. I know they want their money. Believe that. I think it's funny how none of them have shown up yet. Something is going on. Trust me.

Ski would've been here by now," Dro explained.

"Calm down, babe. You're working yaself up for nothing. Just relax. Everything is gonna be fine," Danielle said, standing behind Dro, massaging his massive shoulders.

Just then, Dro and Danielle heard a loud thud, and the sound of approaching footsteps.

"What the fuck was that?" Dro asked, looking around.

"Babe, it's nothing. What's wrong with you? If the police were coming to get us, they'd be kicking down this door."

Dro went to the kitchen drawer and pulled out his Desert Eagle.

"Danielle, go upstairs and get the rest of the money out of the closet. We gotta get the fuck out of here," Dro demanded.

Even though Danielle thought Dro was overreacting, she still followed his orders and ran upstairs into the bedroom to retrieve the rest of the money. Right as Danielle was running up the stairs, the front door got kicked in.

"Freeze! FBI. Nobody move," one of the Feds shouted.

Ten police rushed the house in blue FBI jackets with their guns drawn. Dro didn't waste any time. He immediately started firing in their direction, hitting a cop three times in the chest.

Dro ran through the living room and out the back door directly into the police. The Feds had the entire house surrounded. Dro's body convulsed as he got hit four times in the chest and fell to the ground. Danielle tried to escape by jumping out the second-floor window, but she got bagged as soon as she landed on the grass. When the police handcuffed Danielle and escorted her to a van, she saw Dro on the ground and started throwing a tantrum.

"Oh my God. DaShaun. DaShaun. You killed him. You didn't have to kill him. Oh, God. You no good sons of bitches killed my baby," Danielle shouted, crying as the police held her back from running over to Dro's lifeless body.

When Boota, Wise and I finally made it to Dro's crib and got the news, we couldn't believe it. I felt so many different emotions that I didn't know how I really felt. I was mad at myself for letting Wise and Boota convince me to go chill with them girls instead of going straight to Dro's crib to pick up our money. In another way I felt relieved that we weren't at the house because if we were there at the time we were supposed to, we would've got caught in the raid. I felt sorry for Dro and Danielle, but I wasn't quite sure if I wanted Dro to live or die. I knew if he lived, he was gonna be facing football numbers, or maybe even a letter. I didn't know anything about the legal system, but I knew that shooting a cop and doing a string of robberies equaled a lot of time.

There were so many unanswered questions. How did they get on to us? How many robberies did they know about? Were they looking for me? How much time was I facing? My nerves were shot. I could barely drive home my hands were shaking so much. After Boota, Wise and I split up; I decided to take the hour-and-a-half drive home upstate to break the news to Michelle. I didn't know how she was gonna react when I told her that I pulled another heist, I loved Michelle more than I loved any woman I'd ever been with, but I didn't give a fuck how she took it. I felt like my life was over. There was going to be no college, no basketball, no marriage, no money and no operation for Michelle's mother. I doubted that Michelle was even going to believe that I had done everything for her, and I didn't care. Knowing Michelle like I did, I knew she was going to leave me. When I woke up that morning, I thought life couldn't get any sweeter. Now just twenty-four hours later, I couldn't imagine life getting any worse.

The drive was the longest and scariest of my life. Every headlight I saw behind me I thought was the Feds, and every cop car I saw, I thought was looking for me. It all seemed like a never-ending bad dream. When I finally made it to my house, I drove around the block five times to make sure there was nobody watching my crib and parked in my driveway, put my head on the steering wheel and gathered my thoughts.

I took the keys out of the ignition and walked slowly to the front door. I glanced at my watch and saw that it was a couple of minutes past four in the morning. I crept up the stairs, entered our bedroom and saw Michelle sitting up in the bed reading.

"Hey, baby. I missed you. I couldn't sleep. I have to talk to you about something really important. There's a plate for you in the microwave if you're hungry," Michelle said.

"What happened? Somebody came here looking for me?" I asked, getting up and looking out the window nervously.

"No. Nobody came here. What's wrong with you? You're acting so funny," Michelle said, noticing my strange behavior.

"Ain't nuffin' wrong," I lied.

"You're lying. You think I can't tell when something is wrong?" Michelle set her book on the nightstand.

"I'll tell you after you tell me what's on ya mind," I stated, staring out the window.

"Come here. Come sit down next to me."

I sat on the bed next to Michelle and she held my hand, "Isaiah, I'm pregnant."

"What? How do you know?"

"I took three pregnancy tests. We're having a baby," Michelle announced, smiling brightly.

"Damn! Damn! I can't be a father right now. I can't," I shouted as I stood and started pacing the bedroom.

Michelle burst out into tears. She ran out the bedroom and down the steps. I chased after her. I was under so much stress that I just said the first thing that came to mind. Under normal circumstances, I would've been ecstatic that Michelle was pregnant with my first child.

"Wait a minute. Come here and lemme talk to you," I said, grabbing her arm.

"Don't touch me. Get ya hands off me," Michelle shouted.

I grabbed Michelle by the shoulders and pushed her on the couch. Michelle looked up at me surprised. She had never seen my aggressive side before.

"Listen to me. Just shut the fuck up and listen. You can't have this baby. You can't. If you were smart, you'd get an abortion and get the fuck away from me. My life is over," I yelled.

"If you don't want me or the baby, just say it. I don't need you. I'll raise the baby by myself. I can't believe you. You're just like the rest of them. I thought you loved me," Michelle shouted, crying deliriously.

When I looked at Michelle's face and saw how hurt she was, it snapped me back to reality. Michelle was my heart. I loved her. I owed her an explanation.

"Baby, listen. I'm sorry. You know I love you. I'm just under a lot of stress right now. Trust me, after I tell you what's going on, you ain't gonna want nothing to do with me."

"Isaiah, I love you. I wanna spend the rest of my life with you. Whatever it is, we can work through it," Michelle said as she wiped the tears from her face.

I got on my knees and held Michelle's hand and started pouring my heart out. "A'ight, listen. Remember when I when I told you that I was gonna get the money for you mom's corrective surgery?"

"Yeah. What does that have to do with this?"

"Everything. Listen. Earlier that night, Dro called me and asked me to do him a favor and pull one last jux with him and the crew. I told him no because I promised you and Snoop that I was gonna get out of the game for good and go back to school. But later that night, after I found out what happened to ya mother and saw how much pain it was causing you, I called Dro back and told him to count me in. I couldn't just sit back and do nuffin' and let ya mother die. A week ago, we pulled the heist and got away. We all were supposed to get like three hundred grand apiece. I was gonna pay for your mom's surgery, put down on a house for us and propose to you. Tonight was the night that we were supposed to meet Dro and get our share of the money, but when we got there, it was too late. The Feds raided Dro's house and arrested Danielle. Dro shot an agent and they shot him. We don't even know if Dro is still alive. The Feds got the money and everything. They're probably on the way right now to come and get me as we speak. Michelle, I love you, but you'd be crazy to still wanna be with me and have my child at a time like this."

"Isaiah, I love you. I'll never leave you. I still wanna be with you." Michelle stared into my eyes and I knew she meant every word.

"Michelle, you're buggin'. You don't know how serious this is. You don't know what you're getting yaself into. This shit is real. If you have any sense, you'd get away from me as fast as you can."

"Do you love me?"

"You know I do, Michelle."

"Then let me come with you. I can't imagine living my life without you. Where are you going?" Michelle asked with new tears in her eyes.

"I have no idea. I ain't got much money…"

"C'mon. Get the baby. We can stay at my mother's house until we figure out a plan."

I went into the baby's room and packed up his baby bag while Michelle went into our bedroom and packed our clothes. After we finished, we jumped into the car and drove to Michelle's mother's house. My nerves were worse than they were before. As I lay in bed with Michelle all night, I knew my life was over. It was only a matter of time before they caught up to us. I knew I couldn't hide forever.

□□□

By October 2001, I had been on the run for two months. I was the last one out of the crew still free. Boota and Wise got knocked the same night I dropped them off at their cribs, and Rule got knocked a week earlier in Manhattan at his cousin's apartment. Rule was the only person who knew the exact location of where I was staying, so when I heard he got knocked, I was shook with fear that he was gonna drop dime on me. But as every day passed, I felt more and more secure that I was safe. Rule and I had been through a lot together. He was a lot of things, but he wasn't a rat. Well, at least I thought he wasn't. I was basically a sitting duck. The Feds were in hot pursuit. They went everywhere looking for me: my mother's house in Pennsylvania, my house in Kingston and even my basketball coach's house. I was considered armed and dangerous. They had a fifty-thousand-dollar reward out on my head. School had started at the end of August, and neither Michelle nor I was able to go. Michelle only left the house to go to work and visit her mother in the hospital. The only time I left the house was to hit the block and stick up niggaz, but now being seen by anyone wasn't safe anymore. People's families would turn them in for fifty thousand dollars. Michelle and I decided to save up a few thousand dollars and move to Canada, but since our funds were limited, the plan was never gonna work.

Michelle and I were sitting in the living room of her mother's house cuddled up watching *106 and Park* when I heard a knock on the door.

The knocking on the door startled me, but Michelle kept watching TV like she didn't hear anything.

"Yo. You here that?" I asked.

"Yeah, I heard it. I'm comfortable right now. I don't feel like moving," Michelle replied, snuggling closer to me.

Michelle never gave me any reason not to trust her, but for some reason her not answering the door made me suspicious. Being on the run was definitely getting to me.

"Michelle, get the door."

"For what? It ain't for us. Nobody knows we're here. It's probably some Jehovah Witnesses or something."

"Michelle, get the fuck up and answer the door," I demanded loudly.

Michelle sucked her teeth, got up and walked to the front door. Before she made it all the way to the door, she asked, "Who is it?"

"FBI. Open up. We have some questions for you," two male voices replied in unison.

My heart felt like it jumped completely out of my chest. I always told Michelle that if the Feds ever came to her mother's house to get me that I was gonna turn myself in because if they could track me down there, they could track me down anywhere. Michelle turned around and quickly motioned for me to go hide in the kitchen. I got up off the couch and crawled into the kitchen and hid behind the refrigerator.

Michelle cracked open the door. "Yes. May I help you?"

"Is there a Michelle Russell here?" one of the agents asked.

"Yes. I'm Michelle Russell. What's the problem?"

The agents flashed their badges. "I'm Agent Creegan, and this is my partner, Agent Tiscano from the Federal Bureau of Investigations. We'd like to ask you a few questions if you don't mind."

"About what?" Michelle asked, playing dumb.

"About an Isaiah Thompson."

"About Isaiah Thompson? Hold on a minute. Lemme put some on some clothes. I'll be with you gentlemen in a minute," Michelle responded, closing the door and running upstairs to the bedroom to put some clothes on.

I was behind the refrigerator, but I felt like I was in it. I was shaking so hard, I was knocking magnets off the door. My whole life was flashing before my eyes. It's one thing knowing that the Feds are looking for you and another thing when they're outside your house. My shook level increased from eight to eighty.

I heard Michelle coming down the steps, and although I didn't know what she was going to do, I wasn't prepared for her next move. Instead of going outside to talk to the agents, she invited them inside. The agents were sitting on the couch almost in the same exact spot I was, just ten feet away from where I was hiding. They were so close that I could smell their cologne.

"So, Miss Russell, tell us what you know about Isaiah Thompson."

"I don't know if his last name is Thompson, but I went to school with a guy named Isaiah at Ulster a few years back."

One of the agents took out a wanted picture of me and asked her if the guy in the picture was the same guy she went to school with.

"Yes, that's him, but I don't understand. I haven't seen him in years. He was just a friend of mine. Why are you guys here asking me questions about him?"

"We heard from a reliable source that you two were an item and that you were hiding him out here at your mother's place."

"Whoever told you that lied to you. I told you I haven't seen him in years."

"Isaiah is a part of a criminal organization called the Go Hard Crew. He and his crew are responsible for fifteen to twenty robberies, not including murders and rapes. He is a very dangerous man. If you are trying to protect him for any reason, you need to tell us. He'll use anybody and do anything to evade us."

"Well, I'm sorry I can't be a help to you guys, but like I said, I haven't seen him in years."

"Is that Isiah's son?" Agent Creegan asked, pointing to Michelle's son playing with toys on the floor.

"No. My son is only two years old. Isaiah and I were no longer together when I had my son."

"Didn't you say that you only knew Mister Thompson from school?

So, you were in a relationship with him?"

"Yes. I guess you could say that."

"So you lied to us. People only lie when they are trying to hide something, Miss Russell. What are you hiding?"

"I'm not hiding anything. I just don't think it's any of your business who I've slept with. I told you before that I haven't seen Isaiah since school last year."

"So, you have a boyfriend now?"

"Yes, I do."

"What's his name?"

"Hector."

"And where is he from?"

"None of your fucking business. You two are treating me like a criminal. What does all of this have to do with Isaiah?"

"Well actually, you are a criminal."

"Excuse me?"

"Lying to a federal officer is a crime. First you said you didn't know Isaiah, then you said you had a relationship with him, but you hadn't seen him in a few years, and now you say that you haven't seen him since last year. Which one is it? What are you hiding?"

"I'm not hiding anything. You guys are confusing me. I don't give a fuck about Isaiah or you guys' investigation. Now please leave."

"Okay, Miss Russell, one more question. What did you say your current boyfriend's name was?"

"Harry," Michelle answered, standing up, walking to the door.

Both agents remained seated. Michelle's story was falling to pieces. They knew she was hiding something, even though Michelle was doing a good job of lying. I was proud of her. As I listened to her lie to protect me, I fell in love with her more than I already was. Michelle was my ride-or-die chick, for real.

"Miss Russell. You've told us ten different stories since we've gotten here. We know you're lying. You just told us your boyfriend's name was Hector, now you say it's Harry. I ought to arrest you right now for lying to a federal officer. Do you know how much time that charge holds? You're starting to make me think that Isaiah is in this house right now."

Michelle started crying. I didn't know if she was going to give me up or not, but I wasn't going to wait around and see. I got up from behind the refrigerator and bolted out the back door.

"Freeze! Don't move," the agents shouted, pulling out their guns as they saw me make a move to the door.

The agents fired repeatedly as I ran out the door and missed. I sped through the backyard like track star Michael Johnson. Shots whizzed by my head as I ran from the backyard to the front of the house and down the block where I had my Lexus parked. I was surprised to see they didn't have the house surrounded. They must have believed that I wasn't there because if they did, I know they would have come more than two deep. I felt underneath the mat on the driver's side and picked up my spare key and started the car.

As I pulled off, the agents stood in the middle of the street and unloaded at my car. They weren't shooting to slow me down. They were shooting to kill. They shot out my windshield and back window. I didn't know where I was going, but I knew I had to get the fuck out of dodge. When they were questioning Michelle, I heard the agents say how many robberies our crew was responsible for, not including murders and rapes. I didn't know how they found out all of their information, but somebody was telling, and their story was accurate. If they were going to catch me, they were going to have to work for it.

I sped down Broadway, doing close to a hundred miles per hour, running red lights. I didn't have a care in the world.

I looked in my rearview mirror and saw that two Kingston police cars were behind me. I cut down a back street and made a couple of quick turns to try and get them off my trail. When I looked through my rearview mirror, there wasn't a police car in sight. I drove as far as I could down back streets, but I had to get back to Broadway if I was going to make it to I-87 to try and get the fuck out of Kingston. I turned down Albany Avenue, and as I was turning onto Broadway, a car slammed into me and knocked me into the divider. As the side of my car was fishtailing, one car came slamming into the front and another slammed into the back of the car, forcing my car into a complete stop. The officers hopped out their vehicles, brandishing their weapons.

"Freeze. Don't move. Put your hands on top of your head," one of the officers shouted.

I looked up at the officer, but I could barely see them due to all of the blood running down my face. During the crash, I had hit my head on the dashboard. I didn't know how bad the cut was, but judging from the amount of blood that was gushing out, I figured it must have been bad. Everything was moving in slow motion. I had an inclination to run, but thought against it. It had been only two months, but I was tired of running. I put my hands on top of my head and surrendered.

It had been six months since my arrest. In April 2002, I was in the bull pen at eight-thirty in the morning at 46th and Broadway in Manhattan at Federal Court. I was so nervous that I couldn't stay still in the small ten-by-twelve cement cell I was being held in. My stomach was in knots, my palms were sweating and my fingernails were bleeding from me biting them. My whole life depended on what happened in that courtroom. The jurors held my life in the palms of their hands. If I blew trial, I was looking at 360 months, which equaled thirty years. I turned down the cop out the government offered me for 240 months, because twenty or thirty years were the same thing. They both were inconceivable. Twenty or thirty years were both like life to me at the time. Life as I knew it was never going to be the same, regardless if I blew trial or copped out, so I decided to take my chances with a trial. The deck was stacked against me, and I was going against the almighty federal government. The Feds had a ninety-eight percent conviction rate. When they indicted you, they had you. I was charged with two counts of conspiracy to robbery and two counts of brandishing a fire-arm in relation to a robbery. My lawyer told me that my chances were slim to none, but I felt like I had nothing to lose. I had a fiancé and an unborn child on the way who needed me. I couldn't surrender.

Dro survived the shooting and took a plea for natural life. If he went to trial and lost, he could've gotten the death penalty. Dro was charged with ten counts of conspiracy to robbery, ten counts of brandishing firearms in relation to a robbery, attempted murder of a federal officer, double homicide and rape.

Boota and Wise each copped out to 360 months and were charged with the same charges as me, plus double homicide and rape. Luckily, I was the only one who had nothing to do with the murder of Smalls and his wife. I was upstate at school, so when the rats told about the situation, I wasn't included because I wasn't there and had nothing to do with it. Lucky for me.

When Roach got caught, he told the government everything he and any of us ever did. Dro, Wise and Boota copping out hurt my chances of beating my case because we were co-defendants, and they made me look guilty by association. I wasn't mad at them though because they all told me what they were going to do beforehand. Plus, they were all facing either natural life or the death penalty. Besides, it wasn't like they told on me.

"Thompson, time for your funeral to begin. Let's go," the marshal said to me as I walked over to the slot in the bars and allowed him to cuff my hands in front of me.

I took a deep breath, picked up my manila folder with my legal work inside it and walked down the narrow hallway leading into the courtroom. When I entered and the marshal uncuffed me, I walked over to my seat next to my lawyer. The first faces I saw were those of my mother and my little sister Sable.

Both of their eyes were bloodshot red from crying, but they forced weak smiles when they saw me. I smiled back at them, blew a kiss, shook my lawyer's hand and sat down. Besides my mother and sister, the rows of seats behind me in the courtroom were empty. That day was the first court appearance that Michelle ever missed. Since I'd been in jail, Michelle and I had grown even closer than we were before I went in. Michelle wrote me daily, visited three times a week and never missed a court appearance. She was my rock. I had to convince her to go to her mother's funeral instead of attending my first day of trial. Michelle was going through a lot. Her mother passed away the week prior, she was eight months pregnant with my child, and I was fighting a no-win battle with the Feds. I didn't know how she was handling it all so well.

"All rise. The United States District Court for Southern District of New York is now in session. The Honorable Richard J. Kelly presiding," the bailiff announced.

We all stood up as the judge took his seat and ordered us to get back in our seats as the jury filled the courtroom. I established eye contact and smiled at each one of them. The only thing that I was blessed with was a good jury—five blacks, two Hispanics, one Chinese and four whites. Eight were men and four were women. Out of the eight minorities on the jury, all of them said that they had been victims of racial profiling.

I had a plain cheap black suit with some wing-tipped shoes and a red tie. I had my hair cut down to a low Caesar, and I had cut all of my facial hair off. I was twenty-two, but could pass for fifteen. I looked like a choirboy; the complete opposite of the monster the DA portrayed me as in her opening argument. After my lawyer gave a brief, weak opening argument, the prosecution called its first witness.

"The prosecution calls Aaron Henderson to the stand," the DA announced.

Roach came walking from the back of the courtroom wearing a blue Polo sweater and light-blue jeans. As he walked up, he completely avoided eye contact with me. I tried to hold back the disgust I had for him off my face and control my emotions for the sake of the jury, but it was to no avail. I was biting down on my tongue so hard it started bleeding. It still all seemed unreal. When I got my motion of discovery and found out that Roach was telling, it was a shock. He was fearless.

He was Boota's older brother. *How can he look himself in the mirror after this?* I thought to myself as he was sworn in.

The worst thing about it was Roach told for no reason. The Feds didn't have anything on any one of us. The only reason they tracked Roach down was because his stupid ass wouldn't listen to me and cancel the jux. The old white man I was leery of who stood in front of the warehouse across the street from the jewelry store, took down his license plate number and gave it to the police after the store was robbed saying that we looked suspicious. I knew that white man was going to be the one to bring us down. I told Roach over and over, but he refused to listen. It's crazy because in all actuality, it was Roach's fault that we were locked up. Not only was he the DA's star witness, but also his dumb ass was the one who drove his own whip to the jux.

When the Feds jumped out on Roach, he had on a stolen Rolex from another spot, and they matched the serial number to a jewelry store that he and Dro had done previously. After they brought Roach in, they searched his crib in Pennsylvania where his girlfriend and two kids stayed, and found two guns. The house was in his girlfriend's name and they threatened to charge her with the guns if he didn't cooperate. But instead of Roach being smart and letting his girl take the charge and telling them that he bought the watch from a street vendor, he started naming names. He told on me, Dro, Wise, Rule, Danielle and even his blood brother Boota. When he called Dro's crib the night that they ran up in there, he was calling to set Dro up. When Dro asked Roach if he got caught with one of the watches that was all they needed—Probable cause. They put warrants out on all of us. Roach telling was like a domino effect. The only evidence the Feds had on us were from the mouths of snitches. They had no physical evidence. If I was being tried in the state, they would've thrown my case out at the grand jury. Only the Feds could get you convicted by word of mouth.

I sat trying to control my anger as questioning got under way.

"Sir, could you please state your full name for the court?" the prosecutor asked.

"Aaron Henderson."

"And, do you know anybody in this courtroom?" he asked.

"Yes I do. I know the defendant, Isaiah Thompson. I've known him for ten years."

"And have the two of you ever committed any robberies together?"

"Yes, we have. Mr. Thompson and I stuck up a jewelry store in Rhode Island last August."

"And what was Mr. Thompson's role in the robbery?"

"He was the gunman. He held the employees and customers down while I broke the display cases and took the merchandise."

"And to your knowledge, was that the first time he'd ever committed a robbery?"

"Objection, your honor. That is pure speculation," my lawyer shouted, standing up.

"Overruled. The witness may answer the question," the judge said.

"Far from it. Mr. Thompson has been part of several robberies from businesses to street pickups. He's a professional stick up kid like myself," Roach said.

"No further questions, your honor," the prosecutor said.

"Your witness," the judge said to my attorney.

"Mr. Henderson, have you ever been convicted of a crime before?" my attorney asked.

"Yes, I have."

"Could you tell the men and women of the jury for what, please?"

"Twice for burglary and once for robbery."

"I see. And are you hoping to get a reduced sentence for your testimony today?" my attorney asked.

"Yes, I am, but—"

"And the other robberies that you say you know my client took part in, did you witness him in the act, or did someone inform you about them?"

"Someone told me about them, but—"

"Isn't it safe to say that you would say and do anything to get time off your sentence, including lie on an innocent man?" my attorney asked.

"Objection, your honor, badgering the witness," the prosecutor said, standing up.

"No further questions, your honor," my attorney said.

Roach walked off the stand, and the marshals escorted him back the same way he came in. The judge called recess for lunch, and I went back into the bull pen and ate a cold ham-and-cheese sandwich. I thought that we discredited Roach, but my lawyer told me that Roach's testimony was damaging. My heart dropped. As I sat in the bull pen and waited for recess to end, I started to feel discouraged. There was no way I was going to win this trial, I thought. My life was over. I wanted to cry, but no tears came.

After recess, the prosecutor called Danielle to the stand. She came into the courtroom from the same back entrance that Roach came in from. She was wearing a black long skirt with thigh-high boots and no makeup. Out of the seven of us, Danielle was the only one who got bail.

When I read that Danielle wrote a statement on me, I wasn't surprised in the least. I'm not going to say I understood why she was telling, but I expected it. Danielle wasn't built for all that shit Dro had her doing. When I looked at Danielle, I still saw that prissy white-girl-acting nerd I went to high school with. Dro rarely made mistakes when it came to planning a robbery, but the biggest mistake of all was involving Danielle. We used her for casing spots and being the getaway driver because she looked so innocent and sweet looking. Now those same characteristics I loved about Danielle were gonna win over the jury and help put me in jail possibly for the next thirty years.

Danielle wasted no time telling. She must've started telling in the police car. Not only did she back all of Roach's claims, she also added to it. She remembered exact dates and addresses. The worse part of everything is that she told on Dro. She never even wrote him to explain, then got engaged to her so-called best friend Jamal. As I looked up at Danielle on the stand, I felt like spitting in her face—not only for testifying or telling on me, but because of the way she betrayed Dro. I knew Dro had to be hurt.

"Miss Rodriguez," the prosecutor began, "could you please state your name for the court."

"Danielle Rodriguez."

"Miss Rodriguez, can you explain your role in the Go Hard organization."

Danielle took a sip of water, crossed her legs and took a deep breath. "Most times my job was just to go in the jewelry stores, find out the locations, the brand of watches, number of employees, cameras and things of that nature. I was basically the one who gave the layout to them. Sometimes I drove getaway cars, and once I took part in an actual robbery with my ex-boyfriend DaShaun."

"Miss Rodriguez, you graduated high school with honors, never had as much as a traffic violation and both of your parents are teachers. How did you get involved in something like this?"

Danielle took another deep breath, looked down and began crying. I looked over at the jury and they seemed entranced by Danielle. The prosecutor handed Danielle a tissue and she wiped her eyes and blew her nose.

"Miss Rodriguez," the judge said, "we can take a ten-minute recess if you need time to get yourself together."

"No. I'm fine. I want to get this over with now. I did it all because I was in love with my ex-boyfriend. It was an abusive relationship. If I didn't do what he told me, he'd hit me. I did it because I wanted him to love me."

Danielle was lying through her teeth. She should've won an Oscar for the performance she was giving. Dro never put his hands on her. The reason she got involved with the juxes was because she was a money-hungry, good-for-nothing, money-loving skeezer.

"Do you know the defendant?" the prosecutor asked.

"Yes. I've known him since junior high school."

"What was his role in the organization?"

"Isaiah was one of the most heartless and fearless members of the organization. He'd take candy from a baby if he could make a profit from it."

"Have you ever witnessed him commit a robbery?"

"Yes. Several times. I saw him rob a fur coat warehouse with my own eyes and two jewelry stores. I've never witnessed him do any other robberies than those, but I was around several times when Isaiah was talking about robberies that he'd done or was getting ready to do."

"Is Mr. Thompson a violent man?" he asked.

"Oh my God. He's very violent. Like I said before, Isaiah was one of the most ruthless and fearless members of the crew. I once witnessed him knock a sixty-year-old woman out during a robbery."

"No more questions, your honor," the prosecutor said.

"Your witness," the judge called to my attorney.

"The defense rests, but would like to reserve the right to call this witness at a later time," my attorney said.

"Court is adjourned until tomorrow morning at nine A.M. sharp," the judge said.

The marshal came to my seat, held me by my arms, handcuffed me, walked me to the same door that I entered and put me back in the bull pen. Before they took me back to Metropolitan Correctional Center, my attorney came to speak with me and told me that Danielle's testimony was a major blow to us. He said that her testimony was so damaging that instead of cross examining her, he decided to get her off the stand as fast as he could.

My lawyer told me that he didn't see any way possible we could win the case. My first round of fighting with the Feds was almost a KO. I started to think that maybe I made a mistake by going to trial. When I returned to MCC, I couldn't sleep. I stayed up all night trying to figure out how I was going to get myself out of the big mess I had gotten myself into. I came up with nothing.

The next day when I walked into the courtroom, I felt a thousand times better. Michelle was sitting in the front row behind me with my mother and little sister, smiling and blowing kisses at me. I know it sounds crazy, but seeing Michelle gave me strength. I felt like I could take on the world with her behind me. Earlier that morning, my lawyer came to the bull pen with a twenty-five-year-plea agreement. I turned it down without even considering it, because twenty-five and thirty years still held the same definition to me. Life.

The prosecution began by calling Rule to the stand.

Rule came walking out from the back of the courtroom wearing an orange jail jumpsuit. His hair was in a nappy afro, and he had big bags under his eyes like he hadn't slept in months. As he walked passed me on his way to the stand, the nigga had the nerve to nod at me. It took all the restraint I had not to reach out and slam his head into the table. Watching Rule get up on the stand and be sworn in, I felt nothing but hate. I never felt more betrayed in my life. When Roach testified against me, I felt betrayed, but it wasn't anywhere close to the feeling I had staring at Rule on the stand. I knew Roach way longer than I knew Rule, but I was closer to Rule than I was to Roach. Rule was my right-hand man. Since I met Rule, I had been nothing but a friend to him. When he caught the case for shooting Thirsty, I held him down to the fullest. Not only did I send him money and accept all his collect calls, I even took care of his girlfriend Tiesha. We had our little drama, but when he needed me most, I put the money up for the damages to the bar and got him out of jail so he could be there to take care of his family. I had been nothing but loyal to Rule, and here he was sitting on the stand, getting ready to push my wig back. I made a mental note to myself that if I ever got anywhere close to Rule outside the courtroom, I was going to kill him.

As I turned around in my seat to look at Michelle, I saw Tiesha sitting in the row behind the prosecutor's bench. Tiesha was a thorough chick. I wondered how she could still be with and respect Rule knowing what he was doing. It was then that I came up with an idea.

"Mr. Mitchell, could you please explain your relationship with the defendant," the prosecutor said.

Randy Thompson

"Yeah, sure. Ski and me are best friends. We get money together doing anything and everything to make a profit—from selling drugs to stickups."

"I see. So it's safe to say that you took part in robberies with the defendant," the prosecutor said.

"Ski was like my right-hand man. If you dealt with him, you dealt with me, and vice versa. We was like Tango and Cash. I've done four or five robberies with him."

"Could you tell the court the type of places you two robbed together?"

"We robbed Blockbuster video, Domino's pizza, Toys 'R' Us, jewelry stores, hustlers, grandmothers, babies—we basically robbed anything and anyone with money."

"Objection, your honor. My client isn't charged with any of these crimes the witness alleges."

"Sustained," the judge said. "Mr. Mitchell, please only discuss the crimes that the defendant is being charged with."

"My bad, ya honor."

"No further questions, your honor."

"Your witness," the judge said to my attorney.

"Mr. Mitchell, my client is charged with robbing a jewelry store named Weirs Jewelers on August 21, 2001, in Rhode Island. Were you present that day?" my attorney asked.

"No. I wasn't on that job, but—"

"And you say my client is your best friend. Why are you on the stand testifying against him this morning then?"

"Because I was subpoenaed by the district attorney."

"No, I think it's a little more than that, Mr. Mitchell. Aren't you cooperating with the government hoping for a sentence reduction?" my attorney asked.

"Yes, but, uh—"

"And isn't my client the only one out of the seven of you who were indicted on this case who took his case to trial?"

"Yes, but—"

"So it's safe to say that this is your golden opportunity to get him back?"

"No. It's not like that."

"Isn't it also true that you've always been jealous of my client?"

"Hell no. Why would I be jealous of him?"

"Maybe because you know that he was having an affair with Tiesha, your girlfriend and mother of your newborn."

"What? I knew it, you no-good son of a bitch. I'mma kill you. That's why you gonna get fried, you mothafucka. You ain't never going home. I hope you get life."

"Order in the court. Order in the court. One more outburst like that Mr. Mitchell, and I'm going to have to remove you from my court-room," the judge said.

"No more questions, your honor. Get this filth out of here," my attor-ney said.

As Rule was escorted out of the courtroom, he made several lunges at me. I played like I was scared for the jury. The courtroom was in a frenzy. My plan worked to perfection. I always knew that Rule thought I fucked Tiesha, and I used it against him. He reacted just like I thought he would. Members of the jury were shaking their heads and whisper-ing to one another while Rule had to be forcefully removed from the courtroom. Between Rule's violent outburst and his long rap sheet, I felt like my lawyer discredited Rule. I scored my first knockdown in my grudge match with the Feds.

When the DA called the next witness to the stand, I knew I was finished. Tiesha got up and walked by me to the stand like she never saw me a day in her life. Tiesha never witnessed me in the act of doing a robbery, but she knew enough info to crucify me. I knew the jury was going to eat her testimony up. Not only did she have a clean record, she was a woman.

After she was sworn in, the prosecutor began. "Could you state your relationship to the defendant for the court?"

"I'm Mark Mitchell's girlfriend. He's the defendant's best friend. I'm also the mistress and mother to Isaiah Thompson's baby."

"Excuse me?" the prosecutor said.

"You heard what I said. Isaiah Thompson is the father of my baby. It was a secret. Rule found out while he was in jail and vowed to set Isaiah up."

"Miss Hilton, what are you talking about?" the prosecutor said. "You never discussed any of this information with us before."

"It was none of your business."

"Okay, Miss Hilton, have you ever witnessed Mr. Thompson doing a robbery, discussing a robbery or dividing money up from a robbery?"

"No, I haven't. Isaiah wasn't into that life. My boyfriend was, but not Isaiah. He was always at school or playing basketball, that's why I liked him so much. He was different."

The DA lost all color. I couldn't believe it. Tiesha was holding it down as if we planned it together. Her story was going right with ours.

"That's not what you wrote in your statement or said at the grand jury, Miss Hilton. Do you know you could be cited for contempt and sentenced to time in prison for lying under oath?"

"I ain't lying. The only reason I made up those lies about Isaiah was because you promised me money if I lied on him, but I can't do it. I can't send an innocent man to prison. This is wrong."

Tiesha was putting on a performance worthy of an Academy Award. I sat back in my seat with my arms folded, biting my lip to stop myself from smiling.

"That is absolutely not true. Bailiff, arrest the witness. I'm bringing her up on charges," the prosecutor said.

"Wait a minute. The defense has the right to cross-examine the witness," the judge said.

"No questions, your honor," my attorney said.

The marshals walked up to the stand, read Tiesha her rights and escorted her out the courtroom. As Tiesha was walking by, she winked and smiled. Tiesha was a trouper for real. I felt bad that she was going to get time, but I figured it would be better for her to get a couple of years than for me to get thirty. I looked at the jury, and judging by their faces, they were in shock. They looked like they didn't know what to believe. I didn't have to prove I was innocent; the government had to prove that I was guilty beyond a reasonable doubt. So far, the fight looked dead even. After that day of trial, my lawyer came to the bull pen and told me that the government brought their offer down to seventeen years. I figured that if they brought the cop out that far down, they felt like they were going to lose the trial, so I declined the offer. I hoped that my decision wasn't gonna cost me.

When trial started the next day and the jury walked in, I noticed a few smiles and head nods from them. I guess from all the drama that went down the day before, they were starting to look at me like I was the victim. I looked back at Michelle sitting with my mother and sister and winked at her. It took me hours of visits and three fifteen-minute phone conversations to convince Michelle that Tiesha's baby wasn't mine and that I wasn't having an affair with her. For a minute, I thought I was going to lose her for good, but when I was escorted into the courtroom that morning and saw her sitting with my family, I knew she believed me. As the jury sat down in their seats and became comfortable, my lawyer gave me the worst news possible. He passed me a sheet of paper with the prosecution's witnesses for the day, and I saw names I thought I'd never see: Dro, Boota and Wise. I damn near had a heart attack. I was dizzy, my vision blurred, and my throat was so dry that I could barely swallow. The air seemed thin. Every time I breathed in, it felt like I was taking my last breath. I felt like I was having a nervous breakdown. My lawyer asked for and was granted an hour recess to prepare for the new witnesses.

During the recess, my lawyer took me into an interview room so that we could talk. I listened carefully as he spoke from behind the glass.

"Isaiah, you're really in a no-win situation. The prosecution wants you bad now. They're pulling out all the stops. The next three witnesses are going to kill us. We can't win this case. The prosecution is still offering you seventeen years. Taking the plea would be in your best interest."

"I can't do it. I just can't. Seventeen years is too long. My child will be grown by the time I come home," I replied, rubbing the top of my head.

"Isaiah, you're right. Seventeen years is a lot of time, but it's a whole lot better than thirty years. They knew this case was slipping out of their hands. That's why they went to jail and got the rest of your co-defendants. They must have promised them a large sentence reduction because before last night, these guys weren't cooperating at all."

"Listen, I respect your opinion, and I know you're gonna think I'm crazy, but I wanna finish this thing out. I don't like to start something and not finish it. Tell the Feds to take their offer and shove it up their ass. Fuck 'em," I said loudly to my lawyer who was trying to put a battery in my own back.

"Okay, Isaiah. It's your life." My lawyer stared at me like I was crazy and got up to go back to the courtroom.

I knew I was in a no-win situation, but something inside me told me to ride it out. I knew that Dro, Boota and Wise were scheduled to testify against me, but I couldn't believe it. I had to see it with my own eyes. I wanted to look them in their faces while they told on me.

When I made it back to the courtroom and the DA called Dro out, I immediately started to regret my decision. Dro walked by me like he had never seen me a day in his life. His head was freshly shaven and he had on an all blue MCC jail suit with a pair of Air Force Ones. After he was sworn in, we caught eyes for a moment, but I couldn't read him. He had a blank stare on his face like he didn't have a care in the world. Before he turned his face from me, I swore I saw a slight smirk. Out of everyone, Dro had the most dirt on me. Wise and Boota could only tell about the robberies, but Dro could tell about me killing Paula and Thirsty. If that came out, I'd never go home. After everything happened at

Thirsty's house, Dro told me never to tell anyone what happened. Now I was hoping he lived up to his end of the promise.

He was sworn in, and the prosecutor began. "Could you tell us your full name for the court, sir?"

"DaShaun White."

"Could you tell us your role in the organization referred to as the Go Hard Crew?"

"I was the leader."

"And what was your job description?"

"I picked out the stores we were gonna hit, found out how much the merchandise was worth we were stealing, made getaway plans, fenced the jewelry and distributed pay. I also picked out who the participants who would be in the robbery.

"So, is it safe to say that you know everything that went on in the organization?" the prosecutor asked.

"Yeah. Definitely."

"And Mr. White, do you see anyone from your organization in the courtroom today?"

Dro stood and looked around the courtroom for a brief moment then answered, "No. I don't."

The courtroom was in bedlam. People where whispering to one another, jurors and marshals were conversing in separate groups, and the prosecutor looked like someone just stole her dog. I couldn't believe it. At first I thought I heard wrong, but when I listened to the reaction of the courtroom, I knew I heard right. I looked behind me at Michelle, my mother and little sister, and they were all smiles.

"Order in the court. Order in the court," the judge yelled, banging his gavel.

"Mr. White, I'm going to ask you one more time. Is there anyone in this courtroom who was in your organization?"

"No. There isn't," Dro said.

"I interviewed you last night at the jail, and you wrote a completely different statement than the one you're saying. You said that Mr. Thompson was a member of your organization," the prosecutor said.

"Yes, I did, but I was forced into saying that by you and the FBI. Mr. Thompson had nothing to do with our organization and you know it. You're trying to frame him, and I can't help you and send an innocent man to prison."

The courtroom got loud again, and the judge calmed it down.

"Mr. White, do you know that you can be charged with perjury?"

"Yes, I do, and that's why I'm telling the truth. You're a prosecutor. Do you know that putting false evidence on someone is illegal? I'm pressing charges on you and your office."

"You lying son of a bitch," the prosecutor screamed. "You are gonna rot in jail for this."

"Watch your language in my courtroom." The judge admonished. "Language like that will not be tolerated by anyone. Are you done with the witness?" the judge asked.

"Yes. No further questions."

"Your witness," the judge said.

My attorney stood. "No questions, your honor," he said.

"Marshals, you may remove the witness," the judge said.

As the marshals escorted Dro past me out the courtroom, Dro gave me the same evil smirk that I saw earlier when he first got on the stand. I never felt happier in my life. I knew Dro couldn't get on the stand and tell on me. We went back too far and he was too gangsta for that. We were raised with morals and principles. I was glad that I declined the plea because my chances were looking better than ever. For the very first time since I went to jail, I started thinking about what I was going to do when I went home. If Dro got to the stand and lied for me, I knew Wise and Boota were going to do the same. Dro always planned everything thoroughly.

After Dro got off the stand, the judge called recess for lunch. By the time court resumed, I was feeling like I was on top of the world. I couldn't wait for the prosecution to call Boota and Wise to the stand. Their testimonies were going to push me right out the door.

Boota came from the back of the courtroom with the same slow bop he had since I met him in junior high. When he saw me his eyes lit up, and he smiled at me so much that I had to break eye contact with him for fear that the jury would think something was up. Boota had on a blue MCC jail jumpsuit with a pair of white-and-blue Air Maxes on to match. Even in jail, Boota had to be fly. As Boota was getting sworn in, I looked across at the DA. She looked like her world came crashing down. If she knew better, she would've never called Boota to the stand. It was only going to get worse for her.

"Please state your full name for the court," the prosecutor said.

"Raymond Henderson, also known as Boota Bless," he said.

"Mr. Henderson, did you take a plea agreement?"

"Yes. I did," he said.

"Could you tell us what you confessed to?"

"I copped out to two counts of robbery, two counts of brandishing a firearm, double homicide and rape."

"Is it true that you were part of a close-knit group called the Go Hard Crew?"

"Yes. I guess so."

"Could you tell us the members of the crew?"

"Sure. That's easy. Me, Dro, Wise, Snoop—God bless the dead— my brother Roach and Danielle," he said.

"Anyone else?"

"Nah. That's it."

"Are you sure?"

"Bitch, how many times are you gonna ask me the same fucking question? I said no," he said.

"Mr. Thompson wasn't a member of the crew?"

"Isaiah? Are you crazy? Isaiah is more of a bitch than you. Only thing that nigga ever stole was a basketball."

Boota had the whole courtroom laughing. He always knew how to make a joke out of the most serious situations. I looked back at my mother, and even she was laughing.

"Order in the court. Order in the court. Mr. Henderson, please watch your language in my court."

"My bad."

"Okay, Mr. Henderson. You want to play hardball? Who took part in the Albany robberies?"

"I can't remember off the top of my head, but Isaiah definitely wasn't with us. That bird-ass nigga was probably somewhere shooting jump shots."

"Then why did you tell me yesterday that he did?"

"C'mon, lady. You know you forced me to do that. I decided to say what you wanted me to say just to take a trip away from jail, but you have to be out of your mind if you think I'm gonna tell, especially on an innocent man."

The prosecution knew her case was finished. She had gotten played, and she knew there was nothing she could do to win the case. She took a deep breath, looked over at me and told the judge she had no further questions. So far, the prosecution had called six witnesses to the stand, and three of them said that I had nothing to do with it. The most that she could have hoped for was a hung jury, and I doubted if they would get that.

"Your witness," the judge said to my attorney.

"No questions, your honor," he said.

Boota got off the stand and was escorted back to the same door he came from. As he passed by me he whispered, "I know you ain't think I was gonna rat." He walked away laughing.

By then, I already knew that Dro, Boota and Wise had planned this whole thing out to try to get me proven innocent. Knowing them the way I did, Dro probably came up with the whole plan himself, and to me, that was his best plan yet. Even though the prosecutor knew Wise was going to do the same thing, she called him to the stand. When Wise walked out, he gave me a head nod, a slight smile and got on the stand.

"Please state your full name for the court," the prosecutor began.

"Enrique Santiago."

"Do you know the defendant Isaiah Thompson?"

"Yeah. I've known him since junior high."

"And what would you say Isaiah was most known for?"

"Oh, that's easy. Basketball. He was a real good basketball player growing up. He still is too."

"Didn't you tell me that Isaiah was known for selling drugs and pulling stickups with you and your crew?"

"No. You said that and told me that if I agreed with you, I'd get ten years off my sentence. Remember? I didn't know that you were gonna call me into court. I ain't wit' all this. I can't lie on the man under oath."

"This is absolutely untrue, and you know it. Why are you doing this? I'm going to charge you with purgery."

"Go ahead. You already charged me with everything in the book. Who cares? I'm guilty of my charges, and I can accept my sentence, but I ain't gonna let Isaiah go down for something he had nothing to do with. This is wrong. Fuck that."

The judge gave Wise a stern warning about using profanity in the courtroom before allowing the prosector to continue.

"Does the defendant have you under pressure or scared for your life?"

Wise laughed so hard that his whole face turned red. The prosecutor stood in front of him with her arms folded in amazement. "What's so funny, Mr. Santiago?"

"You. Imagine Isaiah putting pressure on anybody? Only pressure he applies is when he's playing basketball and he's playing defense."

Wise started laughing again so hard that the prosecutor didn't even bother to ask him any more questions. He made her look like a fool. All of them did, and she knew it. The judge asked my lawyer if he wanted to cross-examine Wise, and for the fourth time in a row, he declined. My lawyer had the easiest job in the world. We didn't have to call any witness because the prosecution was putting witnesses on the stand who were clearing my name. Tiesha, Dro, Boota and Wise all testified defending me, but I knew the DA was going to make them all pay for it when she charged them with perjury. Dro had natural life, and Boota and Wise had thirty years apiece, so there was nothing more the DA could do to really hurt them. What's another five years when you already got thirty?

After Wise got off the stand, the judge adjourned the court until the following morning. The next day in the courtroom, the prosecution called Danielle back to the stand, and she fried me even worse than the first time. The prosecution played the videotapes of Boota, Dro and Wise telling them the truth the night before they testified. What the prosecution didn't realize was that they all put me at different robberies not linked to the case. Dro, Boota and Wise had to do that on purpose because they all knew what robberies I took part in and what my role was. My lawyer got the tapes thrown out because he said they were patently irreconcilable and inconsistent due to their content.

That day in court, the prosecution rested and we did as well. I had three character witnesses my lawyer was going to call on my behalf, but he told me that it was best that we send the case to the jury immediately while everything was still fresh on the jurors' minds. The prosecution made their closing argument, and my lawyer did a riveting twenty-minute closing argument that made me seem holier than the pope. As he spoke, I noticed a couple of jurors nodding in agreement. The fight was over, and it was being sent to the cards.

As I was being escorted out of the courtroom, I looked back at Michelle, and she blew me a kiss the same way she did every day when I left the court, but this one felt different. I knew in my heart that the next time I left the courtroom I'd be leaving arm in arm with her, and it was the best feeling in the world. That night back at MCC, I slept like a baby. I was so confident that I was going home that I gave my radio, sweat suits and sneakers out to different people in my tier. It was a wrap.

The next morning the judge called the jury and gave them an elongated speech of their duties and sent them to deliberate. After I had been in the bull pen only two hours, the marshals came and got me and told me that the jury had reached a verdict. It was about fifteen minutes to noon. As I returned to my seat, my lawyer whispered to me that quick deliberations usually meant that the jury had their minds made up for a long time, and in our case that was a good thing. As the jury filled in, I loosened up my tie and took a deep breath. Suddenly there was a large commotion behind me.

"Oh, Jesus. Someone call 911. Michelle's water broke," my mother screamed at the top of her lungs laying Michelle on the floor in the aisle.

When I looked behind me and saw all that blood, I completely forgot where I was. I jumped out of my seat and immediately ran over to Michelle.

"Baby, are you a'ight? C'mon, baby. Breathe. Everything is gonna be a'ight. C'mon, hold my hand," I said, bending down on one knee and holding Michelle's hand.

Just then, two marshals tackled me to the floor, handcuffed me and threw me back in the bullpen. I tried to fight them off, but it was no use. The judge ordered the court into recess until two o'clock. In the bullpen I was a nervous wreck. I couldn't stay still, not because of the impending verdict, but because of Michelle and the baby. I hated that I couldn't be by her side while she went through labor. The marshals were cool though. They kept me posted on everything going on until the ambulance arrived. By that time it was only half past twelve. I had to wait another hour and a half for the verdict. It was the longest time of my life. Finally, in what seemed life forever, the marshal cracked my cell and let me into the courtroom.

When I got back to my seat, my lawyer shook my hand and told me that I was the father of an eight-pound, four-ounce baby boy. Michelle had a C-section, and was doing fine. I was so happy that I felt like crying. But as soon as the jury walked in, my mood completely changed. For some reason, not one of the jurors looked me in the eye as they walked in. My heart dropped. I silently said the Lord's Prayer as the judge ran through a bunch of legal mumbo-jumbo.

Finally, he asked, "Does the jury have a foreman?"

A gray-haired black man stood up. "I am the foreman, your honor."
"And did the jury reach a verdict?"
"Yes. We did."

The foreman passed a paper with the verdict on it to the bailiff, and the bailiff passed it to the judge. The judge read it with an emotionless face, handed it back to the bailiff who in turn passed it back to the foreman.

"We the members of the jury find the defendant Isaiah Thompson not guilty on all charges." The foreman announced.

The words were like music to my ears.

"Thank you. Thank you," I shouted to the jury as I hugged my lawyer.

The judge dismissed the jury and told me that I was free to go. It all seemed too good to be true. My lawyer walked me out of the courtroom, gave me a ten-dollar bill, and told me that Michelle and the rest of the family were at Beth Israel Hospital. Before I made my way down the long steps of the courthouse, I hugged my lawyer one more time and thanked him for everything. I ran down the steps of the court building, and there was a cab parked directly in front of the steps like it was waiting just for me. Nothing could go wrong for me. Everything was going my way.

I opened up the back door of the cab, jumped in the backseat, and yelled, "Beth Israel Hospital. Yo please. Make it quick."

"Nah, but I could send you to hell real fast. Remember me, pai?" the cabdriver said.

The voice sounded familiar, but I couldn't place it. But as soon as he turned around, I knew I was in trouble. It was Candy's brother, Raphael.

Raphael turned around with a nine-millimeter and immediately started firing at me at point-blank range.

I lost count of how many times I was hit. I felt a burning sensation from the neck down. It felt like somebody started a fire inside my chest. I couldn't hear anything, and everything seemed like it was moving in slow motion. Raphael pushed me out of the cab and sped off.

As I lay down at the bottom of the steps staring at the sky, I knew my life was over. My whole life was flashing before my eyes. I thought about everything and everyone who was important to me: Dro, Boota, Wise, Tiesha, Kashaun, Natalie, Snoop, my mother and little sister, and last but not least, Michelle and my newborn son who I was never going to see. I thought about trying to climb up the steps, but decided against it. I was too weak. It was over. I saw a crowd hovering over me, but I didn't recognize any of the faces. I was going to die in front of complete strangers. I heard people screaming and instructing someone to call an ambulance, and another voice asking me if I was okay, but I couldn't speak. Every breath and blink that I took felt like my last. My past had come to haunt me. I stopped fighting and gave in to it. I took one last blink and breath and checked out. No more pain. And then there was darkness.

Coming Soon

Ski Mask Way II

the saga continues...

Ride or Die Chick

by J.M. Benjamin
Available in Stores NOW!

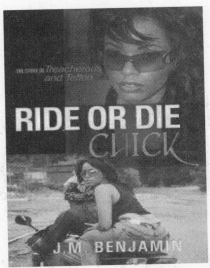

Life isn't easy for Treacherous or Teflon, but when this modern day Bonnie & Clyde duo hook up life won't be easy for anyone seeing paper in Virginia. Bonded by tragic childhoods Treacherous and Teflon grew up hard on the streets of VA. But those same Virginia streets will be suffering losses as ballers from VA or others just visiting the city fall victim to Treach and his Ride or Die chick Teflon!

With their murderous robbing spree sparing no one just how long can Treach and Teflon continue to terrorize the streets of Virginia before they fall victim to the streets again?

Ride or Die Chick, The Story of Treacherous and Teflon is about two people who come from nothing and are willing to do whatever it takes to obtain everything.

This is a modern day tale of Bonnie & Clyde and built on a love that is stronger than that of Romeo and Juliet. A bonafide gangster, Treacherous is confident that he can't lose, as long as he has his ride or die chick!

Ride or Die Chick II

by J.M. Benjamin
COMING SOON!

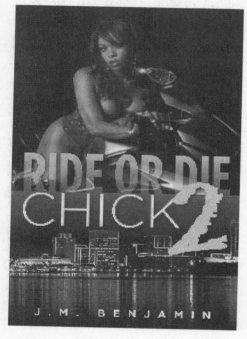

Summer 2008

Down in the Dirty

by *J.M. Benjamin*

Available in stores NOW!

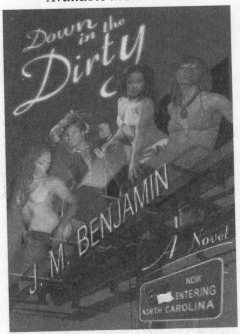

Childhood friends, Keisha, Desiree, Tasha, and Pam quickly learn how to use their beauty and sexual prowess to manipulate men. Each woman has suffered abuse at the hand of a man and they decide to make a life-long pact to get revenge on ballas. These gorgeous but scandalous women turn the tables by making men who cross their path, especially if their not from the dirty, pay for their womanizing behavior.

After pulling several heists and getting away with murder, these ruthless and cold-hearted women will stop at nothing to get what they want—until one of them begins to fall for her prey.

"J.M. Benjamin's freshman novel is pure fire! *Down in the Dirty* takes urban literature to a new high."

–Nikki Turner, national bestselling author of *Hustler's Wife* and *The Glamorous Life*

No Strings Attached

By #1 Essence bestselling author Nancey Flowers

Please accept this invitation to:

Event: Termination of marriage
Reason: Misplaced dick in another woman
Time: 3:40 P.M.
Date: May 20, 1999

Felice Jackson is sexy, single, and satisfied—or so she claims. She is an affluent, thirty-something entrepreneur who is partial owner of the successful firm Jackson and Jackson Financial Consultants. The only problem is her very active sexual relationship with her ex-husband and business partner, Bedford Jackson.

Felice is disgusted with men, but not enough to shut them out of her life physically. She enjoys the touch, smell, and taste of men too much to deprive herself. Instead she decides to stand at the helm of life and call the shots in relationships. If a man can do it, Felice can too. She isn't going to shed another tear for these tired-ass men.

Felice enjoys her no-strings-attached creed—until her secret past collides with her present.

Runnin' Game

by Courtney Parker

"*Runnin' Game* is urban drama at its best!"
–Nikki Turner, national bestsSelling author of
The Glamorous Life and *A Hustler's Wife*

Now that Carter Turner's athletic career is off the ground and running, he has to beat the women off with a stick. Carter is on top of the world…that is until he receives a telephone call that rocks his track career and changes his life forever.

Carter is no stranger to life in the fast lane, with a career destined for gold and a girl determined to ride or die, fate finds favor with this young couple. Only just as the icing is put on the cake, the cake begins to crumble under the weight of Carter's grimy past. With a string of lies straining his relationship and a possible injury threatening his career, Carter is doing what any young player has to do…*Runnin' Game*.

Coming soon

Pole Position

by
Arnold Dorsey-Bey

Fall 2008

Visit: www.flowersinbloompublishing.com
for more upcoming titles and book submission inquiries.